LINE CHANGE

ISRAEL'S A NEW ZONE FOR ETHAN

A Novel By

MARK LICHTENFELD
//

Mazo Publishers

Line Change
ISBN 978-1-936778-53-9

Published by
Mazo Publishers
PO Box 10474
Jacksonville, Florida USA 32247
Tel: 1-815-301-3559

mazopublishers@gmail.com
www.mazopublishers.com

Book Production
Prestige Prepress
prestige.prepress@gmail.com

Cover photograph by Alyse Lichtenfeld

Line Change is a work of fiction. The characters in this story are not based on any particular individuals. However, references to historical events are authentic.

To
Day School Students Across America — *It matters.*

Chapter One

MY VARSITY HOCKEY COACH calls me socially smooth.

That's probably a compliment.

See, I'm a Chicago Jewish Academy guy, and keeping squeaky-clean at CJA requires an insane dedication to behavioral savvy, coupled with a keen awareness of the bearded enemy's next move. You're either sharp or you're doomed.

I'm sharp. Acutely suspicious. I figure the whole world's teeming with foe, so I've made shrewdness my quintessential style. Seriously, it's how I've successfully dodged Rabbi Klepstein's religious radar for the past four years at CJA. For me, school's like hockey—staying safe means playing heads-up. And I play CJA the same way I man the blue line. Steady. Vigilant.

Like keeping my *tzitzis* tucked in when I'm hanging out with the public schoolers at DJ's Rock Club.

Like never being seen in an empty classroom with a living, breathing girl.

And never, *ever* promising Shoshana Kaplan that prep hockey season ends by March, when there's a spring league starting after Pesach.

Yeah, my life works best when I keep things simple. Easy. Drama's for all those other guys who'd rather stay up past midnight pounding the paint off their keyboards for the privilege of spilling these *nobody-cares-anyways* rumors all over Facebook Chat. I don't get that.

Look, I'm not into publicizing emotions. I say blasting your deepest thoughts into social cyberspace is a perfect way to lose control. And that's definitely not my style. I have to be in control. I'm always in control.

Until a half-hour ago. That's when this summer-busting text shows up during the very last period of my very last day of high school. Now, my life is totally out of control.

And it's all because of Dad.

Epic. I'm slogging down California Avenue hauling

this backpack crammed with four years of locker crap, I'm sweating rivers through the polyester fibers of my white, long-sleeve button-down, and it's like I'm not even caring that my face feels like the underside of a greasy Hanukkah *latke*. Truth is, I don't care about anything right now. Well, that's kind of an exaggeration. I mean, I totally care about extricating myself from this early-June nightmare, which is why I've got my brain slaving in full-scale overdrive, analyzing a myriad of schemes to buy me some extra time before my butt's totally fried.

Seriously, I don't know how it got to this. I mean, I always figured the last day of Chicago Jewish Academy would be the greatest moment of my life, a final goodbye to years of ten-hour tortures where twelfth period doesn't even start until the public schoolers are done with dinner.

Instead, I'm huffing home miserable, like a narcissistic graduating senior whose last summer before college is totally ruined.

Because it pretty much is.

I swear, I never saw it coming. But I should have. Dad always said he'd stop at nothing to get me that shot at a full-boat university scholarship. Still, I figured Dad was joking when he told me he dropped by Coach Paulson's office last week and begged him to tell the Maccabi USA big shots that Ethan Conners was the greatest Jewish blueliner since the invention of the electric Zamboni.

Guess that's how this scholarship thing works. You know, Dad gets Ethan's high school hockey coach to schmooze Team USA's manager, Ethan gets picked by Team USA to play the Maccabiah tournament in Israel, and naturally, the international exposure makes Ethan a lock for next fall's roster at Ferris State.

The *roster*. Yup, it's all about free tuition and board for Division-One hockey players. Real smooth, Dad.

Real painful, Ethan.

Look, if anyone would bother asking, I'd tell them I need a summer away from the ice, especially after our North Shore Varsity Flyers made a deep playoff run in the Metro

Chicago High School League. That, and the Skokie Spring League, which would still be going on if the administrators hadn't scheduled our second playoff game for the first day of *Shavuot*, when even the Reform Jewish guys wouldn't show. I mean, no one plays hockey on the very day God gave us the Ten Commandments.

But the worst part is gonna be explaining this to Shoshana. She'll freak.

Which is why I totally bailed on her by sneaking out of school via the alley door next to the lunch room loading dock.

"Wait up, Ethan!" hollers my best friend, Ezra Green, his hands waving like an angry O'Hare ground controller as he turns the corner from Maple and races forward.

"Let's go!" I holler back, staring impatient with both arms folded. I've known Ezra since third grade, and he's one of those guys who's late for everything.

Of course, he's got no idea that *I'm* the one who skulked out early. That's why it's so hard not to laugh as I watch him bust like a sprinter, his long, *tzitzit* fringes jetting out of his shirt like kite strings in a March wind.

"Thanks for slowing," he huffs. "Never even saw you leave."

"That's okay," I say, holding back a smile as Ezra uses his wrinkled sleeve to wipe this sheen of perspiration off his pasty forehead.

"Thank God it's over, Ethan."

"What's over?"

"Are you serious?" He gives me this eye roll. "School. The Academy."

"Oh."

"Waited four years for this," he says.

"Yeah," I grunt with the enthusiasm of a bag of kosher soup croutons.

"Okay, let's hear it, Ethan."

"What?"

"Spill it," he snips. Ezra plans to major in psychology, and he always knows when something's up.

"Look, Ezra—" I hesitate, and then suck this long drag of oxygen. "I've—I've got a situation."

As soon as I say it, Ezra furrows his brownish eyebrows like he's expecting me to spill something heavy. "What happened?" he mocks. "Shoshana changed her status to single or something?"

"Get serious," I carp, shaking my head.

"Well—"

"For starters, forget about Rivky Sandler's Fourth of July party."

"What?" he quips, his eyes beaming ultrasounds right though me.

"You heard me," I say, and now I've got four fingers raking like stubby plows through swaths of my wavy, dark hair. "Look, Ezra. I didn't want to say anything until it was for sure, but my Dad texted me at the end of Jewish History finals. It's a done deal."

"Spare me, Ethan. You're killing me with the suspense."

"Okay—it's just—"

"Ethan!"

"Okay—okay. It's just that I'm going to Israel next month with Maccabi USA. And not by choice, either."

"Cool," he bellows, and I'm wondering how my best friend the psychology major doesn't see that I'm totally grieving. "Just look at it as God's plan for you, Ethan."

"Hello. It's just a hockey tournament," I snap.

"In *Israel*."

"Thanks for reminding me."

"Seriously, Ethan." He gives me this extra-long stare. "It's our religious homeland. Rabbi Klepstein says that even being there for a single day can change everything. Am I right?"

"No."

"Ugh. You're as stubborn as day-old cholent."

I sigh. "Look, Ezra. The only thing that's gonna change is my standing with Shoshana."

"Get real," he says, then shakes his head like he's totally disgusted, which he is. "So why did you agree to go?"

"It's my dad!"

"Your father?"

"I'm serious, Ezra. Dad had Coach Paulson contact Team Maccabi."

"Why?"

"Isn't it obvious? Dad's figuring a little more summer seasoning will make me a shoo-in for second-line defense at Ferris State."

"That's full scholarship!"

"Bingo. It's my father's dream."

"Wow, Ethan. Figured your parents could have afforded tuition anywhere."

"Yeah, well Dad's a cheapskate," I grumble. "Now, my summer's gypped."

He shrugs. "It's more than the money, Ethan. You're the object of your father's athletic fantasies. They say it's tough being an only child."

"Tell me about it."

"So how long you going for?"

"Almost ten—"

"Wait up guys!" shrieks this girl's voice from behind, and when I turn, there's Shoshana and Chaya Levy hustling toward Ezra and me.

"Should I break the news?" whispers Ezra, taunting me with a quick eye wink.

"Just shut up for now." I nudge my backpack into his ribs. "Got it?"

"Okay," he says, and I'm actually trusting him.

I scan back and watch Shoshana trot the final thirty feet or so, the bottom of her long, black skirt sweeping grimy dust films right off of California Avenue's pockmarked sidewalk. The whole time I'm staring, I can't stop wondering how modest-dressed girls can be so sure-footed. You know, expertly negotiating curbs, driveways and potholes without ever tripping over their hemlines. I remember when I had to dress in a Roman toga for the fifth-grade play, and trust me, every step was perfectly calculated to ensure I didn't splatter my face all over the freshly-waxed gym floor.

"Freedom!" chirps Shoshana, as wisps of jet-black hair

blow sideways across her mouth.

The four of us halt at the Lunt Avenue stoplight. "Who's up for Tel Aviv Pizza?" jests Ezra. "Ethan's buying!"

"Something special?" asks Chaya, her fingers brushing a swath of sweat-curled bangs away from her eyes.

"Ezra's just fooling," I grumble, and then stomp the top of his foot.

"Rain check, anyway," says Shoshana. "Got a three o'clock scheduled at Madam Pellier's nail spa."

"Pellier's?" gasps Chaya, her midnight-black eyes perking. "I hear the cheapest manicures start at forty-five dollars."

"Fifty, as of June 1st," corrects Shoshana.

"Fifty dollars for a finger polish job?" I blurt, like I'm forgetting this is the far, North Side of Chicago. "That's—"

"You saying I'm not worth it?" Shoshana's forehead creases angry. "Thanks, Ethan."

"That's not what I meant," I protest.

"Whatever," she mumbles back, and just as I'm swearing to myself that I'll never let her dis me again, she nudges close and caresses my wrist with her fingertips. Mind games for sure, but she's classy and cute. I'm such a sucker.

"Hey, Shoshana," quizzes Ezra. "You working Camp Gan Israel again this summer?"

"We want Moshiach now!" laughs Chaya.

"Zip it," grunts Shoshana. "I am *so* done with that camp cheer."

"So that means you're touring Italy, again," says Ezra.

"No."

"Really?"

Okay, Ezra needs to quit doing this psychologist thing with Shoshana, because I can tell she's getting pissed, and I'm the one who's gonna get dumped on.

"Look, there's no Italy and no Camp Gan Israel either," miffs Shoshana, her dark-chocolate eyes drawing my gaze like she's emphasizing the point or something. "I've got my own plans and can't be tied down for the next two months."

Chaya nods. "Makes sense, I guess. You're leaving for seminary in August, right?"

"August 22. And trust me, I'm planning to make the most of this summer, if you know what I mean."

"Like sleeping in?" cracks Ezra, and we all laugh.

"You bet!" chirps Shoshana, and now she's stroking my arm possessively. "Girls don't have to recite the morning *Shacharit* prayers anyway, so think of me when you two are donning those leathery *tefillin* straps at daybreak."

Before I can answer back, this southbound California Avenue bus thunders past, belching a sick, dark cloud of diesel exhaust which trails us like an April fog for the next half-block.

"Gross!" wails Chaya, her flittering hands racing like fan blades to disperse the fumes. "I am *so* ready for Princeton. You know, the wooded campus and all."

"Good point," I say, nodding.

"And I am *so* ready to hang out with Ethan all summer," declares Shoshana, her charcoal eyebrows slanting serious. "No school, no six weeks of camp brats, and definitely *no* hockey."

"Yeah," smiles Chaya. "Gonna be sweet having the whole summer off, huh Ethan?"

"Uh—"

"For sure!" blurts Shoshana. "Trust me, you'll never see me set foot inside that Skokie Skatium again."

"Guess a break would be nice," I mumble, and when I turn back toward Ezra, he's giving me that look, the one that says she's *my* problem.

"See you guys," says Ezra as he and Chaya bail at Greenleaf Street. So much for moral support.

"Call me, Chaya!" hollers Shoshana. "Maybe you'll come by on Shabbat."

"Will do!" she answers, and now it's just Shoshana and me plodding north toward the other side of Touhy, where the houses are bigger and the girls wax snobbier. Yeah, no grungy alleys or dumpy apartments buildings in *this* neighborhood— just two and three-car attached garages with at least one SUV per family. That's us. Spoiled American Jews, less the New York accent. Oh sure, my parents would hate me for saying this, but it's the pathetic truth. Sorry Mom and Dad.

Shoshana smiles. "I'm so excited," she says, still clutching my wrist. "I think my parents are gonna say *yes*."

"Yes?"

"You know, Ethan. The cabin."

"Cabin?"

"Get real. I'm talking Minocqua. North Woods. First weekend in July."

"Oh yeah," I say, stalling for time because I know where this is heading, and it's not where I want it to go. "So — I'm — coming with you to Wisconsin?"

"Well, yeah," she scorns, her eyes spilling anger. "I mean, we've only talked about it every day since Pesach."

"Uhh —"

"Calling Ethan Conners!" she shouts, her palms shaking my shoulders like she's training for the coconut pickers' Olympics or something. "Do you have any idea how difficult it was to get them on board? I mean, we're talking Orthodox families here."

As she's squawking, I'm doing the calculations in my head. "Ehh, first two days in July, right?"

"Something like that," she shoots back. "What's the big deal, Ethan? Not like you've got a game or anything. Thank God that's over."

"And my scholarship means nothing to you?" I retort. "Look, Shoshana, hockey's been a blessing for my family, as if you didn't know."

I can tell that flusters her. She's giving me this pouty look, and then she rakes her hair back so tight that it's got to kill. Everything's tense, no one's saying a thing, and my head's starting to pound from the rhythmic melody of Nike soles shuffling along this ugly section of crumbling sidewalk.

"Sorry, Ethan," she says, finally breaking the void. "Look, it's gonna be beautiful. Even romantic. Dad's probably gonna let us take his boat out on the lake. I *know* you're excited."

"Yeah," I lie.

"Now you're with the program," she says.

"Of course," I say back, and I'm thinking to myself that it

really would be cool to hang out with Shoshana in the North Woods, even with her parents hovering.

Thing is, I'll be about six thousand miles away, but it's probably best to spare her that detail for now.

"Wanna stop by later, Ethan? Maybe you'll change your mind about Madam Pellier's when you see the way her artistic mastery transforms my fingers."

"I'll call you after *Maariv* evening prayers, Shosh. Around eight-thirty."

"It's a plan," she says, and just as we're about to split at Chase Street, she stands on her tiptoes and pecks me on the cheek, more formality than emotion.

"See you," I mumble, and then she disappears behind Mrs. Saperstein's symmetrically-trimmed juniper hedges.

Now, I'm slogging alone. Just another block-and-a-half to Fairfield Lane, and all five-feet-ten-inches of me is being anchored down by a backpack full of emotional anvils. *Nice going, Ethan Conners. You can body-check an Evanston winger halfway across Lake Michigan, but you can't spill the sordid truth to a skinny, seventeen-year-old motormouth who'd sell you down the Skokie River the day she meets a college guy that doesn't play hockey.*

I turn north on Fairfield and angle a shortcut through the Rosenbergs' dandelion-infested front lawn. Nobody's outside right now and that's a good thing. I'm not looking for company.

I skulk toward the front door of our four-bedroom colonial, steamed at Dad for ruining the first half of summer and hating myself for stupidly prolonging the misery. Guess that's why I told Shoshana I'd call her first, figuring it would be better *not* telling her in person. I mean, if I'm gonna crash and burn, I'd rather not give her the satisfaction of watching me slither.

That's not exactly being socially smooth.

But right now, that's Ethan Conners.

Chapter Two

"YOU'RE WHAT?" SCREAMS SHOSHANA, and I'm thinking there's no way a trill that loud could audibly penetrate my cell's tiny earhole.

"Trust me," I scream back, spraying angry saliva all over my snazzy, new Galaxy S-III display screen. "It wasn't my decision."

"I can't believe this!" she hollers. "The cabin! Rivky's Fourth of July party!"

"Maybe your dad can rearrange it until after I get back from—"

"Look, *E-than*," she interrupts, totally condescending. "October, November, December, January and then all the way till June. Count 'em, Ethan!"

"You mean—?"

"Nine friggin' months! Never batted a lip, Superjock. Two years—kept my mouth shut."

"Look, Shosh. It's the last thing I expected. But my dad's right."

"Right?"

"About international competition helping my chances."

"I don't care about—"

"Well I *do!*" I scream, and then slam my bedroom door shut, which I probably should have done two minutes ago.

"Does it matter this is our last summer together?" she scolds. "All you care about is hockey, Ethan."

"Oh yeah?" I counter. "For a Jewish girl you're pretty darn ignorant about cash."

"Take that back, Ethan!"

"It's not all about *you!*" I holler. "There's a full-boat at Ferris State on the line. That's like twenty-five-thousand a year if I make the team."

I hear her huff, and then the phone pretty much explodes in my ear.

"Shoshana?"

Total silence.

"Shoshana?" I call out one last time, like I don't know she's already hung up on me. Great.

Social drama. I hate this. Seriously, I had all day to devise a defensive battle strategy against Shoshana Kaplan, but right now, my chest feels like it's been splattered by an emotional grenade that just annihilated my summer. Pathetic.

I exhale deep. I'm so emotionally whacked that I let my body lean backward like a human Eiffel Tower until I finally crash hard into the mattress. Of course when my head hits the pillow, my green, knit *kippah* explodes off my scalp, goes airborne, and lands somewhere in the dusty labyrinth behind my headboard. Unbelievable.

Guess what? I'm not budging. My body's perfectly molded into this spaghetti-stained Macy's comforter, so I'll just fish the *kippah* out with the blade of my hockey stick later.

Like much later.

Like maybe tomorrow morning before *Shacharit* prayers. Better yet, school's out so maybe I'll sleep in. Maybe I'll just blow-off morning prayers altogether. Maybe—

"Ethan!" hollers Mom from the other side of my door. "You okay? Sounds like a war zone in there."

"Yeah," I grunt, and I'm thinking how would Mom even know what a war zone sounds like? I mean, the closest we've ever been to a real war zone was when we visited Ground Zero two years ago, unless I'm gonna count our four family trips to Israel. You know, the kind of trips where these armed tour guides lead a bunch of Chicago big shots in single-file lines from our sleek tour buses to the lobbies of four and five-star hotels, even though everyone knows that local security pre-screens our destinations since the last thing Israel needs is an attack on a busload of snotty Americans.

"Just let us know if you want to talk," shouts Mom. "We *are* your parents, Ethan."

"Whatever," I mumble.

Of course, Mom knew I was arguing with Shoshana, but I'm not allowed to bring up her name. That's because Mom and Dad don't believe in casual dating for religious kids, even though I've seen high school pictures of Mom in this sleeveless blue prom dress that would quickly turn Rabbi Klepstein's beard from coal-mine black to Santa-Claus white.

There's something else. Dad hates Shoshana. He calls her *The Criminal*, and I'm pretty sure he's referring to that night last March when Shoshana gouged the blades of my brand new Bauer X-40s into the California Avenue sidewalk, just because our playoff game against Lake Forest went into double-overtime and I was three hours late to Elisheva Goldstein's *Purim* party.

Guess Dad's got a point.

I'm just too cool to tell him.

But this time, it's probably best to let Shoshana stew. That's because *I* messed up. I mean, Shoshana's been talking about Wisconsin forever, and I've totally ruined her summer plans, so I'm not gonna blame her.

Still—we're talking *full scholarship*. It's what every senior prays for. And every parent's dream, too. The stakes are enormous. Shoshana's *got* to understand.

Or maybe not. Real sobering, I think to myself as I flip on my side, my eyes gazing at these evening streaks of burnt-orange sun peeking through parallel slits of my bedroom's dusty mini-blinds. Yeah, the cleaning lady's definitely been shirking.

Stay on point, Ethan. And the *point* is Shoshana. I swear my mind's vacillating back-and-forth, kind of like the way Coach Paulson paces the bench when we're killing a penalty in a tied game late in the third period. Look, Shoshana's got every right to be sore.

Just wish she wasn't such a bitch about it.

"Ethan!"

"Everything's okay, Dad."

"Just checking," he hollers, and then I hear him hopping back down the stairs. Perfect.

I figure I'm safe from further parental interrogation, so I reach for my MP3 and jab the plastic buds into my lobes. There's a Scorpions ballad airing on the Loop. *Still Loving You.* Real sweet and emotional, the singer exuding this totally insane passion. It's making me wonder why I don't feel those kind of romantic earthquakes when I'm with Shoshana. Attraction? Maybe. Ballad-like love? No way.

But that doesn't get me off the hook. You know, this Maccabi hockey thing. Seriously, I can't blame Shoshana for going off the deep end. She's pissed, big-time, probably kicking herself for letting me buy her that slice of Tel Aviv pizza at the Academy's Spring *Purim Shpiel* two years ago. I swear, I wasn't even thinking about landing a girlfriend that night, though Shoshana looked totally incredible—her tight, black sweater and gray, knee-length pencil skirt totally pushing the Academy's dress code, but hey, it was *Purim*, and everyone knows the annual *Shpiel's* not exactly a school-sanctioned event.

Still, I should have been up-front with Shoshana from the start. I mean, who ever heard of an Orthodox guy playing hockey in a public high school league anyway? Poor Shoshana.

When the Scorpions song fades to commercial, I perk my head off the pillow. Wow! That song. Those killer lyrics. When did *I* ever become so sentimental?

"Ethan?" Darn. It's Mom and Dad knocking on the door.

"Come in," I grunt.

Mom starts staring at my head. "Where's your *kippah?*" she says.

"I've got enough problems," I mumble.

"Look son," says Dad, shuffling toward the bed, his blue eyes waxing compassionate. "I know this puts a tiny dent in your summer."

Tiny dent? Okay, I believe with all my heart that Hashem has a plan for every Jew. Rabbi Klepstein even says that we're not supposed to question God's path in our lives. So right now, I'm wondering if I should keep my mouth zipped and blindly submit to Dad's decision.

No chance.

My head explodes off the pillow. "This whole tournament's stupid," I protest. "I'll be competing against *Jews*. It's not like NCAA hockey."

"It's ice time," says Dad, staring at me like I'm an idiot.

"Looks impressive on your resume, too. Anyway, the *goyim* at Ferris State won't know. Just tell 'em it's an international tournament. Yeah, sounds good off the lips. Real good."

"Your father's right," chimes Mom, nodding. "It's a small sacrifice for your future."

Sacrifice, I think to myself. I'll tell them about sacrifice, starting with the Academy. Like those ten-hour days. Like Rabbi Klepstein's totalitarian dress code. Like there's a total of sixty girls in the *entire* school. Sixty! And I hear about it every week from my neighbor, Mike Culvertson, too. Yeah, Mike's a public school junior who's always boasting that there's a thousand girls at Lake Shore High School. Thing is, it's true! I saw for myself when I tagged along with him to a couple classes last year at Passover break. I think that's when I started hating Mike.

I look up, then beam real nasty at Dad. "Fine, we're going," I snap. "When are we leaving?"

"*We're* not."

"Again, Dad?"

Mom stresses her eyebrows into black, hairy worms, and then gives me this stare like I'm supposed to know what's going on. "Uncle Joseph," she says.

"Uncle Joseph?"

"Hip replacement June 28," mutters Dad, shaking his head.

"You know he'll be eighty next August," hisses Mom, like I'm supposed to remember a detail like that when my summer's in total shambles. "Think he's gonna be driving himself out of Northwestern Hospital?"

I can see where this going and it's not going the way I want, so I quickly change the subject.

"Fine, I'm traveling solo." I give them this weak, half-smile. "Guess it'll be cool rooming with some new guys anyway."

Mom slowly removes her gold-rimmed glasses. Bad sign. "Ethan—"

Dad cuts her off. "You're not staying with the team," he blurts.

"What?"

"Tel Chai Youth Hostel's ninety dollars-a-night per guy," he says. "Waste of money. Got to arrange transportation, too."

"So where—?"

Mom butts in. "Chana Borochov's."

"Borochovs'?"

"You remember, Ethan. Chana's my best friend from Columbia. You met her at your *bar mitzvah*. She lives in Kiryat Shemona, a couple miles from the rink."

"And where's Kiryat Shemona?"

Dad sighs.

"It's a small town up north," explains Mom, double-glancing at Dad for support. "Look, Ethan, I'll give it to you straight. It's not exactly the kind of place to visit on tours. Small, run-down and terminally poor. But Chana would just die if she knew you were up there and *not* staying with her."

My teeth start plowing symmetrical anger rows into my bottom lip.

"Gonna be fine," nods Dad. "Borochovs' got a couple of kids your age."

"Yeah," says Mom. "Chana raves about her sixteen-year-old daughter. You're probably not gonna want to leave," she jests.

"Sure," I nod back, thinking this is one piece of information Shoshana doesn't need to know.

"*In-ter-na-tional* tournament," mutters Dad, like I don't know the word. "Gonna make you a scholarship lock."

Mom nods. "It'll be good for you."

"The scholarship?"

"The trip. Kiryat Shemona," she says, using her fingers to sweep a pile of pretzel crumbs off my dresser. "When you were born, I organized lots of important *chesed* projects for the town. Gonna be nice to see the place for yourself."

"Cool," I retort, even though right now I don't want to hear any more stories about Mom's Twentieth-Century charity stuff.

Dad's forehead creases serious. "A little roughing it's good for the soul, Ethan. Makes you appreciate America."

"Whatever," I say, and then give him that look, reminding him that he's messed up my life enough for today.

"It's only for ten days," says Mom, practically reading my mind.

"Which happens to include July Fourth," I counter.

"A week out of your summer," spouts Dad. "Remember, training camp starts right after Labor Day, and you better believe the walk-ons are aching for a chance."

"Dad—"

"Or maybe you're just not hungry for the scholarship, Ethan. That's fine, don't mind your old man. I'm sure Oakton will be happy to have you."

That's *community college* he's talking about, which pretty much ends the conversation.

"Fine," I growl.

"You'll survive," scorns Dad, and then he and Mom lope out of my room.

I take a deep breath and plop my spine back down on the mattress, resigned to accept my fate, convinced that God had this all planned out for me anyway. Sure, it was Dad who loved hockey and helped bust my butt to make it this far. But it had to be divine will that Friday nights in Chicago were prep basketball nights so hockey never conflicted with Shabbat. Dad said it's always been this way, ever since the sixties when the Bulls played on Fridays and the Blackhawks skated on Wednesday and Sundays. Whatever. I'm just glad the high school hockey schedule worked so well for an Orthodox guy.

And that's going to be a problem next year at Ferris State. The NCAA, I mean. Seriously, I checked last year's schedule and there were a couple games on Friday nights. When I mentioned this to Dad, he said it was all arranged for me to stay near the rink on those nights so I wouldn't have to drive anywhere on Shabbat. Apparently, that satisfied Mom because she's never said a thing about it. Either that or she's totally oblivious.

By the way, did I mention that Dad's really a Reform Jew in disguise? You know, a twice-a-year-at-synagogue

Jew when he met Mom at Columbia. *Bar mitzvah* at thirteen, atheist the morning after. Trust me, I've heard stories about how Grandma and Grandpa Blumenthal nearly disowned Mom until Dad studied for a year with Rabbi Sherwitz who reluctantly pronounced him a *learned* Jew. Mom's parents hated our last name, too. To this day, Dad's always reminding people that *Conners* is a corruption of *Groenerz*, courtesy of a derelict civil servant at Ellis Island.

Still, I wonder if I could ever do what Mom and Dad did. You know, partaking in a virtual intermarriage. Look, I may not always pray three times a day, and sometimes I forget to bless after meals, but when it comes time to settle down, I just couldn't imagine marrying a non-observant Jewish girl.

Back to reality. And right now, reality is that my post-high school summer is majorly messed up. Stirring, I lift my head off the pillow, while my eyes prowl these thin, graying shadows leaking onto the plaster ceiling. I'm not trying to sound narcissistic or anything, but it's like, this social stress is killing me. You know, all this turmoil over scholarships, relationships and cancelled Fourth-of-July plans. Suddenly, I feel my fists tightening, and now I'm wailing on my pillow like it's an Evanston winger that just slashed the crap out of our goalie. I hate it when I'm not in control.

Funny how everyone thinks I'm so smooth. That *Ethan Conners has it made.* Thing is, I sometimes wish I could take a shot at garden-variety normalcy. Away from this hockey fast-track. It's like, I never had a chance to think for myself, cause Dad's had this scholarship thing planned since was I was a first-year squirt playing on Skokie's AAA travel team. And it was a social hardship, too. Dad never let me skip a single practice, which meant no Sunday matinees in the winter. No pumpkin-picking during October tryouts. I even had to miss Jake Epstein's winter *bar mitzvah* bash at the premier water park in the Wisconsin Dells. Ouch.

Seriously, I could use a year off. Even six months. Okay, a semester.

But it's not gonna happen. The scholarship is Dad's dream. And God commands me to honor my father.

Anyway, I'm not so sure I'd survive an entire winter without my regular fix of ammonia-scented ice rink refrigerant wafting through my lungs. Sick.

Well, that's the positive spin. Which lasts all of two seconds. Truth is, my life's like a shattered pane of Skatium plexiglass right now, and there's nothing I can do about it.

Miffed, I start doing this headlock thing to my pillow, fling it against the bottom of my dresser, and then grin like a kindergartner at the delayed explosion of grayish-brown dust wafting sideways over the floor.

This is definitely *not* the way I wanted to start my summer.

Chapter Three

SO I'M HALFWAY TO ISRAEL, 35,000 feet over the Atlantic, and this El Al flight is packed tight. Lots of families, tons of kids, and even a few guys garbed in Maccabi sweats. Naturally, I've been trying to weed out the hockey players, looking for anyone my age flaunting an NHL hat or jersey. There's this zit-faced Samson with a Brian Urlacher buzz cut back in 32C who looks pretty ferocious. Just add skates and I'd love to pair with him on defense.

It's actually pretty late to be jetting to Israel. I mean, our first practice is Monday evening, which is officially tomorrow according to Chicago time. Problem is, there is no tomorrow because it's already midnight in Israel and this flight lands in Tel Aviv at 7:00 in the morning. *Monday morning.* Talk about jet lag! Look, if you're not *shomer shabbat,* you leave on Friday or Saturday and get a couple days to recover. But that's not an option for an Orthodox guy like me who can't travel on the Seventh Day. Sure, Mom and Dad could have booked me on a Thursday flight, but I wasn't cool about spending Shabbat with the Borochovs since I don't really know them. Bottom line — the connecting flight from O'Hare to Newark boarded at six in the morning, and after doing the mental math, it looks like I'll have been sleepless for twenty-three hours when we land in Tel Aviv. Stupid.

And I'm nervous, too. I mean about my equipment. God, I hope my gear makes it through. I've never flown with my hockey bag before, and I'm suddenly sweating waterfalls just thinking about my stuff getting lost. I'm not talking clothes and underwear. It's my skates that worry me. It takes a couple months to break in a pair of Bauer X-40s, and it's not like there's a ton of hockey pro shops in Israel. And my sticks — a pair of Christian pro-flex aluminums topping a cool bill apiece. Don't let me down, El Al.

I arrive on-time five hours later, and the first thing that happens is this mouthy Ben Gurion passport officer blitzing me with a verbal once-over like nobody's business.

"*Hockey kerach,*" I explain, trying to bust through her brain that I'm here for the Maccabiah hockey tournament, though her *Sephardic* complexion tells me she's never heard of the sport before.

"*Eyn mishpacha b'aretz?*" she counters, as if every visitor is supposed to have family in Israel. "*Mah oseh po b'levad?*"

I guess I can't blame her for getting suspicious, since I'm an eighteen-year-old guy traveling alone. But my family's history is squeaky-clean, so she's got no choice but to finally wave me through. I'm actually thinking I should apologize to the rest of the line behind me, but instead I bust forward, figuring I better beat feet to the luggage claim before someone confiscates my oversized bag of reeking hockey gear.

My heart's pounding out of my chest as I slalom my way down this polished-tiled corridor. I probably look like a sleepy-eyed purse snatcher the way I'm cutting around slow-moving bodies and oversized umbrella strollers, but Dad would simply obliterate my existence if my hockey gear got pilfered before I even left the airport.

Five seconds later, I blow out this mammoth exhale as I spot the baggage terminal straight ahead. I can see my sticks circling around the conveyor belt, and the CCM bag's coasting shotgun. Nice. My stuff's on the opposite side of the slow-moving loop, so I skulk over to the corner and start scoping out the locals. Lots of people standing around, but I've got no idea if the Borochovs are here.

"Ethan!" hollers this frizzy-haired lady with a phlegmy voice and a mouthful of white teeth like rectangular sugar cubes. I give her a double-take, figuring it's got to be Mrs. Borochov, though she looks a lot thinner than the last time I saw her at my *bar mitzvah.*

"Thanks for meeting me," I say, just as this dark-haired, bronzed and slender teenage-beauty steps right next to Mrs. Borochov. Intrigued, I crack a half-smile at her, and she responds by flicking her long eyelashes twice and then gives me this fiery scowl that could melt a downtown block of Lake Street elevated support beams.

"You've never met my daughter, Danit," chirps Mrs.

Borochov, smiling. "She kept me company on the drive. Left about four in the morning."

Guilt trip, but I force a grin anyway.

"Hi," I say, turning toward Danit, and when she grunts in response, I'm figuring it definitely wasn't her idea to tag along.

"Danit, help Ethan with his bags while I pull the car around front."

"That's okay, Mrs. Borochov," I protest, but she's already busting for the exit, and now it's just me and Danit standing around like a pair of wax zombies.

"I'll get my stuff," I say, and then dart over to the carousel, happy to ditch Miss Personable if only for a couple minutes. I swear, she's kind of scaring me, and I don't think she likes that I'm donning this *kippah* either.

A couple minutes later, I'm back with gear in tow. Meanwhile, Danit's staring lasers at my hockey sticks like she's never seen a pair of Christian aluminum Pro-Flexes, which I'm guessing is true.

"*Bo eetee*," she growls, like she just came out of surgery. "Come."

I'd rather not go anywhere with this jezebel, but I figure I'm six thousand miles from home and it's not like I've got a choice, so I follow her past the glass exit doors and inhale my first drag of outdoor air for the first time since leaving Chicago almost twenty-four hours ago.

"How far?" I ask, trying to make conversation.

She doesn't acknowledge me. Bitch.

I keep following her past this triple-wide line of cabs, buses and vans idling along the circular arrival driveway. The humidity's stifling, the heat's sucking the breath right out of my lungs, and I'm desperate to unload this thirty-pound bag of disgusting hockey gear.

Finally, Danit angles toward a dusty old compact car with an open hatchback. It's a Hyundai, something called a *Getz*, but I've never seen that style in the States.

"That's everything?" asks Mrs. Borochov.

"Yeah," I say, panting.

Now, Mrs. Borochov's gawking at the sticks like she knows they won't fit.

"*Naseem b'cholon*," mumbles Danit, insisting there's room through window. She's spilling scowl everywhere as she opens the front passenger door and then jams the Christians blades-first into the back seat.

"*Mah o-sah!*" hollers Mrs. Borochov. "What are you doing?"

Danit edges herself into the front passenger seat, rolls her window down, and carefully guides the stick-tops through the opening. Of course, that means there's a pair of six-inch-long butt-ends angling through the window, and all these people are staring, which makes me feel like a total idiot.

"I'm sorry," I say, though it's definitely *not* my fault. I mean, you can't even find cars this small in Chicago.

"Don't worry," reassures Mrs. Borochov, and I can tell she means it. But when Danit has to keep wriggling her skinny butt around my pair of Pro-Flexes and then starts fumbling her fingers to untangle the seat belt strap, I know I'm not scoring any points with her.

Welcome to Israel, Ethan.

Chapter Four

FOUR HOURS LATER, we're still motoring north on Highway 90, and I'm thinking Mrs. Borochov somehow missed the border and we're driving through Lebanon. I mean, I'd never been farther north than Tiberius, and we passed there nearly an hour ago. Antsy, I sneak a peek at Danit up front, and she's still slouched immobile in the passenger seat with these black, MP3 earbuds glued into her lobes. She hasn't said a word since we left Ben Gurion, and that's irking me too.

Mrs. Borochov edges her head sideways and gives me this quick glance. "Welcome to Kiryat Shemona," she chirps, as we approach the first traffic signal in the last twenty minutes.

"I've never been this far north," I say, relieved that we're still in Israel, even though I'm staring melancholy at this ugly sidewalk strip mall of tiny falafel stands and grungy pizza shops.

Mrs. Borochov catches me gazing. "Yeah, it's not exactly where I envisioned myself when your mother and I graduated Columbia," she says. "But after nineteen years, I couldn't dream of living anywhere else. Gritty, tough working-class people. Mainly Russian and Moroccan Jews."

"Not your typical, suburban crowd," I joke.

"Right on," she says, nodding. "Kiryat Shemona started as a development town—a defensive outpost sandwiched between Lebanon and Syria. Lots of terror in the early years."

She cuts a left at the next intersection, and then we ascend this hilly rise toward a cluster of dingy, high-rise apartment buildings.

"But not so much anymore, Ethan," she continues. "Things have been pretty quiet since we crippled Hezbollah in the 2006 war."

"You know, I always remember hearing stories about Mom's Kiryat Shemona *chesed* projects," I say, even though I'm suddenly clueless on the details.

"*Chaval*! That *was* a horrible tragedy," croons Mrs. Borochov, like I know what she's talking about, which I don't.

"Believe me, we've had more than our share of martyrs over the years."

"We should only know good things, Mrs. Borochov."

"Yes we should, Ethan."

I'm staring through the dust-caked front windshield, and from the corner of my eye, I see Danit stirring. She's etching her spine tighter against the seat, and I'm guessing that means we're almost at the Borochovs' house, even though all I see are these sooty, high-rise apartments.

"Your father e-mailed the team schedule," says Mrs. Borochov. "We'll get you to the Canada Centre tonight at 6:00."

"Canada Centre?"

"About seven or eight minutes north of town," she explains. "Built by the Canadian Jewish community. Nice pool there, too."

"Sounds great," I mumble, though what I really want to do is crash. I'm craving sleep and now I'm thinking I probably should have left Thursday. I mean, there's no way I'm gonna be ready to hit the ice in six hours.

A couple of sharp turns and then we pull into a rutted, blacktop parking lot behind this six-story apartment building framed in ugly, light-brown cylinder bricks which reminds me of those pictures of the old Cabrini-Green projects in Chicago. Seriously, everything's spelling ghetto—open windows, mismatched drapes and graffiti all over the place. Wow. I can't believe I'm going to be staying in a dump like this. My friends at home wouldn't believe it, and I'm thinking I should e-mail a picture to Shoshana, just to pound it into her narcissistic skull that I'm definitely *not* on vacation.

Mrs. Borochov slows into this half-shaded parking spot and kills the ignition. When she pops the hatchback, I'm quick to fish out my black CCM bag. Meanwhile, Danit's already slipped out the door and she's hotfooting it out of here. Bitch.

I start balancing my bag across my shoulders, then slog around to the passenger side and reach for my Christians.

"Ouch!" I holler, nearly blistering my fingers on the white-hot aluminum shafts. Thank God that didn't happen to Danit or she might have socked me.

"Ethan?"

"It's fine, Mrs. Borochov."

Okay, right now I'm hot, tired and miserable, and I'm also getting annoyed by these intense stares from a squad of little kids playing kickball in the parking lot.

"*Tee-staclee!*" shout a couple of ragged-looking brats, gaping wide-eyed at me and my stuff like I'm Duncan Keith or something. As if they would even know.

Turning away, I keep following Mrs. Borochov toward the back entrance, and I'm hoping they live on a low floor because there's no way I'm setting foot inside any elevator in this building, assuming there's even a functioning one to begin with.

"Let me help," says Mrs. Borochov, as she pulls open this rusted, steel door.

"It's okay," I insist, my voice echoing loud through the murky, concrete hallway, which kind of reminds me of one of those prison documentaries we watched in sophomore social studies.

"Third floor," she says, and as soon as I hear it, I purposefully bust past the elevator towards the grimy, cement stairs before she even has a chance to talk me into riding up. I hate elevators.

But this stairwell's no better, and the hike up sucks away my breath like a summer afternoon in Miami, though it probably doesn't matter since I'm already caked with a week's worth of sweat.

"Turn right," bellows Mrs. Borochov, as I hit the third-floor landing. "Number 305."

Slowing, I let Mrs. Borochov take the lead, and when she finally pushes open the steel apartment door, a fresh burst of cool, dehumidified air punches me right in the face.

Feels great.

"Shalom!" hollers this middle-age man. The guy's sporting bushy, gray hair framing a pair of pale cheeks, which ridiculously belies the scorching, Israeli summer.

"Ethan," says Mrs. Borochov. "This is my husband, Yuri."

"*Na-eem ma-ode*," I say, giving him the formal Hebrew *hello* and extending my hand.

"Nice to meets you," he answers in reasonable English, his eyes totally drawn to my green, sweat-stained *kippah*. "We glad you come stay with us."

I'm peering around the apartment like a starving panther. Yeah, this family is totally secular. I mean, there's not even a *mezuzah* on the front door post.

"Yuri, *la-azor lo*," orders Mrs. Borochov, telling him to help me.

Mr. Borochov doesn't even grimace as he grabs my overweight CCM bag and plunks it down in the first room on the right.

"Sit down, Ethan," says Mrs. Borochov, directing me to this plush, brown living room couch. "You need something cold? Coke? Water?"

"Coke's fine," I answer, lunging my spine tight against the thick cushion and seriously trying to relax my road trip-stiffened muscles.

Mrs. Borochov scampers into the kitchen, and I'm suddenly all alone for the very first time in the last twenty-four hours. Eyes gazing curious, I'm surprised how nice and cozy this apartment's decorated. The place has ambience. I might even describe it as *serviceably-spacious*, especially considering the building's scuzzy exterior appearance. Seriously, it looks like a decent three-bedroom spread with a functionally-sized kitchen, and a living room-dining room area large enough for a Shabbat table seating twelve. Nice balcony, too. Yeah, the whole setup reminds me of my aunt and uncle's condo in Morton Grove, minus the sick aroma of Uncle Issac's stale cigar smoke.

A couple minutes go by and then Mrs. Borochov comes back out, all smiles. She's balancing this wooden tray crammed with fresh-cut fruit and a fizzy, cold glass of cola. I'm starved, and I'm about to grab a fistful of purple grapes, but then Danit and Mr. Borochov bust back into the living room and decide to park themselves on these matching, white-cloth reading chairs directly across from me.

"So you tell me about this sports thing," asks Mr. Borochov, his bushy eyebrows flashing curiosity.

"Hockey?" I say, and then I take a sip of soda. As I press the glass against my lips, I see Danit staring at me with these evil, dark eyes, and it's making me super nervous. There's a tense second or two, and now I'm feeling totally awkward, like I'm going to spill or drool or something like that.

"Yuri's family made *aliyah* when he was a baby," explains Mrs. Borochov. "Hockey's pretty much unknown in Israel — at least until the past few years. Trust me Ethan, it's not like in the States."

I want to tell her I've pretty much figured that out. You know, being gawked at like a pale-faced circus freak wherever I'm lugging my Christians.

"So you play hockey for Maccabi tournament, no?" says Mr. Borochov, scratching his scalp. "Where does Jewish kid learn sport like this?"

Now, all three of them are staring, and I'm starting to cake with perspiration.

"Been playing since I was six," I explain, my fingers nervously massaging this cold glass of cola. "Nearly seventy-five ice rinks around Chicago. Everyone skates."

"Your mom tells me you've locked up a full college scholarship," brags Mrs. Borochov. "Just because of hockey."

"*Mah zeh* scholarship?" queries Danit, and now I turn and start eyeballing her, ready to check out her reaction.

"Scholarship means the college pays for everything," explains Mrs. Borochov. "Tuition, room and food."

Bingo! Danit's mouth drops to her cheap, leather sandals, her eyes spilling rays of envy. She looks up, trying to steal my gaze, but I catch her in the act and then she snaps her head sideways, like she's embarrassed that I caught her checking me out. Nice.

I turn back to Mr. and Mrs. Borochov. "Look," I say, nixing away a smile. "It's not guaranteed. I mean, I've worked real hard to get recruited, but I've still got to make the team. That's why Dad sent me to Maccabiah. You know, to work on my game and everything."

"But it's honor to be selected," insists Mr. Borochov, and then he stuffs this fistful of purple grapes into his mouth like a chipmunk hoarding seeds in October.

"Yeah," I say, nodding.

"Ethan's one of the best Jewish hockey players in America," boasts Mrs. Borochov. "That's the only way to make Team Maccabi USA."

Great. They're all gawking at me again, and now this annoying fly starts buzzing my cheek. I know everyone's watching, but I'm too nervous to shoo it away with my hand, so all I can do is twitch my eyes and it's not doing a bit of good.

Mr. Borochov glances at his watch. "What time you need to be in Metula, Ethan?"

"Metula?"

"You, know, Canada Centre."

"Oh, probably by—"

"Six o'clock," interrupts Mrs. Borochov.

"Five hours? And you just fly from Chicago?"

"Yeah," I answer, not blaming him for being shocked.

"*Meshuga!*" exclaims Mr. Borochov, telling everyone I'm crazy. "You must get rest. Danit, show Ethan to Lior's room. You don't worry, Ethan. We wakes you by five."

"Thank you," I mumble, and then follow Danit into the ceramic-tiled hallway.

"Here," she grunts, stepping inside this compact bedroom which is about half the size of my room at home. There's a pair of twin beds forming an *L* against the white-plaster walls, and my gear's on the floor next to the bed made up with this ugly, green comforter and single, beige pillow. Bed, Bath & Beyond, anyone?

"Lior returns this evening," miffs Danit, expressionless, like she's never had an American house guest, which I'm thinking is probably true. She turns, and is just about to close the door, so I decide to pepper her with this innocent question.

"How old's Lior," I ask.

"Eighteen, like you," she huffs, and I'm wondering what I ever did to piss her off.

"Look, Danit—"

"He's in Haifa," she snaps. "Full day of pre-army testing."

"Army?"

"Don't worry," she blurts, her brown eyes angled condescending. "You get your hockey rest."

Slam! The door explodes in my face, and I'm figuring I've just been totally disrespected by a sixteen-year-old drama queen. Now, my mind's raging, my fingers curling into a pair of angry, tight fists. Look, it's not *my* fault that Maccabi USA wants me. I never asked to be born in America. And the scholarship—what am I supposed to do, drown in guilt? Abandon the last twelve years of 6:00 a.m. practices, 7:00 a.m. games, and a hundred-thousand miles of car rides and bus trips? Not a chance.

I suck some air-conditioned oxygen and fester, standing here like Joel Quenneville with one foot on my hockey bag and both lips pursed tight in frustration. I don't get it. I'm supposed to be cool. This kind of stuff never happens to me in Chicago. *No drama, remember?* Suddenly, I feel myself getting steaming angry, and I'm fantasizing about telling Danit off. It goes something like this:

Tramp. You think you're so hot, prancing around in that tight, black top like a Middle-Eastern skank. Real nice, Danit. That's exactly why God brought your family back to Israel — so you could disrespect Orthodox guys and dishonor yourself and the entire Jewish people. Sure, the Torah means nothing to someone like you. But I'll bet you can memorize every racy plot from those third-rate novels rotting in the back corner of your closet. Yeah, I'd love to see your ignorant, stuck-up smirk as Shoshana Kaplan shreds you to pieces dissecting ancient Rashi texts, while the best you'll ever do is rattle off the winners from five-year-old reruns of Survivor. You're a piece of work, Danit Borochov.

Wow, that felt great. Invigorated, I fling my Nikes over my scummy hockey bag and sink myself into this green comforter. Nice. I can literally feel the tension exiting my muscles as a gentle equilibrium courses pleasant through my veins. It's great being physically at ease, but that just means my mind's free to dance a thousand thoughts at once. And it does. Mainly hockey, of course. You know, like who's gonna be my defensive mate? Is our goaltender solid? I mean, that's why I'm here. And as I bust a peek at my sturdy aluminum Christians leaning against Lior's bedroom wall, I'm starting to get excited about the tournament. Seriously, it's just about time to rid my mind of Danit's teenage dramatics and focus on business.

My business is defense.

And bringing home Dad's Maccabiah gold.

Chapter Five

BY THE TIME MRS. BOROCHOV KNOCKS on the bedroom door, I've already been awake for nearly an hour. Just a quick catnap—nothing heavy. I mean, I know I needed a decent sleep, but I was too anxious to let myself crash, because the possibility of Danit having to wake me from a deep slumber was simply too embarrassing to fathom.

"Just checking, Ethan," hollers Mrs. Borochov. "Yuri's gonna take you to the Canada Centre at 5:00."

"Thanks," I blurt, yanking open the door so she sees I'm ready to go.

"You sleep well?" asks Mr. Borochov as he passes through the hall in a white, sleeveless t-shirt like my Grandpa Mort wears.

"Oh yeah," I answer, half-lying. Like I'm gonna tell him I spent the past hour scheming a way to get back to Ben Gurion Thursday night so I could bail out of here before the weekend.

"Okay. Twenty minutes we go. Plenty to eat and drink. You take."

"Thanks," I say, and then unzip my gear bag, making sure I've got everything. It's weird. I mean, I've dumped this bag a thousand times before inside trunks, buses and hotels, never once worrying about forgetting a piece of equipment. But now, I'm practically freaking as I hurriedly investigate every pocket and zipped compartment, even though there's probably no way to replace anything around here anyway. *Steady yourself, Ethan.*

Three minutes later, I'm pretty sure I've got all my socks, pads and blade covers accounted for. Relieved, I step in front of this rectangular dresser mirror, using my fingertips like a makeshift comb to brush back swaths of greasy, dark hair. I've got this anal grooming routine where I clip my *kippah* snug just behind the geographical midpoint of my head, and then I cover up with this vintage Blackhawks cap that Dad bought at the Chicago Stadium during the 1992 Stanley Cup finals against the Pittsburgh Penguins. Jake Epstein says they hadn't even invented aluminum flex-sticks back then. Talk about hockey stone age.

I stall for a second and start thinking heavy. What I'm thinking about is that I need to do one more thing before practice, which I better do right now so I don't forget.

I'm talking about a *pick-me-up*, and I've got to have it this instant.

I reach into my carry-on bag, fish out a No-Doz pill, and gulp down the whole thing without any water. Look, there's no way I'm gonna chance a disastrous first impression just because I'm probably the only *shomer shabbat* guy on the team and couldn't leave the States until Sunday. Scholarship's on the line.

Now, there's this powdery taste on my tongue. But I've got to admit that I'm feeling pretty psyched as I grab my sticks and sling the CCM bag over my shoulder. I hustle into the hallway, and when I cut through the living room, I see Danit slumped like a zombie in this cushy chair, her brown eyes zoning at the flat screen like it's a Vizio version of her best friend forever. She's got the volume way too loud as this blond-haired bimbo cracks unintelligible jokes and the studio audience laughs on cue every five seconds. Brainless.

"Good luck, Ethan," she spouts, without turning her face from the screen.

"Thanks," I mutter, as I follow Mr. Borochov out the front door. I am *so* not playing Danit's mind games.

When we get to the Hyundai, Mr. Borochov's looking seriously puzzled at my sticks.

"Don't worry," I say. "We just slide the ends out the front window."

"Okay," he answers, and then watches me jam my Christians into the hatchback. I can tell he's relieved when I finally thread the butt-ends outside the half-open passenger window.

"I'll see about leaving them at the rink," I promise, as Mr. Borochov backs the Getz out of the parking spot and cuts a right toward Tel Chai Road.

"Yeah, we no like America, Ethan. Gas too expensive and parking very difficult. Everyone in Israel drives small car."

"It's no problem," I insist, and then I start thinking of home. You know, all those three-car garages filled with shiny, four-wheel drive status symbols. Sometimes I don't get it. It's like, Abraham the Patriarch was all about modesty, but I guess that doesn't apply to American Jews. God, I hope I'm not hanging in Israel with a chip on my shoulder. Because if I am, Danit's gonna sense it. Maybe she already has. Maybe that's why she's been sizing me up with these ice-cold stares that could freeze-dry a salt water flounder.

We're just about a minute north of town when Mr. Borochov points excited to the right. "Tel Chai Youth Hostel," he shouts. "Maybe other players stay there, too."

I'm peering through the glass, barely able to make out this sprawling campus of modern low-rises which resembles a suburban high school more than a motel. I'm guessing that's where I would have been staying if Dad wasn't so cheap.

"Looks nice," I say, nodding hard though I'm not exactly sure what I'm looking at. Whatever. I can't let myself get too excited because the Borochovs are putting me up for the week, and I'm not looking to insult their hospitality. But the truth is, I'd give anything to be staying with the other guys. And as far as I'm concerned, $90-a-day is a small price to be rid of Danit's condescending stares.

"Maybe you get ride back to Kiryat Shemona with other hockey players, Ethan. If no, we come pick you up. *Eyn bayah,* no problem. Just ten minutes from town."

"I'll see, Mr. Borochov."

"But we come to game tomorrow," he says, his mouth grinning with excitement. "I'm much curious about this sport."

I give him a smile and then slouch deep into the seat. I'm anxious about meeting my teammates, and it's not helping that I'm getting car-sick as I stare through the front windshield at this two-lane ribbon of blacktop curving through trees and shrub. I start sucking in long breaths and try exhaling nice and slow.

A minute later, we pass a brown road sign with big, white letters in Hebrew and English, indicating that Metula's only five kilometers away. My brain quickly makes the conversion to miles. Just about 2.5. Kick in quick, No-Doz.

"This is as far north as you get in Israel," says Mr. Borochov, like he's a tour guide or something. "Route 90 from Eilat to Metula. Longest road in Israel. About eight hours' drive from Egypt to Lebanon."

"Interesting," I say. I mean, I guess that's a good piece of information to know in case I ever return to Kiryat Shemona with my wife and kids, which I'm not planning to do.

Now, Mr. Borochov's smiling to his ears. "You see, Ethan?"

"No."

"Canada Centre ahead."

He hangs a left up a hilly side road, and I'm twisting my head, gazing though leafy forests of spruce and pines for my first glimpse of the famous Canada Centre. Total elapsed time since Danit disrespected me — about thirteen minutes.

"Nice place," croons Mr. Borochov. "I hear there's two pools plus ice rink."

"Cool," I say.

He coasts into the parking lot and then hangs a hard left along this concrete driveway fronting the main entrance. There's one large building about three stories tall, and toward the left, I can see a giant indoor pool, complete with high-dive and waterslides. Still not sure where the ice rink is, but when I glance toward the front door, I notice this small army of high school-age guys toting oversized hockey bags and shiny, aluminum sticks. Big, tough-looking jocks, some of them donning Boston Bruins and L.A. Kings jerseys. Americans, I hope.

"Thanks for driving," I say, forcing a smile at Mr. Borochov even though I'm totally nervous.

"You call us if you need ride, Ethan. No problem."

I nod, then carefully extract my sticks. When Mr. Borochov pops the hatchback, I yank out my CCM bag, swing it quick over my shoulder, and start busting up the sidewalk. Weird, this time no one's giving me rock star stares, and I'm actually missing the infamy of hustling a pair of one-hundred-dollar Christians across God's sacred soil.

I feel this combination adrenalin-No-Doz rush as I strut toward the front door. Dozens of hockey players, parents and siblings are milling around the entrance, and it's totally reminding me of the Skokie Skatium on a perfect, summer afternoon.

Except it isn't.

No, this time I've finally arrived at the holy hotbed of ice hockey. A place called the Canada Centre. And according to Dad, this *is* the Promised Land.

It's where Ethan Conners fulfills his promise to Dad.

It's where Ethan locks up the full-boat to Ferris State.

Chapter Six

THE FIRST THING I SEE when I skulk through the grungy, locker room hallway, is this spiritless line of teenage guys standing single-file next to this steel-skinned door. There's a cheap, MACCABI USA sign scotch-taped to the gray-painted doorframe, and it's pretty obvious I'm in the right place. Not exactly NCAA-style accommodations.

I pick up my head and force out this half grin, making sure not to offer any more emotion than absolutely necessary. Doesn't matter. It's like I'm pretty much invisible to everyone, except for these two guys in the middle who I catch beaming at the fringes peeking out of my shirt and then they check back at each other like *I'm* in the wrong country or something. There's this sudden, silent awkwardness as I approach the end of the line, but then the locker door slowly squeaks open and we all start trickling inside like a brood of stick-toting ducklings.

"*Bra-cheem ha-ba-eem.* That means *welcome*, to you Hebrew illiterates," spouts this stocky, fortyish guy with a husky voice like the inside of a fireplace. He's exuding the appearance of a perfect *schlub*, totally unshaven, garbed in a wrinkled, Team USA warm-up suit, and eyeing every one of us with contempt as we trickle into this musty, cramped locker room. I'm figuring he's our coach, even though he reminds me of the kind of creep Mom always warned me about when I'd be shooting baskets alone at Potawatomi Park on summer nights. I always thought Mom was paranoid or something, but this guy looks like the real deal. Sorry for misjudging you, Mom.

"I'm Coach Weiss," the guy croons, real hoarse and abrasive. "You can call me *Coach* or *Sir*, but nothing else. We absolutely clear, gentlemen?"

I can tell this guy's a total jerk. Still, I'm thinking it's best to stay inconspicuous, so I promise to just sit and listen.

"You're home, boys," he snickers, grinning like a drill sergeant on induction day.

Okay, I'm trying not to pass judgment, figuring a lot of

these kids have already spoken to Coach Weiss on the phone. But not me. All I know is that Dad somehow connected Coach Paulson with this Maccabi lunatic, and that's how my summer got ripped off.

"Gonna be a tough, packed week of hockey," warns Coach Weiss, spraying saliva jets through his teeth. "Yeah, they put us in Pool B with France and Russia, so I'm expecting nothing less than the best game from all of you. Got it?"

"The Russians?" whines this lanky kid with the biggest Bauer hockey bag I've ever seen.

"What about it?" roars Coach Weiss, his face ready to explode in anger.

Suddenly, total silence. I roll my eyes sideways and see the lanky kid turn away intimidated, a glaze of nervous sweat growing along the sides of his forehead. No messing with this coach.

"Just two wins and we're guaranteed silver," snips Coach Weiss, looking down at this sheet which I'm guessing is Team USA's roster. "And I'm warning you now, none of you's returning to the States without a medal hanging from the scruffs of your bony necks. Do we understand each other?"

"Yes sir," we collectively grumble, and I'm just staring at Coach Weiss like he's a bad dream or something. Yeah, this guy's a real piece of work. Kind of like a breathing time-warp from one of those black-and-white war movies. God, I hate barking drill sergeants. I despise the whole culture of dehumanizing recruits. No way I'd ever join up.

This kid sitting next to me turns. "Pretty crass," he whispers.

I nod. "If I wanted to enlist, I wouldn't have busted my butt for a D-1 scholarship," I hush back.

My heart drops when I peek up and see our fire-breathing coach staring dragon eyes right through me. Great. Now he's gonna chide me in front of everyone for not paying attention. I look down and cringe, my muscles tense as steel cables. Just get it over with.

But it doesn't happen.

"Maccabiah's allotting ninety minute practice slots

and we're gonna use every last second," snickers Coach Nightmare, eerily diabolical though I'm thanking God he quit staring me down. "Yeah, your high schools swore you're the very best, and guess what? I'm kind'a looking forward to seeing for myself. Yup, that's *ninety* minutes to impress me."

There's a tall guy with a Kings cap rolling his eyes toward me like this can't be happening. I shake my head back at him, acknowledging our pain.

"Get to know each other while you're suiting up," orders our dictator-in-training. "See you on the ice in twenty."

There's about a dozen of us in the locker room, and we're all staring in disbelief, absolutely silent until we're sure Coach Jerk has vacated the premises.

"Who dug this guy up?" smirks the tall guy in the Kings cap, which pretty much solidifies him as the captain in Team USA's pecking order.

"And my girlfriend thinks this is a vacation," cracks this stocky guy with a curly, brown afro that reminds me of those old John Travolta movies from the seventies. "Seriously, all she's worried about's that I'm gonna hook up with a bronzed, Israeli babe."

"Yeah, show me," laughs the lanky kid, who I'm thinking can't be a day older than sixteen. I'm also assuming he's our goalie since he's flanked by these white, rubber-scuffed Mission Commander SE leg pads and a pair of giant, Easton goalie sticks that probably caused an acre of clear-cut. "Last decent female I saw was this bitch at the Ben Gurion passport counter," he says.

"Here's a secret," says this guy to my left who's wearing a Philadelphia Flyers t-shirt and waxing totally sarcastic. "There's this Olympic-sized pool about a hundred yards down the corridor. Just tell some bikini-clad sweetie you're from Team USA, and she'll be hooking up with you quicker than Jonathan Toews wins an overtime face-off."

That gets the room going, the laughter easing our anxiety. Bonding, I guess.

But it's obvious Coach Weiss is all business, so everyone starts attacking their hockey bags and spreading out stuff which hasn't seen a speck of daylight this side of the Atlantic. We're cramped—the locker room's totally undersized—nothing but a square cubicle with wooden benches affixed to the concrete walls and a long rack of rusting hooks for a dozen shirts or jackets.

There's a steady chorus of mumbling as we start strapping up shin guards and lacing skates tight. It's weird being with totally new players, and I can't stop my head from popping up every few seconds to steal gazes at the guys. Look, I'm no Don Cherry, but I think we're packing a strong team. Just twelve skaters and a goalie, but that means two sets of forwards and defensemen plus a floater each way, which translates to plenty of ice time. Dad's gonna love this.

Changing quick, it's kind of interesting that for the very first time, I'm not harboring the tiniest sliver of self-consciousness when some of the guys beam surprised at my *kippah* and stringy *tzitzit*. I mean, we're a team of Jews, even though there's no chance any of these guys are *shomer shabbat*. Whatever. Maybe I'll have the guts to explain to everyone that we're here in Israel because the Torah says we're supposed to be here. Maybe I'll even tell them that the Torah requires us to wear fringes.

Or maybe not. Yeah, it's probably best not to wax Biblical just yet, at least not until I establish myself as Team Maccabi's Twenty-First Century Bobby Orr.

Once everyone's laced up and ready to go, Kings-Hat-Guy starts taking control of the locker room. "Guess we should all reveal our names," he says. "I'm Jake Lowenstein from Birmingham."

"As in *Alabama*?" jests the guy in the Flyers jersey sitting next to me.

"Hey, we got ourselves a geography genius," spouts the Kings-Hat-Guy, and when he lifts his butt off the bench, I swear he's about six-foot-four in skates.

"What's with the L.A. cap?" I chime, curious.

"Just like the colors, *Menachem*. That's all."

A couple guys snicker at the Orthodox jibe, and I'm thinking it's pretty sad that the others don't get it.

"Name's Ethan," I growl, aiming my Christian blade on a beeline toward his crotch. "Ethan Conners."

That pretty much garners his attention—and the respect of everyone else in the room. *Nice move, Ethan.*

Another thirty seconds of clockwise formality, and now, everyone's like family. And not all East-Coasters either. Turns out the guys hail from all corners of the United States. There's Mitch Zuckerman and Jonathan Spevak from southern California, Ryan Mills and Aaron Klein from New Jersey, Noah Richman from somewhere in Florida, Ari Freedman from Denver and Jeremy Bloom from Philly. That's our offensive line-up, if I got it right.

On the blue line, there's me, Lowenstein, Matt Pinsky from Milwaukee, Clayton Gross from St. Louis and Benji Schneider from Nashville. Funny how all our defensemen come from the Central time zone. Oh, by the way, our goalie, Mendy Siegel, is this Minnesota monster who's sweet on reminding us that he broke all the Minnesota high school records for goaltending excellence at this prep school near St. Paul. Didn't ask Siegel where he's playing college, but if half of what he says is true, I'm hoping he's not skating in NCAA's Midwest Conference.

"You guys ready," says Bloom, bouncing anxious on his blade tips. "Room's starting to stink."

"Let's scram," agrees Lowenstein. "Zam's probably off the ice."

We hurry out of the locker room and start snaking single-file through this long, musty hallway. I'm bringing up rear, and when I scan ahead, all I'm seeing is this disorganized, motley crew of American jocks cloaked in a dozen different colors, mainly NHL-replica sweaters. I'm figuring Coach Weiss is gonna hand out our game jerseys later, but it would have been nice if Maccabiah could have given us matching practice pullovers.

"Aren't you a sorry-looking set," barks Coach Weiss, taking mental notes as we penguin along the mat toward the rink door. "Oh, don't tell me—you all just got off the plane."

Of course, when he says it he's staring right at me, and I almost want to tell him it's true.

But I don't.

"Give me ten!" screams Coach Sadistic, and we all know that means ten hard laps. Thank God I'm riding this No-Doz high.

"This isn't even fresh ice!" wails Siegel as he cuts his goalie blades into the soft, gray surface, and the second I push off behind him, I'm thinking the very same thing. Ruts and grooves everywhere, this ice reminds me of Warren Park's open-air rink *after* a Sunday morning pickup game. Guess they don't have personal injury lawyers in Israel. Whatever. I'm just promising myself to be real careful so I don't blow out a knee—and the Ferris State cash.

Five minutes and a dime of laps later, I'm sucking serious wind and my legs are like kosher jelly. I'm figuring everyone else feels the same as we coast counterclockwise and nervously await Coach Horror's next version of torture on ice.

"Scrimmage!" he yells, and that's practically Hanukkah in July for all of us. "Time to find out exactly what I've got."

Coach pairs Lowey and me defensively with Zuckerman, Mills, Spevak and Klein up front. That means the other side's got the extra blueliner, so I'm thinking Coach is checking out Lowey and me as a defensive pairing, which would be really nice since Lowenstein's obviously been pegged as our number one defenseman.

"Siegel, take the net behind Lowenstein and Conners," barks Coach Weiss. "Don't worry, I'll be switching up the guys so everyone gets a chance to shoot your way."

Naturally, this won't be an official, keep-the-score scrimmage since we've only got one goalie. Still, it's a heck of a lot better than busting balls doing mindless skating drills and high-performance calisthenics.

"Get ready!" crows Coach Weiss as he skates to the players' bench and grabs a biscuit from the puck bag. Then, he does this Aaron Rodgers wind up and chucks the rubber all the way to the far corner near the empty goal.

"Game on!" he screams, and suddenly, Pinsky's skating the puck out of his defending zone. I've got adrenalin pumping and my leg muscles are tightening anxious as I read the play and dig my blades deep into this rutted ice sheet. Can't worry about tearing up my knee right now.

Pinsky's real steady on his skates, displaying strong puck control as he weaves horizontally for an opening. When big, Jeremy Bloom circles through the neutral zone, Pinsky dishes the puck right on his tape, and Bloom doesn't lose a stride. Nice. Bloom's all heads-up as he diagonals toward my defensive zone, so I'm playing extra conservative. I don't know this guy, and there's no way I'm making the first move. But Lowey's showing cool aggression and rushes at Bloom, forcing him wide to the right. Bloom hesitates, and then totally surprises me by meekly dumping the puck into my corner to the right of Siegs.

"I got it!" I scream to Lowey. My head's up as I corral the puck and set up shop behind the net, using the goal as a screen to give my forwards time to circle through the neutral zone. *Great poise, Ethan.*

But Bloom won't commit. He peels back, letting centerman Noah Richman forecheck. Now, Richie's busting right at me.

"Bring it out, Conners!" screams my center, Johnny Spevak, totally impatient.

No one knows it, but I'm stalling behind the goal, just so I can set up for an Israeli *savoir-faire*. Talk about risking it all on the very first shift! But I can tell Richman's gonna bite, so I wait for him to charge me behind the net.

"Go, Conners!" yells Siegel, totally nervous. "Bring it out!"

I'm not moving.

"Conners!"

Richman lowers his shoulder, and now he's busting blades right at me. I'm totally bug-eyed, and trust me, my heart's pumping through my ribs as I calculate the precise moment for my Chicago-style flash. I wait until he's five feet away, and then, at the absolute last second, I ricochet the puck off the bottom of the goal frame and spin sideways, feeling Richie's breeze as he takes the bait and whiffs on his check. I've seen Jaromir Jagr make this move a dozen times, and it works just as well for me. I mean, Richman's six feet past the puck before he ever knows what happened. *Sucker!*

Now, I'm in the clear, so I start skating the puck around the left side of the goal. Richman's far behind me, which means it's a five-on-four going our way. Beautiful. When I start attracting traffic, I pick up my head and see Zuckerman uncovered on the right, so I feather this Gretzky-like pass seventy feet into the neutral zone, leading Zuks perfectly. Zuks vacuums the biscuit in stride, and with a cool flick of the wrist, powers the puck just under the cross bar, right into the back of the open goal.

"I'm gonna hang you by those fringes," murmurs Richman, brushing behind me near center ice. He's majorly pissed, and I'm loving every bit of it. Score one for Chicago!

When Lowey gives me a wink through his facemask, I'm feeling this rush of emotion spilling through my veins. Yeah, *number two's* now mine to lose.

"Try it again!" blasts Coach Weiss, as he chucks another rubber disc into the very same corner. "Remember, we ain't the Minnesota Wild. Stay away from the dump-and-chase!"

Now, the entire northern border know's that Richman's gonna set up a shot on this rush. That's good news for me, because it means their defense has to quarterback a play from the blue line, leaving Lowey and me to concentrate on clearing traffic in front of Siegs, which is a lot easier than being chased into the corner by a rushing forechecker. And just as I think that, Richman carries the puck across our defensive blue line and then peels the rubber back to Pinsky on the left point.

"Forwards, move!" hollers Coach Weiss, prompting Bloom and Richman to weave circles through the slot. Meanwhile, Pinsky slides the puck to Schneider on the right point, and I'm figuring he's gonna crank a one-timer, so I focus on the floating offensive traffic in front of Siegs while I keep position just to the right of our goal.

Suddenly, big Bloom parks himself two feet in front of Siegs, practically daring me to move him away from the crease. But I'm not backing away from anyone, so I start nudging Bloom hard with my shoulder, fighting for body position. It's a real physical battle, and I'm not concentrating on anything else. That's why I don't see Schneider freeze our left-winger with a pump-fake, and then dish the puck cross-ice to Pinsky who's got this twenty-foot cushion of open shooting lane.

"Shot!" screams Siegel, and the instant he says it, I jerk my head towards the point, barely making out Pinsky's towering backswing. That's when Bloom decides to body me sideways with his hip, and now I've totally lost sight of the puck which I know is coming my way, and Dad's always telling me that a good defenseman never loses sight of the puck.

Suddenly, *thud*! I feel this sick sensation of frozen rubber on bone.

I'm pretty sure my right leg's severed.

There's this split-second delay before my right ankle buckles, and now the pain's sucking the oxygen from my lungs. When I hear Coach Weiss trilling nervous blasts from his whistle, I'm thinking this has to be *serious*.

"Where'd you get it?" quizzes Lowey, eyes flashing concern.

"Side of the ankle," I moan between clenched teeth, and any hockey guy knows that's the unprotected sweet spot between the skate boot and shin guard.

I'm thinking this is what it feels like to be shot. Hurts like heck, but my mind's telling me it's just the first shift of the first practice. That's why I refuse to bleed pride, so I get up real stubborn, bearing as much weight as possible on my left skate and hobbling to the bench before the other guys get a chance to offer help.

"Easy, Ethan," orders Lowey from the ice.

I pretend to ignore him as I step off the rutty surface and park my butt on this long, plastic players' bench. Ripping off my helmet, I start gazing at my right sock, and I'm getting scared just thinking about the damage underneath. Look, I've been downed before—what defenseman worth his salt hasn't? But this time, the stakes are astronomical. Visions of a retracted scholarship suddenly haunt my brain, not to mention the fact that I may have traveled all this way and pissed off Shoshana for nothing. Yeah, I'm already imagining the phone call to Dad. You know, when I tell him I got injured on my first practice shift, and he's got to re-book me, *with penalty*, on the next flight out tomorrow. *That* would sting.

Here comes Coach Weiss, his eyes beaming like an ER surgeon at my leg.

"Unlace your skate," he orders.

"I'll be okay," I lie.

"Now, Conners!"

I nod timid, then slip off my X-40.

"Let's have a look," he grumbles, as I slowly roll down my sock.

"It's nothing," I insist, staring at center ice.

There's a couple seconds of total tension, and I can practically feel Coach Weiss's molars grinding together like fresh sheets of coarse sandpaper.

"You're done for today, Conners."

Now, my stomach free-falls.

"Just go home and ice it," he grunts. "And be ready tomorrow. You and Lowenstein are my starting blueliners."

I look up, and he's actually giving me a half-smile. I'm loving his diagnosis.

"Okay, Coach," I nod, suddenly feeling like I've been handed a new lease on life. Then, I mumble a quick *thank you* to God, pick up my Christians, and glide slow across the ice.

"Sorry Ethan," says, Pinsky, opening the rink door leading toward the locker rooms.

"I'm a shot-blocker," I smirk. "Nothing gets through to Siegel this week. You can count on that."

"Like your style," he says. "Like it a lot."

Chapter Seven

A COUPLE HOURS LATER, I'm plastered like a hoser rag doll across the Borochovs' living room couch, icing my right ankle with a semi-frozen water bottle while the flat screen Vizio's blasting some Israeli knock-off of American Idol. Of course, I've got no choice but to stare like a zombie at the television and it's pretty disheartening that I'm struggling to follow along, especially with twelve years of private, Jewish school under my belt. But the phlegmy consonants are spewing fast and slurred, not at all like those perfectly enunciated dialogues that Mrs. Rimzel made us listen to in the Academy's intermediate Hebrew class.

When the show goes to commercial, Danit starts ambling around the kitchen with her classmate, Gila. Now I've only known Gila for about twenty-five minutes, but it's pretty obvious she's not like the girls I'm used to seeing in Rogers Park. No, Gila dresses like she just walked out of a Victoria Secret magazine shoot, and it's actually making me uncomfortable. Naturally, neither Danit nor Gila have attempted to say a word to me, but they have been scoping me out like I'm this lazy, exotic specie of suburban-American brat, and I'm thinking they'd both have a serious attitude change if they ever blocked a Matt Pinsky slap shot with their skinny ankles. Bitches.

I catch Danit eyeing me.

"Hey," I say, turning.

She smirks. "You want we call doctor?"

"No."

"Ice skating dangerous," giggles Gila, and right now it's all I can do not to whip this half-melted Neviot water bottle right at her gold-studded nose.

"Don't hurt anyone with those sticks," mocks Danit, and then she and Gila disappear into the hallway. I swear, if they snub me one more time —

Just then, the front door squeaks open. It's Danit's older brother Lior, and this other guy about the same age. I'd met

Lior for just a second when I got back from practice, and he was totally cool. Glad he's here.

"Hey, Ethan," says Lior. "Ron and me's going for a falafel run. You coming?"

I'm thinking traipsing through Kiryat Shemona can't be good for my ankle, but I'm only here for a week, so it's stupid to waste the night away in front of this idiot box. Besides, my water bottle's leaking all over the couch.

I reach for my Blackhawks cap. "Let's go," I say.

"We come too!" hollers Danit, and when Lior nods in approval, I'm thinking it's going to be a long night.

Fifteen minutes later, we're at this outdoor food drag, all five of us parked in filthy, plastic chairs while we wolf down baskets of five-shekel falafel specials and watch traffic cruise up and down Route 90. It's a total pig-out fest and no one's talking. Real awkward, even a bit tense. I mean, it's like falafel idol worship or something. Seriously, Lior's got this two-handed grip on his pita like a football center readying a shotgun snap. To his right, Ron's sporting thin, tan streams of tahina sauce dripping from his lips. Even Danit's showing no shame, inhaling lettuce shreds like a ten-year-old sucking up spaghetti noodles. Gross.

I turn between swallows, eyes staring up and down the sidewalk. Man, this place is grimy. Litter's everywhere, waxed wrappers and cigarette butts accumulating nasty in the curbs. Even worse, this whole, football-field-long block of falafel and pizza shops is offering up a stinking haze of disgusting odors like a Labor Day barbeque on steroids. It makes Devon Street seem like paradise.

I'm spacing to the left when this movement captures my gaze. Mice or rats, I think. *No, wait!* It's a family of black and gray kittens. Real puny and emaciated, not like our overweight housecats in Chicago.

One of the kittens senses me staring. It gets startled, cries out a pathetic *meow*, and then the whole litter scampers into the bowels of this concrete jungle like chipmunks by a backdoor stoop. This is *so* third world.

Danit peeks her head up. I turn too. Coming our way is

this greasy-haired girl with bronzed skin almost as dark as the black spaghetti-strap top barely covering her slinky frame.

"Ayelet!" hollers Danit, and the girl responds by smiling to her ears. She shuffles right for our table.

"Shalom, Ayelet," greets Lior, reaching backward to grab an empty plastic chair. "*Na lashevet.* Sit."

"*Todah,*" she says, and I'm loving her throaty voice. Then, she beads her dark eyes right at me. "*Me zeh?*"

"This is Ethan," answers Lior. "He's from America."

She grins, giving me a half-smile, and I'm making sure not to stare at anything except her mocha-skinned face. I mean, no one dresses this way unless they're at a private beach. At least that's how it's supposed to be.

"*Yafe,*" giggles Gila, winking at Ayelet.

Look, I'm not gonna lie. Danit's friends are exotic. Totally exotic. But in the back of my mind, I'm wondering if they've actually got fathers at home. It's not like I'm saying they should be donning long sleeves and even longer skirts like Shoshana and the Academy girls, but hey, they're still daughters of Zion, and they should at least learn how to honor themselves.

"You got girlfriend?" quizzes Danit right at me, as another pair of perky, tanned girls wave at her from the sidewalk.

"Sure," I say, unconvincingly.

"Moran! Racheli! *Bo alenu!*" shouts Danit, telling them to come over.

Oh God, these two are stunning. Drop-dead radiant. Nicely sculpted with long, dark hair spilling over their shoulders, the taller one showing evenly-spaced blond highlights. They're both wearing these charcoal-black halter tops and matching tight, mini-*mini* shorts that must have been painted on their legs. No exaggeration.

Okay, let me put it this way—it's bad enough that Danit, Gila and Ayelet could never make it through the Academy's front door dressed as they are. But Rabbi Klepstein would have these other two girls arrested if they came within fifty feet of the Academy's *parking lot*.

"*Na la-hakeer,*" spouts Danit, as the smoking twins

approach. "*Zeh* Ethan Conners from Chicago."

I crack a smile. "*Na-eem ma-ode*," I say, testifying to my intermediate Hebrew proficiency. "*Ani m'sachek hockey kerach b'tournament Maccabi*," I explain, telling them I'm here for the hockey tournament, and I'm hoping they know what *tournament* means because I've got no idea how to say it in Hebrew.

"*Mah?*" retorts the taller one, like she didn't comprehend a single word. Now, I'm totally embarrassed.

But then, Danit mouths something quick and suddenly, both girls smile.

"Hello," says the smaller one, her voice raspy, but confident.

"Uhh—hi," I stutter, and then my tongue pretty much freezes. *Not cool, Ethan.*

God, I wish she would say something back. *Anything.* But she doesn't. Instead she just smiles wider, and now I'm trying not to stare at her teeth because her overbite is slightly awkward. Too bad—she's got a nicely-featured face, but I'm guessing orthodontics isn't the top concern in a downscale town like this. Maybe that's why she's showing so much skin.

The weird silence continues, and I'm not liking it. I mean, all of Danit's friends are suddenly gaping my way, probably trying to figure out why an American hockey player's holed up in this gritty town smack in the middle of summer. Whatever. The real problem is that I've never hung out with a crowd of girls dressed like secular, sorority skanks, and I'm thinking they'd all pretty much freak if I pulled off this Blackhawks cap and exposed my *kippah*-plastered head.

I turn back to the group and accidentally lock gazes with Ron, who's sucking up the rest of his pita like a beaver with a tapeworm. Suddenly, the entire thing vanishes through his teeth and then his Adam's apple starts pulsing real slow. Disgusting.

"Ethan, we want that you see something," buzzes Lior, spitting out specks of salivated pita with every *s*. "It's important."

Yeah, right. But I don't have the guts to tell him that this town's a glorified dump, and nothing here could possibly interest me.

"Just up the hill," spews Ron. "*Katyusha* destroys my family's flower shop."

Except that.

"C'mon, Ethan!" barks Lior, nudging my shoulder.

"We no want to come!" remonstrates Danit, eyes flashing indignant.

"No problem," says Lior. "We'll catch you girls later."

More walking can't be good for my swollen ankle. But it's not like I've got much of a choice. Aggravated, I get up slow, fish a pair of hidden falafel balls from the guts of my pita, and wolf them down quick.

"Follow us," says Lior.

I scope back to make sure I didn't leave anything on my chair. Of course, our table looks like a garbage dump, and I'm thinking we should clean up this mess, but everyone's already scattered and I'm not the least bit surprised.

I can hear Danit and her friends giggling like mindless seventh-graders as they skulk over to this newsstand, staring down the glossy covers of some trashy fashion mags. Meanwhile, Lior and Ron start hustling me in the opposite direction along Tel Chai Road, right past this old, beaten-up strip mall and a filthy, outdoor fruit market. We hang a left and then ascend a crumbling sidewalk along a hilly street just a block or so from the main drag. That's when the neighborhood starts resembling a war zone, the wood and steel skeletons of mangled buildings reminding me of old pictures from the Great Chicago Fire.

Ron smirks. "What do you think, Ethan?"

My eyes bulge. Is this guy for real? I don't even know what he's staring at.

"My *abba* bought this place twenty years ago," mutters Ron, real somber. "Best flowers in the north."

Confused, I'm guessing part of this rubble must have been his family's flower shop or something. "What happened?" I ask.

"Rockets!" snaps Lior, peeved.

"From Syria?"

"Syria?" Now Ron's face is spilling shock.

"It's the *Hezbollah* from Lebanon!" shouts Lior.

Great. I've just confirmed to everyone that I'm an idiot.

"You *meshuga*," hisses Ron.

Lior nods. "That's because American Jews don't see this stuff on their five-star tours of Israel."

"That's not true," I rant, lying.

"No matter," utters Lior. "Now you know for yourself. See how we live in border town like this. Yes, *Eretz Yisrael* is not such a place of milk and honey. At least not up here."

I want to ask Ron if his family rebuilt somewhere else, but I'm scared to press the issue and even a bit ashamed to hear the miserable truth. Meanwhile, we're all staring at this relic of destruction, and I'm thinking there's a total disconnect between me, an Orthodox Jew living the cushy life in modern exile, and these gritty, secular Israelis holding on in the face of horrible adversity.

Go figure. Three-times-a-day I'm praying about returning to God's land.

Ron and Lior are living it.

And it's definitely not all milk and honey.

Chapter Eight

NEXT MORNING, I'M WATCHING the first slivers of dawn peeking through Lior's bedroom window, and it gets me thinking that now's a perfect time for some quick, *Shacharit* prayers on the balcony. Rolling off the mattress, I slip on my nicely-folded blue Polo, fish out my *talit* bag, and skulk like a thief into the dark hallway.

Perfect. The apartment's dead silent, and that's good, since I'm not looking to have the Borochovs freak out when they see me wrapped in *talit* and *tefillin*.

I tiptoe into the kitchen, gently pull on the sliding glass door, and carefully step over the scuffed, aluminum threshold. The attached balcony faces north and it's not very large, but there's enough room for an old barbeque and a pair of plastic lounge chairs squeezed between the brick wall and the rusty, metal overlook. Curious, I step to the edge, lean my gut against the peeling-brown rail, and scan my eyes back and forth like an owl hunting for dinner.

The town's a total pit. But the natural scenery's not bad. This place is basically in a valley, enveloped by the green, Manara Hills just a half-mile to the west, and the Golan Heights off to the east. If you look at a map (which I hadn't but Mr. Borochov explained it this way), Kiryat Shemona is sandwiched between mortal enemies — Lebanon, just a mile northwest, and Syria to the east. Actually, Mr. Borochov told me the Syrian border used to be much closer until Israel captured the Golan Heights in the Six-Day War. Whatever. I'm from Illinois and the only enemy we have is the Green Bay Packers in upstate Wisconsin. That's about all I know of war and terror.

Wow, it's hot on this cement balcony. I'm noticing how quickly the sun rises over the Golan, and I suppose I shouldn't be surprised that this valley's broiling so early in the morning. Now, I'm having second thoughts about *davening* out here, not really looking to sweat up my *talit* and *tefillin*. It's humid, too. Real nasty. Yeah, maybe the Canada Centre *is* the place to be, even though it's so bone-chilling cold in that dump.

Zoning, I turn my head toward the west. One good thing about those cliffs is the way they swallow up the western sun. It's like, by 7:30 in the evening, the valley's already in shadows, probably an hour earlier than the rest of Israel. Reminds me of summer afternoons at Uncle Mayer's coach house in the long shadows of the John Hancock tower, except that my uncle's property is probably worth more than this entire town.

Suddenly, the glass door slides open. I turn quick and there's Danit, dressed like a slob and downing a can of Diet Coke with the style of a long-haul driver at a Tennessee truck stop. When she swallows her last swig, I'm pretty much expecting her to chuck the empty can over the rail.

She doesn't. I'm surprised.

"Nice view," I say, making small talk.

"*Ha nof, ya-fay*," she grunts.

At least Danit actually agrees about the nice view. But it's weird that she responded in Hebrew. It's like she's programmed to play these mental mind games, and I'm thinking, *you knew I was out here, so why bother following me if you don't want to talk?*

"Great neighborhood," I mumble back, intentionally staring into her chocolate, half-Russian eyes. Now, I'm playing the game too.

She catches me glimpsing, but I don't care. Then, she purses her lips, furrows her eyebrows, and beams at me wicked.

"Something wrong?" I spout, and I can tell she's shocked by my direct interrogation. Hey, I'm picking up Israeli style quick.

"Arrogant Americans!" she miffs in English, shunning her head.

"What?"

"You stare at my city disgusted, like it's some kind of slum to you!"

"What are you talking about?" I say back, knowing this is about to get heavy.

"Listen," she scorns, still refusing to face me. "No one tells you to come here and pity us."

"What are you—?"

"We're a border city," she rants, and then she turns at me wide-eyed, like a rabid coyote in a California Avenue alley. "Government founded Kiryat Shemona as refuge town for immigrants. And we're first-line defense in case of Arab attack from Lebanon. That's why Americans look down at this place."

"You're psycho!" I rave in her face, not caring that I've probably startled half the neighbors.

"You Americans should—"

"Get real!" I scream, cutting her off. "Look, Danit, I don't care about your pathetic little town. Got it? I'm just here for the Maccabiah tournament. And the sooner I get out of here, the happier everyone's gonna be."

There's a deadly silence, and then Danit starts turning slow, eyes flashing hurt. I'm thinking she's about to apologize.

Instead, she spits at my shoe.

Now *that* practically stops my heart. I'm too shocked to say anything back, and she takes full advantage of my hesitation by spinning sideways and huffing inside. Wow. I'm figuring Danit thinks I just offended *her*.

You know, I've never actually seen a girl spit before. I mean, a thing like that could never happen in Rogers Park. Just thinking about Shoshana doing it makes me laugh. Impossible.

I do a one-eighty toward the railing and stare back out at this lovely city. Okay, at least I'm alone again, but I'm feeling totally uncomfortable. Seriously, I'm pretty much trapped on this balcony because as much as I want to blow-off praying and get back inside the air-conditioned apartment, I'm just too shell-shocked to skulk into Danit's terrain. Peeved, disgusted and seriously angry at Dad, I'm suffocating in some kind of self-conscious anxiety, like there's this poisonous cloud enveloping me in arrogance, and every Israeli sees it. Guess that's why I'm feeling emotionally isolated, and the truth is, I wish Coach Weiss had scheduled an early-bird practice so I could ditch this cylinder-blocked mental ward. Yeah, right now, I'd give anything to be at the Canada Centre.

But that's fantasy. And loitering in this early-morning heat is God-awful reality. Still, I've got to start *Shacharit*, so I force a peek through the sliding door. Great, the kitchen's empty and dark. There's no Danit and I'm figuring she's back in bed like everyone else, so even though I'm not in the mood for *davening* right now, I succumb to Orthodox guilt, throw my *talit* over my head and wrap *tefillin* quicker than those *yeshiva* guys at the Touhy Avenue Kolel. I'm rushing because I'm panicked at being caught, and sweat's already pooling under my head strap before I even start the eighteen benedictions. Talk about sprinting through the *siddur*.

Ten minutes later, I'm practically peeling my prayer shawl off the base of my neck. Seriously, that was probably the quickest *Shacharit* this side of the Jordan. I'm sweating and pretty much miserable, but at least I've fulfilled my obligation. And even though I'm cramped in this cement balcony stained mean with Danit's evaporating spit, the truth is that I'm still within the Biblical borders of Israel, where a Jew's prayers are supposed to merit the utmost respect to *Hashem*, our creator.

Davening in the Promised Land. A real comforting thought for sure. Just wish there was some way to explain it to a secular, sixteen-year-old vixen named Danit.

Chapter Nine

IT'S 10:00 A.M. AND I'M BACK IN BED, crashed in a virtual coma atop this flimsy mattress. Bad news—I think Danit put some kind of curse on me during our bickering on the balcony, because right now, my right ankle's throbbing. I can't move. Throw in the second day of jet lag and I'm pretty much a zombie—spoiled American-style of course.

"Ethan!" Ron and Lior burst into the bedroom, startling me from a pleasant daydream. You know, the kind where it's a beautiful autumn Sunday at Ferris State, and I've got nowhere to go, with all the time in the world to get there. "Get up, Ethan!"

Reality check—I'm a prisoner of Dad's scholarship fairy tale, wasting my Fourth of July holed up inside this puny, ratty apartment that wouldn't even qualify as a Section 8 rental on Chicago's South Side. Seriously, the living room air conditioner sounds like a lawnmower's empty fuel tank gasping for fumes, and this tiny bedroom reeks from a combination of moldy plaster and putrid hockey bag. *Welcome to the third world, Ethan.*

"Let's go!" bosses Ron, totally impatient, like it's *his* apartment.

"Where?" I protest.

"The city pool, dumb-ass. Opened five minutes ago."

"No way," I counter, wishing I could explain how an eighty-mile-an-hour slap shot's torture on the ankle.

"You're coming," scolds Lior.

"Listen, guys," I moan, lifting my head off this paper-thin pillow. "You know what it's like being hit—?"

When I cut myself off in mid-sentence, they're both staring at me like I'm speaking Aramaic or something.

I see Ron peeking at my bag. He's surveying the contents, and I'm wondering if he's oblivious to the stink. Then, he reaches for one of my black hockey gloves and starts caressing the padded finger slits like he's stroking a puppy's head.

"I don't get this sport," he says, eyes spilling confusion. "How long you play?"

"Since I was six," I say, forcing back a yawn.

"Six?" croons Ron.

"Look, hockey's totally popular in the States," I explain. "Probably fifty rinks in Chicago. Every neighborhood's got one."

"It's crazy," chimes Lior, his tanned head bobbing with exaggeration. "*Nu*, I've seen it on the television. Guys flying down the ice, killing each other. It's like soccer with sticks, played on this frozen field."

"Not quite *that* violent," I remonstrate.

"Good to hear," says Lior, smiling sarcastic. "So let's go, Ethan, no?"

"Yeah, okay," I grunt, like there's even a choice.

"Hot girls, too!" brags Ron. "We introduce you as our American friend — the hockey player from Chicago."

He turns to Lior and grins wicked. That's when I know I'm gonna be the bait for their female fishing expedition. Hey, I can handle that.

Fifteen minutes later, we're approaching the entrance to Kiryat Shemona's outdoor water hole, and I'm not impressed. Sure, it's a real large municipal pool with swimming lanes and a pair of faded blue high-slides. But the ambience is *so* trailer park. Trust me, I'm not being super-snobby — that's usually not my style. But this place looks like a cheap time warp from some 1960s movie. I'm talking an old guy parked in a lawn chair, taking admission fees and making change from a tin box atop a plastic card table. And don't even get me started on the locker room — just an old, grimy cavern framed by peeling, wooden beams — the kind of dilapidated dump that the Chicago Health Department would have shut down even before the discovery of chlorine.

"They got working lockers or an office for my phone?" I ask, like the naive tourist everyone knows I am.

"Ehh, no one brings stuff like that here," scoffs Lior.

Great.

"Yeah, they steal everything," nods Ron.

"They?"

"That's why there's no more lockers," he says. "Too much hassle for management."

"Thanks for telling me," I sneer. "Now, I can't go in the water."

"Sorry, Ethan," mutters Lior.

Beautiful. The morning started out like crap and it keeps getting worse. Can't wait to see what the afternoon's got in store.

"C'mon, let's find a spot," says Lior.

I shake my head, then exhale frustrated through my nose. Seriously, this just isn't right. I mean, back home we trust Jews. My cousins in Highland Park never worry about having their cell phones or MP3s stolen at their brand-new municipal water park. But here, in the State of Jewish refuge, there's Jews stealing from other Jews and no one seems to care. It's as if the Eighth Commandment is hopelessly irrelevant in God's holy land.

We slog back outside, and the first thing I notice are all these ancient chaise lounges sporting ribbed fabric caked with decades of yellow sweat and tanning cream. Totally gross.

"Too crowded," complains Ron, eyeing a cluster of mobbed tables near the high-dive. "Just follow me."

I'm not getting it. It's 10:45 on a Tuesday morning, and hundreds of spots are already taken. Doesn't anyone have summer jobs around here?

I'm hustling to keep up with Ron and Lior as they double back toward the shallow section, but there still aren't any vacancies. Seems like the only threesome of empty chairs is way out by the far northern corner next to the kiddie pool.

And that's where Lior's busting. Looks like he's about to stake a claim.

"No good," mutters Ron, his head spinning side-to-side.

"*Mah pee-tome?*" grunts Lior. "You don't like it, you find something better."

That pretty much shuts Ron up, but I'm guessing they're both pissed at me for taking my sweet time crawling out of bed. Too bad.

I'm surveying the scene, my brain spinning optimism. I mean, the kiddie pool isn't Gold Coast real estate, but it's not like we're the only ones parked in this half-acre of steerage. Yeah, lots of bronzed girls soaking up sun like *sabra* solar panels. Lior notices and so does Ron, and they're both smiling. Crisis resolved.

"You stay with the chairs," orders Ron, stripping off his black t-shirt and flaring his caramel-tanned biceps.

"Yeah, no problem," I say, like there's even a choice, and now I'm starting to understand why they didn't warn me about bringing the phone. Real sneaky.

I start lazing on this rutted-vinyl chaise lounge, watching Ron and Lior jet past the kiddie zone toward the Olympic-sized pool which is mobbed thick with hundreds of bodies. Suddenly, Ron accelerates toward the edge and then dives head-first into the water, nearly clobbering an old lady with his flying feet. Wow! If anyone pulled a stunt like that at the Oakton Oasis water park, they'd be instantaneously muscled off premises by a squad of burly lifeguards, no refunds given.

But it's not just Ron. It's everyone. Pushing, shoving and swearing. No manners. No class. Right now, I'm zoning at this day-after-Thanksgiving waterslide line, and it's all cutting and butting. Turning to my left, I'm glaring astonished as a mother or sister — I'm not really sure — ignores this naked toddler who's squatting in the concrete corner and doing his business like it's his private bathroom or something. Behind me, a stoned squad of tattooed teens sporting black-inked *chais* are laughing and passing around this two-foot-high hookah or bong. I'm not about to ask for clarification.

Disgusted, I turn back, close my eyes and give myself up to this Middle-East sun. Thoughts stirring fast, I'm actually wondering where the heck I am, as if this is the same Israel Mom and Dad *schlepped* me to all those times before. Now, I'm figuring they intentionally secreted me from all this riff-raff. You know, just five-star hotels and sanitized half-Anglo suburbs. Maybe Danit's right. I *am* a spoiled American.

A minute goes by, and then I start feeling my whole body

frying like a human falafel on this gross, chaise lounge. Even my *kippah* feels like it's about to combust. Antsy and bored, I fish out the cell phone from my Speedo pocket. No way I'd ever leave it unattended around here, but maybe Ron or Lior will agree to watch it for a few minutes so I could test the water later. That's assuming they ever return to our little island in the kiddie zone.

I'm cradling the Samsung in my palm, the dark plastic warming fast from the almost high-noon sun. Zoning at the screen, I'm wondering how much it would cost to text Shoshana right now. I mean, I'm not the type of guy to pad her bill or mine with international roaming charges. 3:30 a.m. in Chicago—do I dare text her? Do I even want to?

Okay, I plead guilty. I mean, I shouldn't even be thinking about Shoshana right now. Look, I've always considered myself reasonably elevated, but it's just not possible to ignore these bronzed, Israeli girls parading around in the skimpiest bikinis ever. *Willpower, Ethan.*

Bored and sweating buckets at the same time, I'm thinking I should try socializing with one of these teenage beauties, but the thought absolutely intimidates me. Besides, I've probably got nothing in common with these Kiryat Shemonans, except for being Jewish. Frustrated, I exhale long and start sinking back into my chair.

Suddenly, the sun disappears from my face.

"*Atah Amerikayee?*"

Stunned, I glance up over my left shoulder. And standing over me's this prettiest Israeli girl ever. I mean *amazingly, terminally pretty.* She's about sixteen or seventeen, and I'm guessing five-foot-three with liquorice-black hair, mocha eyes and this jet-black bikini showing off a dark-chocolate tan—the kind you'd never see in Chicago.

"Ehh, *ken,*" I say, fighting for words and stalling long enough to plan a follow-up sentence in broken Hebrew. "*Ani gar b'Chicago.*"

She smiles, her overlapping rows of pearly-white teeth glistening sun sparkles like a celestial disco ball.

"*Lo hayitee b'Artzot Ha-breet,*" she says, telling me she's never been to the States.

"*Chaval*," I say, telling her that's too bad, while simultaneously fantasizing that she'll park herself next to me on Lior's chaise lounge.

She does!

"*Mah oseh b'Eretz Yisrael*," she asks. "*Yesh lacha kroveem po?*"

"*Lo*," I say, telling her I don't have relatives here and wondering how I could possibly explain ice hockey to a Kiryat Shemona local. But I have to try. "*Ani m'sachek hockey-kerach b'America. B'shavua hazeh, yesh tournament gadol, Macccabiah, eytzel merkaz Canada b'Metula.*"

She gives me this puzzled stare after I tell her about the Maccabiah tournament. Whatever. I know my Hebrew's not the best. Just ask Mrs. Rimzel for proof.

"*Zeh mi-en-yan* — how you say — *interesting*," she spouts, and then wraps her fingers tight around my left wrist.

Cool. I'm telling this perfect *ten* I play hockey, and now she's pouncing on me like I'm a two-shekel pita special. *Nice going, Ethan.*

I sit up in my chair. "*Mah shmech?*" I ask, figuring I should know her name.

"Shayna."

"Pretty," I say, changing to English. "*Shmee*, Ethan. *Na-eem ma-ode.*"

"Ethan?"

"Uhh — yeah," I stutter, wondering to myself what, exactly is going on here. For sure, Shayna's cute, and she's staring sweet donut holes right through my eyes. Still, I'm not about to trust her, or anyone in this place just yet. That's probably why I'm sliding my fingers across my pocket, feeling for my Galaxy S-III.

It's there.

"Ethan, you buy us Cokes," she bosses, in throaty, broken English.

"Uh — sure," I say, just before she walks her fingers up my arm. "Wait here."

I bust off this sweaty lounge and hustle toward the

concession stand near the front. When I come back a long minute later, our gazes lock and she's smiling *so* pretty.

I hand her a sixteen-ounce Coke.

"*Todah*," she says, and then sucks up a three-second swig through this long, green straw.

I can't let her catch me staring, so I start shifting my eyes back-and-forth, like I'm checking out friends, even though the only people I know here are Ron and Lior, and it's not like I really want them muscling in on me and Shayna right now anyway. But even when I'm faking it, I still have this smoking vision of Shayna imprinted in my brain. Oh, man, she's prime. And that overbite. Real nice, though it would never fly in Chicago. But I'm guessing Israelis aren't so hung up on snobby expectations of soap opera vanity.

I don't like this conversational lull. "Tell me about Israeli life," I say, leaning toward her. "What's exciting in Kiryat Shemona?"

"You," she grins, and I'm thinking English isn't her best subject.

"Ehh—I'm just here 'till Sunday," I explain. "Tournament ends Thursday night. That's if we make it that far."

"*Sababa!*" she chirps, and then she starts stroking my arm the way you'd pet a cat.

It's weird. I've got no idea where this is heading, and I should be basking in the moment, but instead, my gut's telling me that Ron and Lior schemed this whole thing up as a practical joke. Seriously, Shayna doesn't know a thing about me. Not that I don't deserve this kind of attention after suffering through four years of slim pickings at the Academy.

I suck in a long breath of courage. "Maybe we can go out tonight, Shayna." Oh God. I can't believe I've just asked her on date, but everything's moving so fast that it kind of slipped out.

She smiles. "*Sababa!*"

Is that all she can say? Better make sure she's really wants to meet tonight. "*Rotzah l'hee-pagesh b'leila hazeh?*"

"*Ken*, Ethan. *B'eyzo sha-ah?*"

"Seven-thirty — err — *sheva v'chaytzee* in the *canyon* food court," I say, brimming with confidence in my colloquial Hebrew.

She stalls, slurping up cola the way a smoker sucks a nicotine drag. Smooth.

"*Me-vee-nah?*" I repeat.

"I understand," she mumbles, kind of shy. "7:30. It will be good."

Okay, I know I'm paranoid, but I can't kick this thought of Ron and Lior videotaping me as I'm waiting forever at the food court, both of them holding their laughter while I'm checking my watch in utter frustration. Shayna's *got* to be in on this.

Or maybe not.

Just when I'm bursting inside, thinking everything's great, my heart suddenly free-falls. Team USA's first game is *tonight*!

"Wait!" I holler. "*Slicha*, Shayna. I totally forgot. I'm playing tonight at 7:00."

"Oh," she whines, looking perfectly sad.

"I'll — I'll be back by 9:00," I stutter, hoping to mend the damage. "And the Canada Centre's only five minutes away."

She smiles. "I come with."

"What?"

"Sounds fun, Ethan. I never know this hockey."

"I don't — "

"You pick me up."

"But — "

"I think it's gonna be fun to see this."

"Look, Shayna," I say, real serious. "I don't have a car."

"No?" she gasps, her dark brows furrowing disappointed, which makes me feel like sludge.

"Tell you what," I say, thinking quick, and now she's smiling again while her elongated fingers clench my wrist. "Maybe — "

"Yes, Ethan," she interrupts.

"Look, Shayna. I'm staying with this family on Yehuda HaLavi Street." I say it, figuring Mr. Borochov won't care if he shuttles an extra body to Metula. "Come by at 5:30. They'll drive us to the rink. *Me-vee-nah?*"

"*Sababa!*" she bursts, totally ecstatic, and I'm still wondering if this is all a clever setup.

But I'm hoping I'm wrong, so I grin, set my drink on the shady cement under this chaise lounge, and quickly scan the surroundings. Then, I turn back to Shayna. "You come here with friends?" I ask.

She nods. "They get along without me, Ethan. Unless you want that I should leave."

"No way," I insist, though honestly, I could use some alone time, just to digest everything that's been going on.

She doesn't answer, and now there's this heavy spell of silence which makes me feel real awkward. Stalling, I reach back down for my cola and start fiddling with the clear plastic lid until the suspense finally forces my tongue to roll out anything audible.

"So tell me about life in Kiryat Shemona," I stammer, just like a nervous seventh-grader at a *bar mitzvah* dance party. I am *so* pathetic.

"Oh, not so exciting like America," she says, her eyes looking up as she takes this long drag through her straw until she sucks bottom. "I think you don't want to hear."

Actually, I do. It's like, I'm starting to trust this girl, and she's definitely intriguing.

"I think your town's beautiful," I say, half-lying. "Nestled by the mountains like a perfect Colorado landscape. I'm telling you, Americans pay millions for scenery like this."

"*B'emet?*" she says, giggling.

"*B'va-dai,*" I affirm, though I don't have the heart to explain that the millions only happens *after* somebody razes all those filthy-ugly apartment projects. *Watch it, Ethan. She probably lives in one.*

"Tell me about your house," she queries, changing the subject.

"It's nothing—"

"And your girlfriend?"

Whoaa! Where did *that* come from? Okay, now I'm paranoid

all over that Shoshana has set this whole thing up. You know, a tiny cell phone secreted in Shayna's bikini-top about to become a long distance lie detector. Yeah, this could be like one of Rabbi Klepstein's code-of-conduct stings. As always, I've got to be careful.

I shake my head. *"Eyn li chavera,"* I blurt, bearing false testimony in the holy language, which totally guarantees my descent to the other side of heaven.

I look up. Shayna's smiling wide, spilling a mouthful of teeth, a few on the bottom crooked. Yeah, I'm thinking I just made her day, and she pretty much confirms it by sliding her hips onto my chaise lounge and nudging her knee against mine. Her sun-roasted skin is hot to the touch, but it feels real nice just the same.

"Atah yafe," she whispers about two inches from my ear, giving me an armful of goose pimples. Emotionally intoxicated, I'm trying to think of something cool to say when —

The rest of my Coke suddenly explodes like an Indonesian tidal wave in my face.

As soon as it happens, I'm stunned senseless, my eyes half-blinded by a shower of tiny ice chips melting into my corneas.

"What the — ?"

"Beat it, *Amerikayee!*" screams this six-foot mass of Israeli bruiser. The guy's towering over my chair and he's majorly pissed.

"Mah pee-tome!" blasts Shayna, fuming.

"What the f — ?"

"She's with me!" he hollers, cutting me off again. "What you do here? Go!"

I'm glaring at Shayna, hoping for an explanation. Nothing.

But at least her eyes are blazing indignant. *"Mah a-see-tah,* Gilad?" she snaps, and I'm thinking she's gonna rip this jerk's dark, bulbous nose right off his face. *"Ta-geed li! Ta-geed li!"* she yells, mists of saliva shotgunning from her mouth.

I'm sitting here, totally paralyzed, waiting for the two of them to duke it out.

"*Boi eetee!*" he hollers at Shayna, and then he grabs her arm like he's a Chicago policeman leading a druggie to the municipal lockup.

She turns, grits her teeth, and gives me this quick glance like she's calling for help or something. No chance, I think to myself. This guy's all muscle.

Two seconds later, they're gone, vanishing in a crowded maze of sweaty bodies near the main section of the pool. Meanwhile, I'm practically glued to this chaise lounge, my face and shoulders sticky with cola syrup, my brain trying to figure out what the heck just happened.

I turn. No one around me is paying the slightest attention. It's as if they know it's a total setup.

And now, I'm betting it was, too.

Exasperated, extremely paranoid, and drowning in guilt, I fill my lungs to overflowing with an extra-long ingestion of searing oxygen, gritting my teeth hard in frustration. "Sorry, Shoshana," I mutter half-audible, as though she's standing right next me. "Guess I really deserved this."

Good thing she's half-a-world away. And now, I'm thinking I better not come home.

Chapter Ten

EIGHT HOURS AND A HORRIBLE sunburn later, I'm tensed up at the Canada Centre's red-line face-off circle, donning my new lily-white jersey with the big number 22, and waiting for the referee to drop the puck. It's Team USA's very first game of the Maccabiah tournament, and Dad would be proud to know that I've earned the starting assignment, pretty much like Coach Weiss hinted after yesterday's practice. It's cool being paired with Lowey who's right there to my left, his dark eyes burning confidence through his facemask, like this game's just another midnight rat-hockey scrimmage at the Birmingham ice rink.

Guess I should also mention that we're opening against Team France. I mean, how tough can a bunch of sissy French nationals in powder-blue uniforms really be? Not very, I'm thinking.

And that's a good thing, because playing a contact sport is going to be particularly painful in my current physical state. I'm talking throbbing sunburn, bruised ankle and this incredible jet lag. Oh, did I forget to include extreme emotional imbalance? Yeah, that whole incident at the pool still stings like a surgeon's knife carving figure-eights through my guts.

I'm waiting at center for the ref to drop the puck. And waiting. I'm generating megawatts of nervous energy as I rock back and forth on my blades, antsy for this game to start. Okay, what's the deal? This has to be a joke. It's like that Metro playoff game two years ago when some parent forgot to bring the national anthem CD to the scorer's table, and we're standing at center ice like zombies for the next five minutes while the rink manager tries to locate a Star Spangled Banner knockoff disc from the main office.

Maybe that's the problem—there's only a Hatikvah CD. Meanwhile, my fingers are twitching right through these nylon hockey gloves. Anxious, I look up, stealing a glance at the French left-winger. His blue eyes are glaring angry, like he's peeved at his parents for ruining his European summer.

Hey, I know what you mean, Claude. So let's understand each other—the sooner we start, the quicker we're done.

"Let's go, zebra," I grunt, figuring he's a foreigner and won't understand my American-style disrespect. And get this—he's wearing *gloves*. Sure, it's cold in here, but *come on!* Tell you what, Mr. Referee—try skating in the Lincolnwood rink on a sub-zero January night. Then I'll cut you some slack. Meanwhile, I'm just praying this guy's not Israeli. I mean, sporting gloves in July won't do much to scare Hezbollah terrorists.

The official's still loitering at the center ice dot. It's like, he's doing this impersonation of a Grant Park statue, minus the usual crush of overweight pigeons. Angry, I check back toward the penalty bench. There's a guy fiddling with the door latch, driving his wrists against the metal handle in two-second intervals. Looks like the door's not flush with the boards. Told you this rink's a dump.

Okay, now my on-ice ADD's kicking in, and I feel myself losing focus fast. Turning, I peek at the crowd. There's about fifteen rows of bleachers stacked steep along the west side of the rink. And the place is *packed*. I swear, every player must have brought ten friends and family. Passionate fans, too—there's a dozen French flags swaying back-and-forth and maybe half as many Stars and Stripes.

Craning my head sideways, I'm surprised to see the Borochovs through the scuffed plexiglass by the far curve in our defending corner. Pretty much figured Mr. Borochov would just return after the game, but I guess he went back to pick up his other half. Nice. I'm actually liking that they're here, though they look pathetically clueless, like they've got no idea what's about to happen, which is probably true. Too bad Lior and Danit didn't tag along, but I really don't blame them. I mean, it doesn't get any worse than freezing your bones inside an ice rink on a cloudless, summer evening. That's why there's never more than fifteen bodies warming the Skatium's plastic bleachers on a Sunday, late-afternoon spring league game. Looking up at these packed stands, I'm thinking I should be grateful.

Suddenly, the referee's whistle tweets sadistic, killing my daydreaming. I snap my head forward, not really believing that he's going to drop the puck. But when I see him cock his wrist, I know play's about to start.

Splat! The puck lands nice and flat. Maybe this zebra *does* know his stuff.

Zuckerman's centering for Bloom and Spevak and he wins the draw clean, squirting the puck back to Lowenstein on the left.

"Over here!" I holler, reading the play as a pair of French forwards converge on Lowey, which leaves me wide open on the right side of our defensive blue line.

Lowey's fishes me the rubber without looking up. Smooth.

"Bring it up, Conners!" shouts Coach Weiss before Lowey's feather pass even reaches my blade.

Playing right defense as a lefty, I corral the puck in perfect stride, then shake off the forechecking left-winger with a pee-wee-style deke and bust across the attacking blue line in full momentum.

"Let it go!" roars Bloom, drawing traffic toward the French goaltender. "Shoot!"

I'm already halfway between the blue line and the top of the circle with about ten feet of cushion between me and the nearest Frenchie defenseman. Shifting my weight to my front skate, I take this massive backswing, and Pierre reacts by skulking timid to his left, safely out of my line of fire.

Slap! I launch a Brent Seabrook rocket, the puck clearing the French defenseman's stick by nearly a foot as it cruises 80 m.p.h. toward the net.

Thud! This loud boom echoes solid leather. Of course, I can't see what happened because the slot's crammed with bodies, but it sounded like all leg pad to me. Meanwhile, everyone's yelling, and there's a mad scramble in front of the crease. Still, no whistle.

A half-second elapses and suddenly, the crowd starts roaring.

Somehow, we scored.

"Way to clean up the rebound!" screams Spevak, hockey-glove-high-fiving Zucks.

Lowey and I skate up to join the celebration. We're both smiling as we glove-tap our forwards like sparring boxers.

"Nice set-up Lowey," I say.

"Assists for each of us!" he laughs, showing rows of teeth through his white face mask.

Gliding back toward center, I look up at the clock. Just thirteen seconds elapsed. Wow! Quickest goal since Jason Greenberg scored five seconds into last winter's playoff game against Deerfield High School. Yeah, I've got a good feeling about this game. Real good.

By the second intermission, I'm surprised anyone's still waving the French flag. Like I predicted, it's more of a slaughter than a contest, American power trumping European finesse. And even though Coach Weiss ordered us to quit running up the spread against Team Croissant once the score was 8-0, he must have known his sermon of compassion wasn't going to make a deep impression on a motley crew of teenage goons looking to pad individual stats. Yeah, one period left and Bloom's already tallied twice, Klein's got a hat-trick and Lowey and I are *plus-six*. Nice.

With the score 12-0 to start the third, there's really nothing to play for, and both teams know it. At least Maccabiah's implemented the mercy rule, so the clock's not going to stop for the rest of the game. Of course, that means I'll get only three or four more shifts, but I don't care. I'm thinking I just want to get this drubbing over with and then hang out with Ron and Lior or maybe even laze alone on the Borochovs' living room couch.

Looks like the refs want to get moving, too. They're hustling both teams to line up at center, and trust me, no one's complaining. The zebra with this half-shield drops the puck quick, and you can tell neither team's giving much of an effort. Exactly fifteen minutes later, the horn wails and it's finally *game over*.

Actually, *game's* a serious overstatement. A 14-0 blowout, Coach Weiss had us dropping three-deep all period, just to guarantee Siegel's shutout. And now, lining up for the obligatory post-game handshake at center, I'm looking into these French kids' expressionless eyes, sensing that none of them really want to be here. They seem absolutely demoralized, lazing pouty-lipped like a dying school of Cajun cod, probably itching for a quick elimination so they can head off to the coast for some sun and fun. I don't blame them.

Okay, I'm not the kind of guy to say *I told you so*, but if Dad were here, I'd definitely remind him that a Jewish hockey tournament's not exactly NCAA competition. I mean, Team France isn't one-tenth of the Michigan State Spartans. Just sayin'.

But I swear, if I'm ever an advertising CEO, I'm definitely hiring the guy that persuaded these French sissies to *schlep* all their equipment from Paris. Now, that's real marketing genius.

Chapter Eleven

CHILLING AT THE BOROCHOVS' after the game, I'm parked on this couch, thinking I should call home and tell Dad about our win. It's 1:30 p.m. in Chicago and Dad's probably back from lunch, so it's as good a time as any to broadcast my *plus-seven*, all-star stats.

I get up and stroll into Lior's bedroom, swiping my Samsung off the dresser. "Darn!" I grumble to myself. Phone's out of battery. So I start hunting for Dad's 220-volt converter which should be in my carry-on, but after two minutes of frantic searching, I'm absolutely convinced that it somehow got lost between Newark and Tel-Aviv—more than likely on the grimy floor of that El Al 747.

Either that or I never packed it.

Aggravated, I trudge back toward the couch and I should probably ask Mrs. Borochov if I can use the land-line, but everyone's still milling around the living room, eyes glued to the flat-screen. And *everyone* includes Danit and her Victoria Secret poster-girl friend Gila. No way I'm gonna call home in front of *them*.

"Sit down, Ethan," says Mr. Borochov, as he pours a clear glass of cola, heads of caramel-colored foam spilling over the rim.

"Soon as I find my electrical converter," I say, and then bust back to the bedroom before Danit gives me another condescending stare.

Okay, maybe I'm a little sensitive, but I swear Danit and all her friends are festering with sick envy toward Americans. And *I'm* American. Seriously, I thought we were allies, that every Israeli wouldn't be able to do enough for their Jewish cousins in exile. But it's not like that, and I'm guessing it's got something to do with the army. I mean, here I am, this eighteen-year-old spoiled American guy traveling six thousand miles just to play in a glorified hockey tournament, and now that I think that to myself I guess it does sound totally pathetic. You know, post-high school summer without a care in the world. Icing a full-boat scholarship to a top university, just because I can balance myself on a one-eighth-inch strip of stainless steel.

And then there's Ron and Lior. They've just graduated, too. But there's no college scholarships in their rough-and-tumble world. Even worse, they're not going to college. At least not for three more years. Oh sure, they'll be leaving home in September, just like me. But they've been drafted for three-year stints in the IDF. And even though Ron and Lior have never exuded the slightest disrespect toward me, I can just sense it everywhere Danit goes. There's envy in her fiery, brown eyes, subsuming her since we met yesterday morning at Ben Gurion. And I'll bet this *kippah* doesn't help either. I mean, it's part of my essence, but I'm doubting Danit sees it that way. For her, my knit-green skull cap probably smacks arrogant, like being religious is easy when you're living the rich, American good life. Maybe she's got a point.

Of course, *wealthy America* gets me thinking about Shoshana. It's weird that I feel like I've totally cheated on her by the way I've been mentally ogling all these racy locals. Seriously, my conscience pleads guilty, even though I'd like to think our relationship doesn't even rise to the level where either of us can actually be *cheaters*. God, I hate when my mind gets filled to overflowing with these kind of mental gymnastics, which is probably why I'm still convinced the whole Shayna thing was a candid-camera setup, no doubt being posted all over You Tube for Shoshana Kaplan's sadistic pleasure. Out of sight, but suddenly drowning my mind, it's like Shoshana's more palatable from the other side of the world. Talk about a messed up relationship.

That settles it. Now, I'm fishing my fingers deep into my carry-on, feeling all around for that plastic plug converter which I'm convinced is hiding inside a rolled up sock or something. I'm not leaving this room until I find it.

"Got it," I mumble to myself, feeling all ecstatic that I've managed to locate the thing so quickly the second time around. Now I can call home in private.

I plug the Samsung's cord into the converter and push

the silver prongs into the wall outlet. There's this lame, melodic chime, and then the screen lights up all powder blue. Smirking, I plant myself atop Lior's dollar store mattress and scroll down to Shoshana's number.

That's right, I'm putting Dad on hold. Sort of. I mean, for some crazy reason, I'm thinking I owe it to Shoshana to finally call her. Sure, I've shot her a few generic e-mails from the Borochovs' computer, but like I said, there's still this dark cloud raining guilty showers on my soul. For two years, Shoshana's put up with my crazy schedule of six-month prep leagues and off-season power skates, and now I'm rewarding her by ditching her on our last summer together, just to placate Dad by playing in a Middle-Eastern hockey tournament. Yeah, I wouldn't blame Shoshana for being too pissed to answer.

But I've got to try. So I press the Galaxy S-III tight into my palm, punch in the overseas code, and follow up with Shoshana's cell number, all the time figuring it's early afternoon in Chicago and she's probably at the Lincolnwood Mall, bad-mouthing me to her friends while she tries to catch the eye of a guy who's never laced up a pair of Bauers.

The connection goes through quick and scratchy. Suddenly, I hear that familiar, American ring tone. My heart's pacing fast, my hands clamming nervous. Two rings so far—she's letting it go to voice mail, a clever way of showing me she's miffed. Shoshana, Danit. Yeah, not having much confidence with females right now.

Four rings. Still no answer. Come on, Shoshana. When the call transfers to voice mail, my brain's suddenly a Hewitt-Packard processing instantaneous calculations—like whether I should leave a message and what to say if I do.

There's the beep. I'm going for it.

"Ehh—hello from Israel," I stammer, trying to sound cool, like I'm hanging on the Mediterranean beach instead of holed up in this Section 8 apartment. "It's Ethan. Just chillin' here in Kiryat Shemona before our next game."

I pause. Did I really say *chillin*? That's not cool. It's lame.

"Sorry I missed you," I continue, all anxious. "I'll—I'll e-mail you later, Shosh. Bye."

Click. I exhale in absolute relief. Sure, I've been kind of a jerk, but the truth is I'm not planning on missing her next year anyway, and I'm guessing she knows it.

Lior pops his head in. "*Shoshana*?" he mocks, grinning.

"She's from back home," I say, still not trusting him.

"Girlfriend?"

"Yeah."

He leans his spine against the oak-stained door frame, nodding gently. "Doesn't sound like much to me."

"What?"

"Tell me about her, Ethan."

"Like?"

"Like, what makes her special?" he asks, like he's grilling me on a trashy, afternoon talk show, and I'm thinking this is too weird for one guy to be asking another guy.

"I don't know—"

"She cute?"

"Uhh—yeah."

"Skinny?"

"Well—"

"Hotter than Danit?"

"That's enough!" I holler.

Lior looks stunned, and now there's this heavy silence cutting real tense. Aggravated, I prop up my back and sit board-straight atop the bed, exuding total confidence as I stare deep into his dark-featured face.

"I'm sorry for prying," he says, relaxing his eyes. "Guess I'm just a little bit, how you say—*envious.*"

"You mean, jealous? Of what?"

"You, Ethan. Life in America."

Oh God, he's just like his sister. Now Lior's plastering me in guilt, too.

"Look," I counter, irritated by all of this. "What's so great about the North Side of Chicago, anyway? You ever been there, Lior? Ever plodded down California Avenue into the face of a sub-zero Arctic wind howling off Lake Michigan?"

"God-willing, Ethan."

"What?" I rant, shocked.

"You're blinded Ethan!" he rants back, and then parks his butt next to me on the bed.

"Look, Lior, I don't know what's infecting everyone around here, but it wasn't my idea to come to Israel this summer, so cut me some slack and get your sister off my duff too! *Maveen?*"

He grits his teeth. "Maybe *you're* infected, Ethan."

"Me?"

"Infected by how you say — *privilege.*"

"Spare me, Lior. Am I supposed to sob now?"

"That would be a good start," he retorts.

"Don't go all emotional on me," I huff. "You guys are supposed to be tougher than that."

Now, Lior's forehead's showing these angry canyons. "Maybe we'll talk after your little sister's *bat mitzvah* party gets trashed by a Hezbollah raid."

"That happened?" I blurt, my eyes bulging. Okay, *this* needs clarification.

"*Chaval,*" he says, nodding. "When sirens go off, everyone rushes out of dining hall. The band, too. Mom and Danit planned it for months and then terrorists ruin it."

The way he tells it makes me feel sick. It's practically unimaginable. I mean, who thinks about such things in Chicago? Seriously, the worst *bar mitzvah* tragedy I can remember was when Mendel the Juggler choked on this black olive during Shmuli Rosenthal's party at Tel Aviv Pizza.

"Four years later and Danit's still angry," scorns Lior, picking this cuticle on his ring finger, like he's totally anxious.

"Ever think about coming to the States?" I ask, hoping to ease the tension.

"Are you *meshuga?*" hollers Lior, like I've just asked him to join the pom-pon squad or something.

I sigh. "Israel's a free country, Lior. Heck, hundreds of Israelis live in my own neighborhood. Seriously, after hearing your story, you've got every right to come over."

Now I know what I said makes perfect sense, so why's Lior staring at me like *I'm* the one with the problem?

"It's not so simple, Ethan."

"What's not so simple? Yossi Grossman's family just moved from Haifa to this bungalow on the other side of Greenleaf. And Chaya Rabinowitz and Marty Stern—"

"*Yeradim!*" he wails. "A curse on those who take their families from the Land."

"What?" I definitely didn't expect *that*.

"Don't play dumb, Ethan," he grouches, without looking up. "We don't cut and run."

Now *I* feel like a jerk.

"Sorry, Lior. That's not—"

"Look," he interrupts. "Maybe we're not so religious like you, but that doesn't mean we're ignorant."

"I didn't mean—"

He cuts me off again. "God gave us this land, Ethan. And just because we don't pray three-times-a-day or keep strict Shabbat doesn't mean we're not gonna fight for our heritage."

Lior's fiery-brown eyes are burning howitzer holes right through me. He needs me to answer, but I'm totally tongue-tied, afraid to make an ever bigger fool of myself.

Which is why I'm letting Lior's dirty, disgusting sermon of truth hang like soiled laundry right in front of my very nose. Oh, I get it now. Guys like Lior and Ron are all about sanctifying God through IDF service, and they wouldn't have it any other way.

And then there's me, and just about every other American Jew, pretty much clueless about real-life sacrifice. Like keeping Shabbat in Chicago's gonna protect God's Promised Land from another terrorist attack. I am *so* worthless.

"Look, Ethan." Lior's voice mellows, like he's ashamed for stunning me. "For us, being Jewish is more than a daily race to keep the 613 *mitzvot*. Understand?"

"Sorry," I mumble, my eyes flashing anxious. "I mean about what I said. I—I should have known."

"Ethan," he says, reaching his arm around my shoulder. "Let's just say we're partners."

"Partners?"

"Seriously, Ethan. We stay to fight, but we're nothing without American support."

I force a guilty grin. "You mean it?"

"Well, for some of us it is a bit demoralizing. You know, losing three years while our Jewish brothers in America party at university."

"Sure," I utter, my half-smile masking a wounded conscience.

"Guess it's all a matter of how you say—*perspective*," explains Lior. "You know, some of us serve proud—others resentful. And then there's those who flee to America, avoiding army altogether."

While he's saying this, I'm staring, unblinking, wondering what I would do if I was standing in Lior's sandals, facing basic training right after *Rosh Hashanah*.

I think I know.

And I'm seriously ashamed.

Chapter Twelve

WHEN COACH WEISS CHUCKS the puck into my defensive corner at next morning's 7:00 a.m. scrimmage, my sleepy eyes are fighting to focus on the bouncing biscuit. I start gliding head-down toward the end boards, and it's like my brain's totally out of hockey, my thoughts stupidly flirting with Shayna.

That's *flirting with disaster.*

Crack! Jeremy Bloom's right shoulder practically bulldozes a tunnel through my ribs. A second later, I'm collapsed on the ice and everyone stops skating.

"You're gonna get yourself killed!" wails Coach Weiss, clouds of hot breath seeping from the corners of his mouth.

"I—I was looking the other way, Coach," I stutter. "Settin' up a quick outlet for Spevak."

He knows it's a lie.

"Second line out!" he barks. "Take a powder and catch your wind, Conners!"

"Yes sir," I say, and then dog it to the bench where I drench my throat with squirts of lukewarm Neviot.

"Better keep out of Bloomie's way!" shouts Lowey from the ice, grinning a mile wide through his facesmask. "The guy's totally solid!"

"Thanks," I mutter back, and it hurts to breathe when I say it. Winded, I park my rear on the bench, and keep sucking drags of this musty oxygen which tastes like propane from the Zamboni's exhaust. As the poison fills my lungs, I'm letting my eyes wander toward this giant Coca-Cola clock on the south wall. Of course, the big red logo gets me all hot and bothered about sticky syrup, Shayna, and everything else that happened yesterday at the pool.

"You okay?" asks Richman from the other side of the bench.

"Yeah," I grunt, still doubled over in pain, and pretty much not caring about hockey right now which isn't a good thing, because if I can't keep focused on the game, I'm practically setting myself up for a serious injury. *Wake up, Ethan!* God-forbid I get hurt here. I mean, Ferris State isn't guaranteeing my scholarship. Picture the conversation— *"Dad, my spleen was crushed at practice because I was daydreaming about this girl I'd met at the Kiryat Shemona pool."*

Guess that's called a one-way ticket to Oakton Community College. Lesson learned.

Two shifts later, I'm back on the ice, hustling for all I'm worth. When practice ends, I'm absolutely drenched, sweat cascading like melting icicles off my brows and gray clouds of steam vaporing from my head, just like you see in the NFL when the camera cuts to sideline shots of exhausted linemen skulking the sidelines on a Soldier Field January.

"Rest up boys!" shouts Coach Weiss, his eyes spilling satisfaction at our early-morning effort. "Win tonight and we're advancing straight to the championship. That's a guaranteed medal."

As Coach's prophecy echoes across the rink, I'm gliding toward the locker room, eyes scanning the empty stands like a love-struck idiot. Not that I really expected Shayna to magically appear in this refrigerated dump at 7:45 in the morning, but just considering the possibility is kind of intriguing. I mean, the only thing she knows about me is that I'm hanging at the Canada Centre this week, so if she wants to find me, it's got to be here.

Keep dreaming, I think to myself. Meanwhile, I just want Zuckerman's dad to rush me back to the Borochovs' place so I can shower quick and look decent again. And then, I'm planning to get lazy. Real lazy. Like vegging all day in front of the flat screen, and resting my body for tonight's big game versus the Russians. No traipsing to third-world water parks with Ron and Lior. No mental mind games with Danit. Just an entire day devoted to absolutely nothing.

Nothing. Right now, that sounds real good.

Thirty minutes later, I'm squirming liked a hooked flounder atop Lior's cut-rate mattress, my eyes fixated by this tarantula-sized web of cotton-white dustballs hanging from the corner of the plaster ceiling. I'm pretty much exhausted after that grueling practice, and since Lior's gone, I'd love to crash another three hours or so before I shower, but Lior's room's already sheathed with brilliant streaks of sunlight filtering through the eastern window's stringy curtains, and there's no way I can sleep in this theater of brightness.

Hey, check this out. My legs—they're loose! And my ribs, too. Not much lingering pain from Bloomie's sledgehammer shoulder. Nice. And a bit strange. I mean, I woke up yesterday virtually immobilized, my entire body stiff as a pane of plexiglass. Practically had to force Ron and Lior to hoist me out of bed.

But now, my limbs feel like boiled strands of extra-long spaghetti. What gives?

Shayna, that's what. I mean, she's pretty much all I've been thinking about, and I can't ditch the feeling. It's like, I'm hopelessly infatuated by her exotic, bronzed face, the perfect touch of her fingers, and the burning gaze of those rich, mocha eyes. Suddenly, I can totally relate to the emotion from that Scorpions' song. *Still Loving You*, right?

Reality check, Conners. There's no chance of seeing her again. And why would I even want to, especially with that Middle-Eastern King Kong itching to *shochet* me for dinner.

Just then, this melodic chime starts blaring from my reeking hockey bag. Great. Does anyone back home realize it's still summer-vacation bedtime here? I bust over to the bag, swipe away a pair of sweaty shin guards, and fish out the Samsung.

And then, my jaw drops to my socks.

It's Shoshana!

"Hello," I mumble, totally nervous.

"How's it going, Ethan?" she chirps, her voice perky, like she's calling from Metula instead of the other side of the world.

"Pretty good," I answer.

"Yeah, well Rivky Sandler's having this awesome Fourth of July party as we speak. You really *should* be here, Ethan."

"Glad you're having fun," I say, totally forgetting that it's already Wednesday, July 5 in Israel, which is pretty easy to do when you're like six thousand miles from home, and this pretty girl named Shayna's going sweet on you. At least I'm *hoping* she is.

"Is—is everything all right?" stutters Shoshana, her Chicago-accent radiating concern.

"Sorry, Shosh," I answer, suddenly feeling guilty for leaving her solo at Rivky's party and making her play second fiddle to Canada's national pastime—again. "It's early morning here. Gotta keep it hushed."

"Figured you just finished *davening*," she counters. "Thought it was a good time to call."

"7:00 a.m. practice, Shosh. Just got back."

"Well, sorry if I interrupted whatever you were doing, Ethan."

Typical. Now she's getting all pouty on me and I'm feeling like slop. Sure, I know she hates hanging solo at parties. I mean, who wouldn't? And I should probably cut her some slack since she thinks I'm just wasting this week holed up in an Israeli hick town and living out Dad's scholarship dream, when the disgusting truth is that I've spent the past twenty hours daydreaming about Shayna *I-still-don't-know-your-last-name-but-I'm-planning-to-scout-you-out-this-week-anyway*. Man, if guilt were muscles, I'd be Israel's Twenty-First Century Samson.

"Don't worry, Shosh," I say, raking my fingers through my greasy, helmet-matted hair. "I'm just zoning in bed. Glad you called, though. Could have easily crashed and missed *Shacharit*."

"Yeah, I get it," she grumbles, and suddenly there's this real tense silence. Makes me wonder if *I'm* the only one harboring pangs of separation guilt. Or is it separation giddiness? I'm so confused.

"Hey, we're playing the Russians tonight," I blurt, changing the subject. "If we win, we're in the finals. Guaranteed silver medal!"

"Nice," she utters, probably hoping we lose so I can fly back sooner. Doesn't matter. My return ticket's for Sunday night, and there's no way Dad's gonna pony up a $200.00

change fee to El Al.

"Hey, is that Noah Finkelstein in the background?" I ask, eavesdropping on muddled voices filtering through this tiny, Galaxy-III speaker. "Can't believe it's still July Fourth in America."

"Ethan!" she hollers. "It's long distance!"

"Sorry, Shosh."

Now, there's another moment of total silence. Real painful.

"Look, Ethan. I've got to go. Not paying international charges just to hear you breathe."

"Yeah, okay," I say.

"Fly safe. See you next week."

"Thanks, Shosh. Bye."

"Bye, Ethan."

The screen fades to black. She's gone.

I plop the Samsung next to my pillow and then inhale hard, half-ashamed to be relieved that the call ended so quick. Seriously, that was one sorry conversation, and even a fifth-grader could sense the romantic death knells echoing between cell towers. Whatever. Shoshana and I both knew that dating was against Rabbi Klepstein's rules, and Mom and Dad never liked *The Criminal* to begin with. Nuff said.

But I feel sick just the same.

Mentally exhausted, I bring my knees up tight against my chest, wrap both arms around my shins, and then start rocking back and forth atop this dime-store mattress. I'm trying to re-focus, concentrating on my game, even mentally re-hashing Coach Weiss's defensive positioning instructions for our neutral zone traps. Anything to make me forget about Shoshana, Danit and even Shayna. I mean, Dad sent me here to sharpen my athletic skills, not wallow in a terminal rue about two girls I'll never see again and another that'll probably be sore at me for the rest of the summer.

The scholarship, Ethan. Dad's words keep cutting through my skull like a sharpened skate blade slicing through a clean sheet of ice. I'm here for the cash, right? I mean, it's all about God, family and hockey—or maybe the other way around.

Either way, my heart's pumping fantastic rivers of energy, and suddenly, I'm rocketing off this mattress and reaching like an octopus for my *talit* bag. Guess right now, God's first.

Which means I've got to start my morning prayers. Like, real quick. Technically, it's almost too late to even *daven Shacharit*, but the truth is that I was barely able to wake up on time for Mr. Borochov's 6:30 a.m. shuttle to our morning practice at the Canada Centre, and it's not like I'm gonna use God as an excuse for being late because Coach Weiss couldn't care less about prayers. Dog-peed-in-my-skates—no problem. Connecting with God—don't bother dressing.

Anyway, it's not like anyone around here's making me keep a time sheet with the Big Guy. Still, my conscience is scrambling, so I quickly don my prayer shawl like it's a super-hero's cape and then coil *tefillin* around my left arm and over my head. Kind of sloppy, I know, but the door's closed and I've got to *daven* fast.

I take one last listen before I start, my ears perked like a stir-crazy house cat until I'm sure no one's skulking through the hall. Look, the last thing I need is for any of the Borochovs to shimmy in and start ogling me like I'm some sort of religious alien wrapped in fabric and leather. I mean, Lior would have freaked out yesterday morning on the balcony if he'd have busted me in full *Shacharit* regalia.

Don't get me wrong—I love the Borochovs' Israeli hospitality. But talk about secular—this family's the *real* deal.

Chapter Thirteen

WEDNESDAYS ARE MERCHANT MARKET DAYS in Kiryat Shemona, and Lior wasn't kidding when he said this town's gonna be bustling with shoppers. Right now, I'm strolling down Tel Chai Road with Lior, Danit, Gila and a few hundred strangers, and just about everyone's lugging these brown plastic bags filled to overflowing. It's a scorching afternoon and I figured Ron and Lior were planning on dragging me back to the pool today, but now I'm thinking this is a good change of scenery. And with all these people, I'm also thinking I stand a decent chance of running into Shayna somewhere along this crowded pedestrian mall. That's why I agreed to go in the first place.

Staring all around, I'm not sure what we're supposed to be buying, but it's kind of cool to people-watch in a foreign country. And trust me, this part of Israel is totally foreign to me—more akin to a third-world bazaar you'd see on a National Geographic cover. It's amazing how all these canvas tents on Tel Chai Road literally sprouted overnight from vacant city lots, the grimy sidewalks suddenly lined with long, lunch room-style wooden tables manned by pushy, screaming merchants hawking everything from dime store trinkets to ten-pound cantaloupes. I swear, when we drove down Tel Chai Road yesterday, this entire block was nothing but acres of gravel and broken glass flanked by dilapidated ruins of concrete foundations. Twenty-four hours later, it's the Skokie flea market on Middle-Eastern steroids.

"*Zote mateem li?*" laughs Danit, as she holds this black tank-top over her skinny chest. "*Rock chameesha shkalim.*"

"*Ta-eem!*" yaps Gila, smiling, and I'm thinking just $1.50 for a new top? Wow! The Academy girls shell out $40.00 a pop for the very same kind of threads (with sleeves of course), just because they're stamped with some tony New York imprint on an overpriced Macy's rack.

Naturally, Shoshana wouldn't be caught dead in a dump like this. But these Kiryat Shemona girls—I love their raw simpleness. Attractive. *Real* attractive.

Danit dumps the tank-top back on the display pile. *"Az bo naylech leek-note pay-rote,"* she says, turning toward Lior and me. "We need to get fruit for *Eema.*"

Lior nods. "Mom likes to stock up early for weekend," he explains. "All the produce gets picked over by Friday morning."

That's hard to imagine. I mean, I'm staring at a Soldier Field's length of fresh fruit and vegetable tables patrolled by sleazy hawkers shouting loud and annoying. And these prices—totally cut-rate! I can't even fathom how they grow so much food in such a tiny sliver of coastal plain, but I guess that's why God proclaimed this to be a *Land of Milk and Honey.*

"Agvaniyote, shlosha l'kilo!" screams this old guy with a wrinkled, bronzed face and row of broken teeth like a rotten ear of corn.

"Unbelievable!" I crow, shaking my head in disbelief at all these skyscrapers of boxed tomatoes. "Lior, this stuff's a dollar-a-pound at Lincolnwood Produce."

Of course, Lior's got no idea what I'm talking about, but he's giving me this million-dollar smile anyway. "Israel has best prices and freshest vegetables," he boasts, fishing his fingers through a wooden crate of red and orange peppers.

I turn, watching Danit jostle near the melon rack where she's fighting for body position like Derrick Rose on the baseline. There's definitely a method to the madness, and it's pretty obvious that aggression is key. Nobody survives timid in this town.

"Al teeshcach a-va-tee-yach," she hollers to Lior, telling him not to forget the melons.

"As if I don't know the list," he mumbles to me. "And they've got to be seedless, too."

I love it. Israel down and dirty, not like the five-star Sheratons showing off luxury lobbies and English-speaking bellhops. I'm suddenly angry at Mom and Dad for depriving me of all this.

"Nice," says Danit, peeking at Lior's basketball-sized

honeydew.

"And which of you girls is gonna carry it home?" I joke, smirking at Gila.

"Maybe you," chuckles Danit, turning bashful right at me. "Keep strong for tonight's game."

"Good idea," I say, surprised that she even knows my tournament schedule.

"Darn!" hollers Lior, making a pair of fists. "I forgot Mom's shopping sack."

"*Tee-paysh, tee-paysh,*" scorns Danit, telling her brother he's a fool.

"Don't worry," I cut in. "Seriously, I'm happy to help."

"Guests don't work like slaves," counters Lior.

"Well, *I* don't carry melon *gadol,*" miffs Danit, and I'm thinking it's nice to see her ticked at someone other than *me.*

"Go pick out some lipsticks," mocks Lior, using his hand to wave away the girls. "Ethan and I can handle it."

Gila eyes Lior and scrunches her face into this contorted scowl. Then, she grabs Danit's wrist and pulls her sideways, both of them disappearing into the market chaos.

Lior rolls his eyes. "My sister can be — how-you-say, *beetch,*" he grumbles. "I never understand her."

"Either way, I'm helping with the stuff, Lior. And that's an order."

"Whatever."

"Let's just finish up and get back."

He smiles. "We shop faster without them, Ethan."

"Great," I say. "Seriously, I can use some relaxation before tonight's—"

POW! This horrible explosion suddenly cuts me off wicked, and then the whole world vaporizes in my face. I feel this intense pressure, like a bowling ball pressing into my chest, while my head pounds concussion-like and both ears ring in absolute pain. Stunned and practically unconscious, I'm thinking this has to be some kind of sleep-deprived hallucination, challenging my brain with sticky visions of pulpy produce splattered everywhere. But when I feel my forehead raining splotchy streams of fruit guts while my nose whiffs this gruesome, acrid stench wafting evil through these mangled tent canvases and shattered table displays, I know it's no dream.

It's real.

Silent seconds seem to last eternal. And then come the screams. Pitiful wails. The most horrible manifestations of human emotions I could ever imagine. Still, I'm buzzed. Shocked.

I glance to my right, gagging at this mangled pair of eyeglasses. My God, what's happening?

"Danit!"

That's Lior's holler. When I turn, I see him muscling a collapsed, wooden table off the tops of his shins.

"Lior!" I scream, wailing insane like everyone else.

"Ethan!"

"Over here, Lior!"

There's an old lady curled on her side about five feet to my right. I rush over.

"*La-azor li*," she moans.

I take her tiny hand in my palm. Her legs start to move.

"Ethan!"

It's Danit's voice, but I still can't see her.

"Move!" yells Lior. "The roof!"

My head tilts up, my eyes bulging in disbelief as this filthy, canvas ceiling droops low, the wooden support pole groaning and bending under pressure. That's when the ultimate adrenalin rush kicks in. Hyper, I shovel the old lady's tiny body into my arms and burst forward, just as the support beam snaps clean, and sprays lethal splinters everywhere.

"Ethan!" screams Lior. "You all right?"

"Pretty sure," I answer, breathless, and then I start timidly examining my clothes for bloodstains. I've always read about people who were shot but never realized it until they saw blood. I'm hoping that's not me.

"Ethan! Where's Danit?"

"Lior!" she shouts. "Here!"

"What about Gila?" he yells back.

"*Lo yo-da-at!*"

"Stay with me, Danit!" he orders.

I'm sweating buckets as I slowly turn back to the old lady. She's looking better, and now she's sitting straight up and brushing the dust from her skirt. I think she's okay.

"*Todah rabbah*," she mumbles, gazing right at me. "*Hashem* blesses you."

I'm too stunned to answer, so I just nod in response.

She nods back. Then she stands up and carefully plods forward, sidestepping upturned tables and scattered produce everywhere.

Meanwhile, my body's shaking. I'm trying to muster the courage to look at my arms and legs, and I'm just about to roll up my sleeves, when I suddenly get distracted by these screaming sirens echoing loud from all directions. I'm guessing it's been just ninety seconds since the explosion.

I see Lior and Danit shuffling close.

"*P'goo-ah*," scorns Danit, her eyes beaming angry.

"You mean *rocket*?" I say, totally shocked. "Terrorists?"

"Always Kiryat Shemona," growls Lior.

"Why?"

"Because we're so close to the border," he says, and now I feel like an idiot.

"*Ezra ree-shona!*" screams this burly paramedic, charging into what's left of the market.

"Let's go!" hollers Lior. "Out of their way!"

Everyone's darting toward the street, and that's probably a good sign. I'm bailing too, and totally sweating as I run with Lior and Danit past spilled produce, the cement sidewalk caked with this slippery film of stomped fruit and vegetables. When we finally make it to Tel Chai Road, I turn back, happy that I didn't see any serious injuries and hoping I'm not being stupidly optimistic.

Lior yanks a kleenex from his pocket. "Take this," he says. "Your forehead looks like a modern art exhibit."

"Thanks," I say, but my hand's quivering so hard that I can't keep the tissue pressed to my skin.

"Your arm!" shrieks Danit, ogling the back of my right shoulder.

"What?"

"Blood!" she wails. "Lior. Look!"

Now, my stomach's free-falling.

"Oh, yeah," mutters Lior.

I'm not feeling any pain, but I've got to look.

"You okay?" asks Lior.

"I—I think."

I'm sweating rivers as I crane my neck hard to the right, while my left hand tugs my yellow sleeve over my shoulder.

I see the red. And then my stomach curdles when I feel splotches of wetness.

But I'm not worrying about myself. Instead, I get this sickening vision that it's someone else's blood—maybe from a dead person.

"Ethan. I'll call the—"

"No!" orders Danit. She grabs my shirt and starts pulling it halfway over my shoulders.

"Ouch!" I yell.

"Slivers," utters Lior. "No problem, Ethan. Hold still."

Like I've got a choice.

Just then, Danit turns. "Gila!" she shouts, embracing her friend who looks pretty much unscathed—and still incredibly stunning.

I flinch. "Stop moving!" orders Lior, like he's an army medic-in-training. He's pressing his palm against my right shoulder blade, and now there's a half-dozen bystanders watching him administer a crude, first-aid.

"Got 'em!" he carps. He holds up a trophy pair of two-inch wood shards, the tiny ends stained dark-red.

"*Tza-reech la-azor?*" blurts this *real* medic, busting right at me because he thinks I need help.

"I'm fine. Lior, tell him."

"*Lo*, we don't need. *Hakol b'seder*," announces Lior, motioning with his hands.

I turn back toward Danit, and she's got this real serious look beaming from her eyes. She's definitely concerned.

"I'm fine," I tell her, hating the thought of Danit Borochov worrying about *me*.

She shakes her head. "I can't believe this happens!" she screeches. "Ethan gets injured. *Nu*, crazy thing. I live my whole life here and never even get scratch."

I crack a half-smile, and then make Lior hand me the wooden slivers. Dumb as this sounds, I'm gonna take them home, along with this yellow Izod knock-off stained with my own sacrifice to *Eretz* Israel, which I promise to never wash. Souvenirs of Middle-Eastern hatred, I guess.

"You sure you're okay?" says Gila, showing concern.

"No problem," I answer, even though my heart's pounding through my ribs while my brain keeps processing everything that just happened.

"Ethan's tough," brags Danit, and I'm shocked by the compliment. I try holding my head high and proud, just like a marine at roll call.

"Thanks, guys," I say, masking the nausea stewing though my intestines. Of course, I've never been through anything like this. And it's definitely not like I'd imagined from watching all those news clips on CNN.

It's weird. This is *real* war, and I'm in a front-line foxhole. It's Hezbollah gunning for *me*. Shockingly intentional. Lethally personal. I wish I could explain it better. But I can't. I mean, I thought I knew what it would feel like. You know, when I was six thousand miles away on the living room couch, watching the survivors' expressions as reporters wave microphones into their shell-shocked faces.

But when you actually smell the sulfur and hear the cracking wood, it's suddenly something totally different. There's no time to think. Your brain doesn't panic. You just react. And hope to survive.

I did. And it looks like I'm okay. Physically, that is. *Baruch Hashem*, I think to myself, praying to God that everyone else came out unscathed, too.

Chapter Fourteen

WHEN WE GET BACK TO THE APARTMENT, Mr. and Mrs. Borochov are waiting like a pair of angry Mossad agents, practically interrogating Lior and Danit the second we open the door. The Hebrew's spewing fast and furious and I'm not even trying to understand. Meanwhile, Mr. and Mrs. Borochov keep ogling my red-stained shirt like a pair of September yellowjackets at a Labor Day picnic, and I know just what they're thinking.

"You need to go to clinic," bellows Mr. Borochov, totally agitated.

"I'm fine," I counter.

"And your parents!" cries Mrs. Borochov. "We must call—"

"It's okay!" I interrupt. I mean there's *no* way I'm calling Mom and Dad with Danit parked in this very room. Besides, I'm completely fine and there's no point worrying them.

"It was just a splinter," explains Lior, his voice harping serious. "Ethan's okay. *B'rtzenoot.*"

Mr. and Mrs. Borochov turn, and I'm watching them duel each other with these perfectly grim expressions, like they're not buying Lior's diagnosis. There's a second or two of intense silence, and then Mr. Borochov meekly nods in assent.

"*B'seder,*" he huffs, raking his fingers through thinning swatches of his salt-and-pepper hair. "You let us know if there's a problem. Agree?"

"Of course," I answer back, totally relieved that I won't have to deal with Mom's hysterics just now.

"What time is game tonight?" questions Mr. Borochov, as he sinks himself into the soft, brown couch and reaches for today's *Ha'aretz.*

"Ehh—seven o'clock," I say. "If you could drive me to the Tel Chai hostel, I'll catch a ride with the Zuckermans."

"You rest up until then," insists Mrs. Borochov, still eyeing me suspicious like I'm either injured or about to infect the family with West Nile Virus.

"Okay," I say, and then turn the corner into Lior's room where I give one long exhale before plastering my sorry butt on the springy, twin mattress.

"Wow!" exclaims Lior, following me inside. "Thought my parents were gonna send you back to Chicago for sure."

"Yeah, guess I see their point. You know, it's like I'm *their* responsibility or something."

"And to still play tonight—"

"That's why I'm here," I say, cutting him off. "There's *no* way I'm missing a single shift. They'll have to carry me out first."

Lior smiles. "You're tough, Ethan. Real tough."

"Thanks, I mumble," plopping my head into the recesses of this flimsy, cotton pillow.

"Rest up, Ethan."

A couple minutes go by while I wallow in the silence, my eyes zoning at these same ceiling dustballs which seem to be growing larger every hour. Spacing, I feel my soul drowning with introspection. Okay, so Lior thinks I'm tough. Nice. And now, maybe Danit does too.

A dream of the impossible—maybe I'm not Danit's pampered American malcontent any longer. Just sayin'.

But if it's really true, that may be better than Maccabiah gold.

Four hours later, Mr. Borochov's motoring me to the Canada Centre. He's been sporting this worried look all afternoon, and I'm thinking he's still weighed heavy with guilt for not making me call Mom and Dad after what happened. That's probably why he's driving me the whole way to Metula instead of dropping me off at the hostel. Whatever.

"News report says no one killed," mutters Mr. Borochov, his stubby fingers playing with the radio's volume. "Small rocket, thanks God. Mainly damage to market, not people."

Now that's a big relief to me. Really, I was feeling sick about playing hockey tonight. Didn't think I could possibly keep my head in the game. I mean, I hated thinking that I'd escaped this afternoon's attack pretty much unscathed, while others may have been martyred for their country.

"Lior says this always happens to Kiryat Shemona," I spout, like I'm some kind of big know-it-all. "He told me it's the fate of Israeli border towns."

Mr. Borochov nods. "Not so much recently," he explains, his hands gripping tighter on the steering wheel. "But we do seems to take worst of it, especially with the *Hezbollah* so close."

"Yeah," I grunt, staring through the Getz's dust-caked window toward the Golan Heights in the northern horizon. "Lior even told me what happened at Danit's *bat mitzvah*. Horrible."

Mr. Borochov's eyes drift toward me, and then he nods long and slow. Suddenly, there's this searing silence accompanied by the monotonous rhythm of cheap rubber tires digging into rutted blacktop, and I'm just wishing we'd start talking about something else.

"It's okay," consoles Mr. Borochov, his voice noticeably shaky. "At least no one hurt today. But many families around here not so lucky. Some lose kids, too."

I'm gritting my teeth as he says it, trying to think of something to say back, wishing we'd detour off this subject of hatred and terror. Seriously, I can't even relate to the pain exuding from Mr. Borochov's sullen expression—the pain of knowing Jewish neighbors who had actually been murdered. I mean, who knows *anyone* who's ever been martyred? Such things are inconceivable when you live in the sheltered isolation of Chicago's far, North Side.

And yet here, in Kiryat Shemona, people just go on with their daily lives, as if the possibility of a terrorist bombing is about as likely as a pit bull attack in downtown Chicago. Incredible.

"You want we pick you up tonight?" offers Mr. Borochov, hanging a left off Route 90. "Chana's working late, but I get her around 9:00 and drive up to Metula right after."

I shake my head. "Thanks, but I'll have the Zuckermans drop me off after the game."

"No problem, Ethan. Hey, Lior tells me tonight you play

against my countrymen."

"Maccabi Russia," I say. "And I'm thinking they're a lot better than that team from France."

"Oh, Russians always good at hockey," affirms Mr. Borochov, his left fingers scratching the side of his cheek.

"We'll take 'em," I boast.

"I thinks so, too, Ethan."

Just ahead, I see the white-plastered walls of the Canada Centre peeking over the distant treetops. It's my fourth time driving this way since Monday, and I'm feeling like this straight-shot up Route 90 is becoming as scenically monotonous as the McCormick Boulevard-to-Dempster Street shortcut Dad always takes to the Skokie Skatium.

But then, a squad of these dark-green, flying army gunships buzzes real low, which is something that's *definitely* never happened on the way to the Skatium. Cool.

"Okay, Ethan," says Mr. Borochov, double-parking the Hyundai along the sidewalk next to the Canada Centre's front entrance.

I get out and hustle to the hatchback. "Thanks for the ride," I say, swinging my heavy bag over my shoulder and then scooping up both Christians with a single motion of the right hand.

"You call if you need me to pick you up," says Mr. Borochov. "And be careful out there, too. I thinks this sport can be real dangerous."

I give him a half-grin. "Don't worry. Just a matter of knowing where the puck is and playing heads-up."

"Yeah," he says, real confident, then lets out this husky laugh like he's imitating an ESPN Sportscenter analyst, even though he's probably got no idea what I'm talking about. Must be a guy thing.

"There's a reason why I *schlepped* this stuff from Chicago," I say, rolling my eyes toward my CCM bag. "It's supposed to keep me safe."

"Well, I thinks goalie is smartest player on ice, Ethan. He has so much equipment he could stop rocket propelled grenade and not gets hurt."

I nod. "And my job is to make sure the Russians don't get any of those rocket propelled shots on our goalie. I'm a defenseman, you know."

I flick him a goodbye wave, then lug my way toward the sliding entrance door.

"*B'hatzlacha*, Ethan!"

Chapter Fifteen

I CAN'T BELIEVE I'M SAYING THIS, but right now, the Canada Centre's musty locker room never smelled so sweet. Yeah, just being around the guys and luxuriating in the scent of sweaty jerseys and reeking skates is the ideal remedy for my mental malaise, a perfect escape from terrorist rockets and Jewish survivor guilt.

Lowey's the last guy to straddle inside. I catch him stealing my gaze, and he's staring at me like I've got a Bozo-sized pimple growing on the tip of my nose. It's making me jittery.

"What's up, Conners?" he razzes, dumping the repugnant contents of his oversized CCM bag onto the rubber-matted floor. "I mean, you're looking too damn pale for a Mid-East summer."

"No pool at the projects?" jokes Zuckerman, showing off a toothy smile.

Wow, I must be giving off a pretty awful appearance. Really, I didn't think these stick-swinging buffoons were capable of sensing an amoeba of teenage emotional distress. But now's not the time to freak them out with vivid descriptions of what happened at the vegetable market.

"What is it, Conners?" demands Lowey. "Spit it out."

"Heatstroke," I mutter, and it's the perfect lie.

"Look, Conners," blasts Siegel from the other end of the locker room. "If you're not up it, let Coach know, because I don't want no nauseated defenseman trying to clear the Russians from the front of my crease."

"Shut up!" I erupt, stunning everyone.

Coach Weiss bursts into the locker room, his brown eyes ready to combust. "Enough!" he barks. "You boys get your pathetically-vacant heads in the game or we'll be playing for bronze tomorrow afternoon."

"Coach is right," spouts Spevak, wrapping black tape around his wooden blade insert. "Focus and win. Then it's guaranteed silver with a chance for gold."

There's this big, collective groan, and everyone's nodding

their heads in choreographed synchronicity.

And then, the locker room goes silent. It's definitely all business now, just grunts and breaths as dozens of fingers yank wax laces tight. Nothing like the perfect fit of hockey skates wrapped snug and taught around sweaty feet. I'm *so* ready for this game.

Ten minutes later, I'm digging my blades into the ice for the warm-up skate, physically exhilarated by the Canada Centre's chill sweeping across my face as I bust a pair of counterclockwise laps around the rink. Yeah, hockey's just what I need right now, a perfect cure for the guilt and despondency lingering from this afternoon's nightmare.

But there's still the Russians to worry about, and watching them hustle single-file through the east gate onto the rutty surface, I'm suddenly wishing we'd drawn Israel or Germany for our second game instead. Big and arrogant, these Russians won't even crack a smile as they line up for a complicated passing drill on their half of the ice. Every one these White-Shirts is spilling total discipline, like those Red Army teams from the eighties. Scary.

"What d'ya think?" asks Schneider, brushing up to me near our bench.

"They're definitely not France," I retort.

"Wingers need to bottle them in neutral zone," he mutters. "Take away their finesse game. Kind'a like *Miracle on Ice.*"

"They're tough," I wane, staring lasers at the Russians' precision passing maneuvers. "And even if we beat these guys, we're still gonna have to face Canada for the gold."

"Not gonna be easy," scoffs Schneider as he skates toward our bench, leaving me with a total dearth of optimism.

Five seconds later, the warm-up horn sounds and Coach Weiss orders us to the bench for some final instructions. You know tonight's game is real important, because Coach is all dappered in this navy-blue sport jacket, white shirt and cherry-red tie, and whether he knows it or not, he's looking like Uncle Sam minus the top hat and gray whiskers.

"Play our game, boys. Nothing fancy. No heroes. Got it?"

"Yes sir!" we scream, and I'm suddenly getting butterflies

in my gut, like this is the winter Olympics or something.

"Bloom's line to start with Conners and Lowenstein on the back end. Let's go, boys!"

I love starting, and I'm gliding proud to center ice, intoxicated by the pre-game buzz oozing from the stands. We're the visitors tonight, garbed in our blue jerseys and socks, the letters *USA* stitched in cursive white across our chests like those old uniforms from the 1990s. The Russians are in classic home white, their red letters and pants looking almost like Canada's jerseys when they beat Team USA in the 2010 Vancouver Olympics.

Lining up at center for the Russian and United States national anthems, I can feel my heart dynamiting through my chest. This is a *big* game, and I'm totally nervous. Everything's on the line here, especially the guaranteed medal to the winner. Coach is right — I couldn't bear to come home empty-handed.

When the Russian anthem fades to silence, the crowd starts cheering, just like at the United Center. It's a full house, every wood-splintered bleacher spot occupied by friends and family. I'm figuring that with so many Russians in Kiryat Shemona it's going to be like a home game for the guys from Siberia, but there's still a ton of Stars and Stripes swinging all over the place which is totally warming my heart.

"Win it!" I holler to Bloom, as he glides toward the center ice face-off dot.

Bloom turns and chucks me this solid head nod. Wow. This guy's fearless, incredibly cocky and thank God he's on our side.

Finally, the referee whistles the centers ready and snaps the puck down. It's a crisp, pro-style drop, the rubber lying pancake-flat as Bloomie and his Russian nemesis fight for body position. Bloom turns and uses his skate heel to nudge the puck sideways, squibbing it right to Richman on the wing. Richie looks up and sees he's got nothing, so he makes the smart play by slapping the biscuit deep into the Russians' zone.

"Forecheck!" screams Lowey, as Bloom starts bullying like

a freight train after the rolling rubber.

I'm reading everything through my white-wired cage as I glide careful toward our offensive blue line, refusing to set up at the point until I can get a better read on possession. Look, there's no way I'm going to be caught flat-footed on my very first shift.

The puck's rolling loose in the corner to the right of the Russian goal. Bloomie's barreling forward, edging his body against this lanky, Russian defenseman.

"Support!" cries Coach Weiss from the bench, and suddenly, Richman darts toward the corner, mixing with Bloom and the Russian defender. It's two-against-one and Bloomie reads it perfectly, slowly peeling out of traffic and waiting for a loose puck.

That's when Richman leans hard into the Russian and kicks the rubber sideways to Bloom.

"Boards!" I holler, anticipating the play and calling for the puck just as Bloom gets possession.

Bloomie's got all-star hockey savvy, and the instant he snags the puck he wrists the rubber hard around the end zone dasher. It's a perfect play, the puck tight and flat as it circles behind the net, hugging the boards the entire way. I know it's coming to my backhand, so I angle to the right, corral the biscuit against the dasher, and then fumble to bring it to my forehand.

But this rutty ice won't cooperate. The puck clips a rough spot and turns sideways, then does this high jump right over my steady, three-inch-wide blade. Of course, when this Russian left-winger sees what's happening, he rockets toward me, and I'm figuring I've got about one second to beat him to the bouncing biscuit.

No chance. The winger covers ten feet like a cruising 787, and I see him staring me down like he's going to physically separate me from the puck. Panicked, I swipe a desperation poke at the rolling rubber, punching it back deep into the Russian corner.

And then I'm clobbered.

The echo of brutal contact resonates gruesome as the stocky

Russian slams me hard into the unforgiving side boards. It's my shoulder against stone-hard plexiglass, and trust me, it hurts.

"Out of the way!" heckles the Siberian bruiser, and then there's a whistle as the puck stalls between players to the side of the Russian goal.

"You speak English?" I blurt, staring dumbfounded through his paint-flaked white facemask.

"That's how we talk in Syracuse," he snickers, and then skates away for a line change.

I sigh hard, exhaling a frosty condensation through my cage. My brain's racing, and it takes all of two seconds to figure this out. Yeah, I'll bet the whole team lives in North America. Sure, Russian through ancestry only—one great-grandparent from the old country and a pair of crisp Benjamin Franklins for tournament registration.

"You okay?" asks Lowey, as we hop onto our bench.

"Sure," I say, lying. I mean, that Syracuse turncoat got me right where Lior extricated those splinters, and now my shoulder's throbbing like a butt-boil under pressure.

"Keep 'em back on their feet!" shouts Coach Weiss, leaning over the boards as both teams line up for the face-off inside the Russians' zone.

I plant myself on the plastic bench, right between Lowey and Pinsky. "Would you believe these guys speak English?" I mumble at Lowey. "They're Americans."

"What?" snaps Lowey, lifting up his helmet and squirting this Nile River-long stream of yellow Gatorade down his gullet.

"I swear it's the truth," I say. "The guy that plastered me said he's from *Syracuse*."

"Probably immigrants," reasons, Pinsky. "But it kind of pisses me off just the same."

I look up as play resumes, and the puck still hasn't left the Russians' zone. Textbook. Our forwards are checking aggressive, and our backliners are doing a great job holding the point.

"On goal!" erupts Coach Weiss, as Benji Schneider's slap

shot sails high and wide.

"Tender's setting up real deep in his crease," observes Lowey. "Means he's scared. Afraid to challenge."

"Good read!" hollers Coach Weiss, turning toward us. "Got it defense? If there's no traffic in front, keep your shots high and hard."

"Will do," I mumble, itching to get back in the action.

Ten minutes later, the horn sounds, ending the first period. It's still scoreless, with just a handful of shots-on-goal per team. Both sides are playing tight and boring defensive hockey, and for the spectators, this game is probably as painful as watching the Blackhawks skate against the Minnesota Wild.

"Keep up the trap," orders Coach Weiss, grinning sinister. "We're frustrating their forwards."

Naturally, Coach has his game plan, and I'm not one to second guess his experience. But just the same, it's forcing these Russian-Americans to dump-and-chase, which means I'm constantly backpedaling into our defensive corners, and those kind of extra scrums are murder on my shoulder.

"Pinsky, Schneider, start the period," barks Coach Weiss, and I'm totally content to hang loose on the bench and catch some extra drags of musty oxygen.

Leaning back and scanning the crowd, I see the usual bunch of American fans waving the Red White and Blue, while this one section in the far corner's sporting these weird looking banners which I'm guessing must be Russian flags. When I peer deeper and space extra-serious into the sea of bobbing heads, I'm suddenly thinking about Shayna and the Borochovs, and now I can't stop myself from scoping everywhere for a familiar face, even though I know the Borochovs couldn't come and there's no possible way Shayna would even know about tonight's game. Whatever, it's still nice to dream.

The horn sounds to end intermission, and I'm watching the referees hustle to center. There's this thunderous tempo enveloping the building as the crowd starts buzzing with anticipation. Everyone knows this game's going to be tight, and you can almost taste the thick and heavy tension.

Spevak's centering for Zucks and Klein.

"Win it Spevak!" shrieks Lowey from the bench.

He doesn't. Spevak gets his pocket picked by this lanky Russian who times the drop perfectly, sweeping the puck back to his guy Boris on the blue line.

"Trap!" screams Coach Weiss. "Rush him, Klein!"

I see Klein forechecking hard, but the Russian defenseman reads the play well. He looks up, then peels the puck diagonally up-ice to his left-winger who's already busting forward.

"Careful!" I holler. "It's a set play!"

"What?" yells Mills from the other side of the bench.

"They've adjusted to our trap!" I yell back. "Did you see their winger exploding through the lane?"

"Get back, Spevak!" screams Coach Weiss, as the Russian center slips open near our blue line. "Cover!"

But it's too late. Cracking our strategy, the Russians create extra traffic on the strong side of the neutral zone just as their left-winger sneaks the puck back up the middle to their skinny center. Leaning a mile long with this Mario Lemieux reach, the guy slips between Schneider and Pinsky, corrals the biscuit in total stride, and now he's carrying the mail with less than fifty feet between him and Siegs.

Breakaway.

"Steady, Siegel!" screams Coach Weiss, his hands pressing potholes into the boards. "Don't commit!"

Total pressure.

I'm staring wide-eyed and breathless as the Russian bullets to the net, head-faking like Pavel Datsyuk the entire way. Everything's surreal, the crowd's in a frenzy, and I swear, the action feels like it's happening in extra-slow motion.

But Siegel's cool. I mean, totally composed. He's straddling the top of his crease like Martin Brodeur, daring the guy in white to make the first move.

Beautiful. Siegs' mental mind game is working perfectly. He doesn't flinch in his crease, and that puts all the pressure on the playmaker. Indecisive, the Russian waits a split-second too long to deke, and instead gets himself totally handcuffed before he can even cock his wrists for a shot.

"Atta boy!" screams Coach Weiss, ecstatic.

Siegs sweeps the loose puck toward the near corner, and half the crowd starts cheering wild. Our bench is euphoric.

And the Russians are sleeping.

"Pinsky!" screams Zuckerman for all he's worth, cherry-picking undetected near the red line.

Pinsky's the first guy to the rubber, and he's showing total poise as he corrals the loose puck and picks up his head. Amazing. There's no Russian within thirty-five feet of Zuckerman at center, both Siberian blueliners still caught up in the excitement of the breakaway. What a breakdown of discipline!

And Pinsky's happy to make them pay. He feathers this perfectly airborne pass about six inches off the ice, and when it lands flat at center, Zucks takes the puck in stride. Now, it's Team USA on the breakaway.

"High corner!" screams Coach Weiss, his fingers practically uprooting these strands of gray hairs along his temple.

Zuckerman's chugging past the blue line, and I see him cranking his wrists forward while he switches his weight to the front skate. He's got his head up like the Queen's Royal Guard as he surveys the choicest spot of the four-by-six-foot cage.

But the Russian goalie's poised. He counters by skating out of his crease to cut down Zuck's shooting angle.

Now, Zuckerman's twenty feet from the net. The whole building's hushed tense.

"Shoot!" hollers Mills from our bench.

"He's going five-hole!" wails Lowey.

We're all staring to our left, watching Zuck's stick blade flex like an Apache bow.

Snap! The puck rockets off his left-handed blade and screams airborne, my body english guiding the frozen rubber toward the upper-left corner of the net.

Our entire bench is breathless. Everyone's waiting for the back of the net to bulge. And then—

Ping! The puck dents off the iron crossbar, deflects high

toward the corner, and somehow disappears over the plexiglass. The ref whistles play dead, and to make matters worse, it's a neutral zone face-off.

"Damn!" hollers Coach Weiss, heart attack written all over his face.

"Zucks had him beat!" grouches Lowey. "High and hard, like Coach said."

"Keep at 'em boys!" yells Coach Weiss, motioning for a wholesale line change.

Perfect. I'm itching to get out, so I jump the boards and power directly for the red face-off dot on the Russian side of the neutral zone. Lowey's hustling right behind me.

"Win it," I chirp to Richman at center.

But my mental momentum gets totally stymied, because the ref's waiting to get the Russians lined up correctly. The zebra's just standing at the dot, flipping the puck into his palm like the game doesn't have to end until Shabbat. He's actually looking riled this time, his beady, brown eyes staring lasers at the Russians who are taking forever to get organized because their coach is barking on the bench, probably scolding his players for that last defensive breakdown.

"Get 'em going!" hollers Coach Weiss.

The referee blasts this angry, extra-long whistle, and now everyone's set.

Splat! Another perfect drop. Richie ties up his opponent's stick, but the wily Russian soccer-kicks the rubber sideways, directly to his comrade on right wing who quickly slides it against the grain to his right defenseman.

This time, Coach Weiss isn't screaming trap, so Bloom's forechecking hard, forcing the Russian defender to nudge the puck cross-ice to his partner on the left. That causes our forwards to back off into the neutral zone, while Richman angles toward the Russian puck handler.

"Watch up the middle!" I scream, my eyes glued to the Siberian wingers circling our side of the neutral zone.

Richie backs off his press, and now, the Russian defenseman skates the puck past his blue line. I'm sure he realizes we're not trapping this time, so he looks up ice and tries threading this bomb to his centerman who's busting diagonal toward our blue line. But Richman gets a blade on the pass, causing the puck to bounce over the Russian center's stick and right to our net where Siegel steers it harmlessly into the corner.

"Bring it out, Conners!" yaps Lowey, as Siegel coasts back into the crease.

Hyper, I peel toward the far corner and take the puck behind the net, looking to set up a play. There's this line of Americans standing along the bleachers behind me, and they're pounding their fists against the glass like drunken Hawks fans during an overtime game against the Canucks. I'm loving the spectator intensity, and I start getting these crazy butterflies as I circle left, and thread this thirty-foot pass right to Richie's blade.

"Take it!" screams Siegel, slamming the heel of his big goalie stick into the blue-painted goal crease ice.

Richman motors along the left-side boards, head up the entire way. When the Russian center takes a textbook defensive angle, Richie dumps the biscuit deep and then hustles forward like a speeding Kenworth, letting the Russian defenseman know there's going to be some serious contact in the corner.

It's a perfect, finesse dump, the puck stalling at the curved dasher by the Zamboni door, and the Russian's only option is to use his body as a shield between Richie and the rubber. Meanwhile, Mills is rushing in from the neutral zone for support, and now my blueliner brain's predicting that the Russian defender's gonna ditch the puck quick, unless he's looking to get sandwiched by our hulking forwards.

And that's exactly what Boris does. He pokes the puck forward, just in time for Mills and Richman to peel off before making contact.

From the hash-marks on the left, Bloom's already read the play, and now he's busting behind the net, corralling the loose puck right along the end boards.

"You've got time!" I yell, seeing no White-Shirts within twenty feet of him.

Bloom takes the puck and cuts left, freezing the Russian

defense. Suddenly, he digs his blades hard and kicks up a spray, then pivots the opposite way which buys a couple extra seconds. He's looking up the entire time, and I know exactly who he's beaming at.

Me.

Adrenalized, I'm sneaking in fast from my right point, angling toward the top of the circle.

"Conners!" shouts Bloom, like he doesn't know I'm staring right through him.

That's when he threads this soft, flat pass into the high slot, looking for me to blast a one-timer.

I'm happy to oblige.

My stick's already waist-high as Bloomie's pass radars a direct path toward my blade. Then, with about thirty-five feet between me and the Russian goal, I absolutely let go, my Christian flexing like a Roman catapult as I power the puck in full stride.

It's a rocket—exploding off my blade like a Tiger Woods drive. And it's rising high. Real high. When the nearest Russian defenseman shies his head sideways in self-preservation, I'm figuring I've probably overshot the net.

And then, *Splat!* The frozen rubber plasters the netminder square in the forehead, taking a big hunk of plastic right off his helmet. The guy goes down like he's been clubbed by a Chicago cop, and the crowd goes absolutely silent. A split-second later, the ref blows his whistle, ordering both teams to their benches while the Russian coach darts to his wounded tender.

I can't believe this.

And I'm feeling like total crap.

"Too dangerous, Conners!" barks Coach Weiss. "Keep those shots down."

Like I needed to hear that.

"Concussion," says Schneider, as if he's auditioning for a support role in *House*. "I could tell by the sound."

"They'll never let him stay in," says Lowey. "He's done."

I know it's just a game, but when I see this prostrated body in the red-and-white uniform, I can't help from feeling like a monster. A criminal. The guy's hurt, and *I'm* responsible.

"Hey. They don't have another goalie," blurts Pinsky, staring toward the Russian bench to our right. "What's gonna happen, Coach?"

The rest of us gape at the dispirited Siberians like we're actually surprised they don't have a spare netminder. Of course, neither do we. I hear baggage fees are a fortune for a pair of big, leathery leg pads.

Now, the gate along the far boards opens, and a couple of older men step onto the ice. They're sliding in dress shoes like crippled penguins toward the injured player.

"Doctors, probably," says Lowey. "This is gonna take a while."

I'm staring like a zombie, my conscience totally overloaded by iron anvils of guilt. Seriously, I can't stop watching the medics do their work, and the more I gape, the more I think about this afternoon's explosion. You know, how I escaped unscathed, unless you call a pair of tiny, souvenir shards a legitimate casualty of terror.

So how could it be that *Hashem* saves my butt from Hezbollah, and then causes me to strike down a fellow Jew on the very same day? Incomprehensible.

"They gonna cancel the game, Coach?" asks Mills, unsnapping his chin strap. "I mean, assuming he can't play."

"Or forfeit," says Schneider.

Coach Weiss shrugs. "Amateur hockey rules require teams to have a substitute or temporary goalkeeper on the roster."

Spevak laughs. "Just like us."

"But they don't have a spare," says Bloom, looking totally impatient.

"Gotta dress a skater," explains Coach Weiss, like he's imitating a law school professor. "That's the rulebook definition of a *substitute goalkeeper*. Or else play six skaters."

It's another five minutes of waiting, and then a couple of Russian players escort their injured goalie to the bench. I see the White-Shirts ripping away like hungry coyotes at the poor guy's leg straps, and that's when I realize Coach Weiss was spot-on.

"They're dressing a skater!" I holler.

Coach Weiss is watching, and he's looking pretty emotionless. He's probably thinking the game's about to be tainted.

I'm thinking the very same thing.

Look, beating up on a fake goalie's not gonna command a whole lot of respect. But defeat—that would be totally embarrassing. Suddenly, Team USA's got nothing to gain and everything to lose.

"Huddle up," barks Coach Weiss. He's got both feet planted atop the shiny plastic bench, and we're all pressed tight in a disorganized semi-circle against the boards. "Just play your game, boys. Keep the puck out of our zone and we'll be fine."

I turn. Half the guys are beaming at Coach Weiss like he's out of his mind.

"Does he *not* realize they're playing with a scrub netminder?" mutters Schneider.

"Mind games," mumbles Siegel.

"Oh, one last thing," fires Coach Weiss, his forehead suddenly creasing angry bulldog folds. "No high shots on net. Team USA doesn't win at the expense of sportsmanship. Have I made myself clear?"

There's this collective echo of *yeahs* and *uh-huhs*, and it's obvious everyone's lost their competitive juices. No one wants to be here right now. Pathetic.

We're moping around in mindless funks for another five minutes until the ref finally decides to resume play. I'm so out of it that I don't even remember the score.

I look up. Tied at zero. Boring.

Coach Weiss sends out Richman's line with Schneider and Gross on defense, which means I get to park myself on the bench and stare at the ice. And what I'm staring at is this Maccabiah zebra taking his stance at the neutral-zone dot. Guess he forgot that the stoppage occurred in the Russian zone. Nice attention to rules.

But Coach Weiss doesn't say anything, and it doesn't matter anyway because Richie wins the draw clean back to Gross. Of course, Gross is total heads-up, and the Russians don't even have a millisecond to react before Grossie feathers the biscuit over to Mills on left wing. Mills dekes quick at the blue line, and then dishes the rubber back to Richman who's naturally attracting traffic. There's a big, White-Shirt defenseman closing in fast, and Richman's got nowhere to go, so he wrists this fifty-foot laser through the defender's legs, testing the substitute goalkeeper.

Crack! The goalie gets his stick on the puck and makes the save. But he's using a pair of forward's skates, and he's real shaky on his blades as he fumbles to control the rebound. Kind of reminds me of those old pee-wee games when we'd all take turns playing goal. We couldn't even stop a basketball.

But this is international competition. That's why I'm shocked to see the sub fighting for balance as he reverses into his crease. Meanwhile, this Russian defenseman's panicking, and he blindly swats the puck toward the side boards. Mills hustles to the rubber and gets there first, eyes-up all the way as he corrals the puck and then slides it over to Schneider at the right point.

"You got room!" hollers Coach Weiss.

Schneider cocks his head quick, which tells me he's scheming some kind of shake-and-bake. I see him arc his stick high above his shoulder like he's gonna blast a slap shot. The Russians take the bait, and their defense freezes like a sweaty sock on a Siberian clothesline. Suddenly, Schneider drops his blade back to ice level and snaps a wicked line-drive about ten inches above the ice. Mills reads the play and rushes the slot, smelling a possible rebound. There's rush-hour traffic in front of the scrub netminder, and the poor guy kicks out his left ankle in desperation.

He whiffs. Real lame. This St. Petersburg substitute looks like a guy who's never played goalie before, which I'm guessing is pretty much true.

Look. I've got feelings. And I'm telling you I feel real sorry for the kid as the puck trickles over the goal line and wobbles toward the back of the cage.

And I'm thinking everyone in the building feels the same, because there's hardly a response from the crowd, and not much celebrating from our bench either.

"Keep at 'em!" yells Lowey.

I turn. "You serious?"

He nods heavy. "When I was on JV, we beat Birmingham Central with eleven skaters and *no* goalie."

"Get real," mumbles Spevak, rolling his eyes.

Coach Weiss turns. "Focus boys. No one's handing us a thing. Everyone keep working."

I sigh, and blow out this cloud of CO-2 through my wire cage. Seriously, Coach's pep talk has got to be the mother of mental mind folly. I mean, there's no way these Russians can match up with us minus a netminder. And yet, I know exactly where Coach is coming from. A cakewalk versus France, and now this debacle against a crippled Team Ivan. Sure, going 2-0 into the final is gonna be nice. Problem is, we'll be heading in completely untested.

Forty minutes later, the final buzzer sounds, and we're giving each other the most pathetic high-fives ever. It's a 6-0 blowout, but you'd think *we* were on the short end the way our melancholy expressions radiate through rusty-wire facemasks. When I skate though the handshake line, I can't help from feeling sick about what just happened.

"Nice game. Hope your goalie's okay," I say to every mopey White-Shirt, hoping no one recognizes me as the assailant who ruined their summer trip to Israel.

Most of them just smile back. But the Benedict Arnold from Syracuse is a bit more animated.

"Good luck," he says to everyone he passes.

Nice sportsmanship. Real nice.

Chapter Sixteen

WHEN I WAKE UP THE NEXT MORNING, I actually feel refreshed, like it's the best night of sleep I've had on this trip, which is positively true. Perfect.

I kick the cotton blanket off my ankles and stare toward the ceiling, zoning at these faint traces of early-morning gray spilling through Lior's bedroom window. Antsy, I pull my head off the pillow and crane my neck sideways. The desk clock on the dresser shines 5:50, and of course, I'm thinking I should grab my *tefillin* and *daven Shacharit* before anyone else gets up.

I hustle into the tiny living room, while my mind overflows with scenes of tonight's championship game versus Canada. Visions of victory. Glory of gold. Fantasies of a full-boat scholarship and the total culmination of Dad's parental dream. Nice.

Spacing for a few extra moments, it's hard to believe the tournament's almost over. Such a crazy week. Hockey. Rockets. New friends and hot girls with attitudes. Shayna, too. Yeah, right now I'm thinking it would have been so weird if I'd missed this—if I'd just been rotting lazy with Shoshana at the cabin and never experienced gritty Kiryat Shemona. Seriously, I can't even imagine it. Sure, some of the locals are throwing me odd vibes, but still, I feel like this city's already part of my essence.

The living room's as dark as the Old Orchard theater after opening trailers, so I start fumbling through my *tefillin* bag, using my fingertips to feel for the box with the longer straps. I'm thinking it's almost too early for morning prayers, but there's no chance I'm gonna do *Shacharit* with Danit watching. Rabbi Klepstein likes to say prayer is all about concentration, and trust me, that couldn't happen under Danit's evil eye.

Fifteen minutes later, I'm done. One good thing about all my years of religious school is that I know the *Shema* and *Amidah* by heart, and even Ezra says no one *davens* quicker than me.

I re-fold my *talit*, neatly wrap my *tefillin*, and stuff everything back in the blue velvet bag. Then, I amble into the kitchen and pour myself a tall glass of orange juice. Yesterday's butter-stained *Ha'aretz* newspaper is spread like the *Chicago Tribune* over the kitchen table, so I decide to get all sadistic by forcing myself to stumble through the small-printed Hebrew in this gloomy, dawning light.

I suck my glass dry and peek over at the oven clock which is glowing 6:15 in the morning. Guess it's a good time to call home. Probably should have done it last night, but at least now I can sneak onto the balcony without worrying about any Borochovs eavesdropping on my long-distance conversations. I'm a private guy.

Time for a quick mathematical calculation in reverse. It's 10:15 P.M. in Chicago, right? Wow, still yesterday evening.

And as soon as I think that, my conscience gets sucker-punched by this blocker glove of guilt. Seriously, if yesterday's rocket attack somehow makes the ten o'clock news, Mom's gonna freak. Big time.

That settles it. I skulk back into Lior's room, swipe my cell off the mattress, and then peel for the balcony. Like a surgeon, I use my fingertips to gently slide the door open, and then close it the very same way.

I'm anxious, but I've got to do this. Should have done it yesterday, but I was too cool to worry Mom. *Selfish, Ethan.*

I punch in the international area code and enter our ten-digit land-line back home. The Samsung's pressed like a BOSE headphone against my ear as I stare east over the railing, probably toward Syria, where the first real rays of morning sun are beginning to peek over the distant Golan Heights.

"Ethan?"

"Ehh, hi, Mom," I stammer, hoping I'm not worrying her by calling so early, Israel time.

"Haven't heard from you since yesterday. Your father's dying to know how the team's doing."

"Two wins, no losses. Playing Canada tonight for Gold."

"*Baruch Hashem*. That's wonderful, Ethan."

"Yeah," I say, hoping she doesn't press for details. I mean, even the North Shore Flyers could have trounced Team France and that handicapped Russian-American team.

"Ethan—"

Darn. Mom's testing me by doing that fading-voice thing. She knows.

"Mom?"

"Mrs. Epstein from the *shul* called me all frantic this afternoon. She saw a news report. Something happened in Kiryat Shemona."

"Something—"

"Everyone's worried sick, Ethan."

Now, my stomach's cramping sailors knots of guilt. I should have called home after it happened.

"Look, Mom—"

"Just need to know you're all right."

"Mom—"

"Why didn't you call?"

I hesitate. "I was there, Mom."

"There?"

"They hit the farmers market."

"My God, Ethan! You saw it?"

"I was *in* it."

"And you didn't call? We would have taken the next flight!"

Bingo, I think to myself.

"I'm fine, Mom," I plead, and now I'm feeling real good about not calling home yesterday. I mean, it took nearly an hour to talk the Borochovs out of *schlepping* me to the clinic. No way was I coming off as a pampered American. Not in front of Danit. Not when others may have suffered *real* injuries.

"You're done playing, Ethan! I'm calling Maccabiah."

"Calm down!" hollers Dad in the background, and then he steals the phone from Mom.

"Dad, it's fine."

"What is?"

"I played yesterday. I'm totally okay."

"Great," he mumbles, like he doesn't know what I'm talking about.

"Tell Mom to relax. They say it was just a cheap, home-made rocket. I'm one-hundred percent, and Team USA's playing for gold."

"Beautiful," he quips, and I know that's what he wanted to hear. "I'm giving you back to your mother."

"Wait, Dad. Don't you want to know what it was like?"

"I only care that you're okay."

"But the explosion!" I feel myself getting loud and emotional, which is not something I do in front of my father. Or anyone else.

"You're playing, Ethan," he mutters.

Flustered, I turn toward the brick wall and practically glue my lips to phone. It's like, Dad's going to know how it was. I *want* him to know.

"Listen, Dad," I say, getting angry. "It was surreal. Not like you see on the news. And it freaks me out that there could have been injuries. There *had* to be."

"But not you."

"No, but—"

"That's what's important. Ferris State's a great school for hockey," he says, like the only thing he cares about is my free ride to college, which is the sorry truth. God, I hate myself for thinking that.

But I hate Dad more for saying it.

"Listen, your mother wants to speak to you again," he whispers into the phone. "Tell her you're okay. You know your mother. She's crazy enough to call Maccabi USA and make them send you home."

"Not a chance," I say, but it's not because of the tournament. I don't even care about gold or silver medals right now. It's Danit's mean-spirit that keeps spiking my conscience, and there's no chance I'm gonna let her or anyone around here think that *this* American Jew cuts-and-runs.

"Atta boy," brags Dad.

"I'm staying no matter what," I say.

"You're good as gold," he says back, pretty much emotionally clueless, which is fine by me. Look, he's still my father, even if our priorities are suddenly half-a-world out of sync.

Truth is, if Dad hadn't pushed me on the hockey fast-track, I wouldn't be here right now. And that would be worse than losing to Team France. Seriously, there's something so cool about this trip. It's raw. Rugged. Kiryat Shemona's gripping my soul like a new pair of Velcro shin straps. Yeah, this place is changing me the way none of Mom and Dad's five-star trips ever could.

"Ethan—"

"Mom, I told you everything's fine."

As I say it, I hear Dad hollering again. "Stop worrying everyone!"

"You're telling me not to worry, Lew?"

"I'm fine, Mom."

"Shut up!"

"Mom?"

"I mean your father. Stop interrupting, Lew!"

"Look, Mom—"

"My God. How did I let your father talk me into this?"

"This?"

"Letting you go alone. I should have known more than anyone the danger in Kiryat Shemona."

"What are you talking about, Mom?"

"I swear, Ethan, if anything happens—"

"Answer me," I say, and then my stomach sinks when Danit shuffles mean-eyed into the living room.

"Be careful, Ethan. Please be careful."

"Look, I gotta go," I snap, totally embarrassed that Danit's watching me argue with my mother. "Tell Dad I'll call him after the game."

"That's a promise, Ethan?"

"Promise."

"Bye, Ethan."

I kill the connection, then slowly turn back toward the living room. Darn. Danit's still beaming at me with those condescending dark-chocolate peepers, and it's making me feel like I'm a suspect on the wrong side of a two-way police station mirror.

But then, my heart starts pounding thunder when she steps

forward and slides the glass door all the way open.

"How's it feel?" she says.

"Feel?"

"You American Jews. Spoiled rich. Leave fighting to us while you party at college campus. Amazing. Lior goes three years to *Tzahal* and when he comes out, you're graduated almost."

I swallow hard, and then my tongue freezes solid, like a game puck in the bottom of a snow pile.

"And that *kippah*!" She stares up like a hungry raccoon scouting a fresh nest of sparrow eggs. "Religious Jew. American *dati*. Think you're better because you pray everyday."

"I'm not judging anyone," I counter.

But she is. And this is gonna get ugly.

"Now you see what it's like for us. Every day. Isolated by entire world. And you Americans just send money while we fight. Send your big shot *machers* on sleek tour buses. Surrounded by guards and soldiers!"

Now that hurts. I mean, she's pretty much described every one of my trips to Israel.

"Look, Danit—"

"Go play you're ice games!" she screams, the sunlight illuminating angry mists of saliva jetting through her teeth.

Okay, right now I hate Danit even worse than when I first met her at Ben Gurion. At least then, she was probably being a bitch because she didn't know me. Now, she's being a bitch because she does.

I hear this flurry of footsteps from the kitchen. When I look up, Mrs. Borochov is bursting like a trackster towards the sliding glass door. "Danit! How dare you disrespect guests!"

"*Eema*." Danit looks surprised. She kills a half-second tugging the ends of her hair. "It's the truth *Eema*. We fight, and the rest of world's Jews send money. They don't bother with war and death. But you see—soon as next Hitler shows up in America, they all come here on first flight to Israel."

"Danit Borochov!" Mrs. Borochov's eyes look like a pair loaded tank turrets about to explode. "Money can be very important, too. Israel needs the help."

"*Eema—*"

"Apologize to Ethan."

"I won't!"

"Now, Danit!"

"*Lo, Eema.* I tell you Israel's just a cheap insurance policy paid for by American donations. I hate them for it! I hate Ethan, too!"

My mouth's gaping. So is Mrs. Borochov's. Suddenly, Danit bolts back into the kitchen, and now the balcony's enveloped in this wicked silence.

I stare at Mrs. Borochov. She's biting her lip so hard I can feel the pain. No one says a thing, and I'm wondering to myself what she meant when she defended American money. Just trying to be nice, I figure. Whatever. Everything is so tense. So awkward.

Please, say something, Mrs. Borochov. Anything.

But she doesn't.

"It's okay," I grunt, desperate to break the tension.

She turns slow, and gives me this combination eye roll-head shake thing. "*Slicha,* Ethan. I am so sorry for Danit."

"Don't worry."

"I—I don't know where that came from. Danit—she's not like that. You must forgive us, Ethan."

I nod. "Of course."

Thing is, I don't really believe her. About Danit, I mean. I think Danit is *always* like that. She's cut real mean.

Mrs. Borochov mopes away from the balcony, and now my thoughts start churning like a Zamboni with a hyperactive auger. Would have been nice if Mom had warned me that the Borochovs' daughter was a Jewish vampire thirsting for American guilt. I mean, it was bad enough that I'd messed up my summer with Shoshana. Who needs this?

I do.

I say this because pretty much everything Danit hyped about is true. Seriously, I'd been suppressing those very same thoughts since I first set foot in this grimy development town. It's like, my mind's been drowning in a dark cesspool of overprivileged shame.

I suck a stiff inhale of high-rise humidity and strut back inside.

"Some orange juice?" offers Mrs. Borochov, eyeing me from the kitchen table.

"Thanks. I'll get it."

I swipe my old glass and fill it three-quarters to the top, waiting for a head of pulp which never seems to come. Then, I skulk back onto the balcony. Wow, it's getting hotter. At least the morning sun's partially screened by the top of the next building to the east.

I'm leaning my ribs against this rusty metal rail, my eyes zoning toward the east, where the Hula Valley melts into the Golan foothills.

"Don't get too worked up."

I turn, half-startled, and there's Lior straddling the sliding door's threshold. He's donning this faded, Dallas Cowboys t-shirt, his dark hair still wild with sleep.

"You heard?"

He shrugs. "Look, Ethan. Danit's a, how-you-say, *hardhead*. She has her own opinions."

The term's *hothead*, but I'm not about to correct him.

"I've noticed," I say. "So it's her way or the highway."

"But maybe you give her a chance."

"You mean like cut her some slack?" I'm trying to keep cool, though my eyebrows are creeping to the top of my skull. "Get real, Lior."

Lior bites down on his lip, blows out this marathon sigh, and it's obvious he's preparing a closing statement for the defendant.

Hope he knows *this* jury's out for blood.

"You've got to understand Danit," he says, tapping his foot atop the concrete balcony like a rhythm guitarist on steroids. "She's addicted to American television. Western fashion, too. She's fascinated by rich people."

I cut in. "And she thinks all American Jews are rich."

"Maybe she does, Ethan. And maybe that's why she's bitter around you."

"Me?" I blurt, rolling my eyes.

"Not *you* as a person, Ethan. It's more like, Jewish Americans."

"Yeah, Lior. Been pretty much sensing that since Monday morning at baggage claim."

"Listen, Ethan. You already know what happened at her *bat mitzvah* party. But there's something else."

"Something else?"

He nods. "Last summer Danit spent a week in Jerusalem on this teen program volunteering in the Old City, and all she talked about were the hordes of well-dressed Americans ignoring the street beggars because they were too busy shopping like maniacs at the Jewish Quarter's expensive gift shops."

"Really?" I say, hoping Lior doesn't notice my Adam's apple pulsing.

"And Danit sees what goes on in Kiryat Shemona, too. It's like, whenever border war happens, our city gets surrounded by American journalists and Jewish big shots posing next to tanks and soldiers."

"Typical," I retort, and then I start thinking about our Israel scrapbooks at home. All those pictures of Mom, Dad and me leaning against tanks and standing atop camouflaged Hummers like it's the Museum of Science and Industry or something.

"They think they're so brave," spews Lior, angry. "But Israelis know it's a show. And when peace comes, the cameras disappear. But the poverty and hardship never go away. It's like, no one wants to live on border. No one wants to visit. There's no expensive gift shops here. America's Jews are scared. They don't care."

"Except your mother," I spout back. "She's an American. She moved here from New York."

Lior droops his head, defeated. "I know, Ethan," he tells the pitted concrete. "This is what frustrates Danit. It bothers me, too. Why can't other Americans sacrifice like my mother did? They only come to live in Ramat Gan and Jerusalem. I don't understand."

I do. But I'm too chicken to tell him. It's called haughtiness. Or privilege, if you prefer. You know, posh over grit. College over ideology.

Wait. I've just described myself.

No one's saying a thing, Lior's still sulking, and I'm pretty much done with this subject anyway, so I down my juice and balance the empty glass atop the balcony's rail.

Meanwhile, my eyes are following this old lady on the apartment terrace across the street. She's got arms like Gabe Carimi, and she's fumbling a plastic cleaning bucket near the terrace's ledge. I watch her finally get a solid grip on the handles, and then she starts lifting the bucket up to her chest. I'm hoping she doesn't—

She does.

Amazing. She dumps this pail of gray liquid three stories down to the sidewalk, without ever checking if anyone's in harm's way.

"Lior! Did you see that?"

He shrugs. "It's Israel, Ethan. And this isn't what you call a real polished town."

I nod. "Guess that's what Danit meant."

"About Americans?"

"Jewish Americans."

"You'll get over it, Ethan."

"Yeah, well it's like being punched in the nose with a fistful of truth," I grouch. "Your sister's right. Look at me, Lior. Silver spoons and hockey. If I really think about it, what's the meaning of my life, anyway?"

"What? You're crazy!" He starts beaming at me like I'm a total lunatic. "College. American dream. You've got everything, Ethan."

"What's *everything*?" I holler, just as my arm accidentally brushes my empty juice glass over the railing. There's a three second delay and then, *crash*!

"*Everything* begins with peace and security," squawks Lior, ignoring my clumsiness. "Get it?"

"But it's too sterile," I counter. "You know, Rogers Park. My whole existence."

"So—"

"Here, it's cutting edge. It's like Israel's this living history being played out every single day."

"Fool!" The word explodes out of his mouth. "Where you live, you can walk anywhere, never worrying who's gonna be the next Schalit. Never wondering if the next *Katyusha*'s got a bead for your bedroom. That's what Kiryat Shemona's all about."

The way he says it totally stresses me. "Stop it, Lior!" I scream.

"Stop what?"

"All this preaching!" I holler, sucking anger through my teeth. "I'm sick of it. I'm sick of everyone waxing weird about Kiryat Shemona. Poor Kiryat Shemona. It's like, I'm getting these vibes that you're ashamed to live here. And then there's my Mom's charity work for this place, but I can't even remember why she had to do it. All I ever hear is just *poor Kiryat Shemona*."

"Maybe you should have asked."

"Look," I huff, my right foot kicking frustration along the metal rail's bottom. "I didn't sign up for a guilt trip. You think this is how I wanted to kill my summer? I'm just here for hockey. *Maveen*? It's all my Dad's dream. And a tournament victory's his payoff."

"Sure," he grunts. "But you can dig a little deeper."

I swallow hard.

"Drama's not in my DNA, Lior. Never has been. I'm always the cool guy at school. I own a life that glides forward like waxed skis on Michigan powder. It's the way I like it, too."

Lior turns, his charcoal eyes beaming serious.

"Look, Ethan." He takes a step closer to me. "I admitted this to you before. I know there's—how you say—resentment. It's only natural for Israelis to feel this way."

"Natural?"

"I mean what Danit says about sending money while we do the fighting."

"Oh."

He laughs. "I'm told the mind wanders real easy when

you're hauling fifty pounds on your spine in basic training."

"Guess I'll never know, Lior."

"That's okay," he wanes. "I'll write you about it in few months."

I smile. "Danit told me about pre-army testing. You scared?"

He nods. "Wouldn't you be?"

"Darn right I'd be scared. And you know something else, Lior?"

"Tell me," he says.

"Right now I feel like a pathetic fool. A total loser. You know, coming here to play hockey, just to satisfy my stupid ego."

"That's not—"

"Beating up on other Jews and thinking it's cool. Oh yeah, real dangerous. It's like, Mom and Dad's worst fear's that I'll take a puck in the shin." I shake my head and blow hurricanes of frustration through my nose. "How do you explain that to Israelis living on the edge? Mothers and fathers wondering if God's gonna write their sons in his next book of Jewish martyrs."

"You don't mean that."

"But it's the truth, Lior. You admitted it to my face. You've shown me the miserable reality. You, Danit, and just about everyone else around here."

My words vibe heavy across the balcony, and I'm actually feeling like a jerk for dosing out a soap opera sucker punch to my Israeli host.

But Lior looks as cool as Marc Trestman on the sidelines. He blinks twice, draws a long breath, and then wraps his right arm around my shoulders.

"I appreciate your sincerity," he says, gripping me tight. "Seriously, Ethan, I'll be going to army soon and I swear, what you just said will always stay with me."

That gets my face flushing warm and red, and it's like a cocktail of emotions are suddenly beating down the doorstep to my heart. I'm pissed. Embarrassed, too. And now, I'm faking this hair swipe with my wrist because my eyes are welling heavy, and there's no way I'm gonna show that kind of emotion to Lior.

"Thanks, Ethan," he says. "For being honest."

"Yeah," I mutter to the floor mat, and I'm totally hating what just happened. I'm hating that I opened my soul to Lior Borochov, and I feel like a total wimp for saying what I did.

What happened to *Mr. Socially Smooth?*

When I check back to steal Lior's gaze, I can sense this ultimate seriousness exuding from his eyes. Of course he's scared. You know, three hard years of army. A world of crazies sworn to destroy the Jewish State. Two millennium after Titus, and the fate of Jewish society rests upon the teenage shoulders of Lior and thousands like him. What a burden—something that few American high-schoolers could ever understand. I can't, and I've pretty much admitted it.

"Pool today, Ethan?"

"Sure," I say, loving that he changed the subject. "When?"

"Let's try for 10:00 this time."

"Make it 9:45."

"*Sababa.*"

Lior shuffles back inside, leaving the sliding door wide open like he wants me to follow.

But I can't.

Instead, I reach over and pull the handle shut. Then, I turn and go back to staring at all these grimy, high-rise apartments sprouting like giant, cement cactuses throughout this dusty town.

I'm zoning deep, letting the sun's early rays spill over my face. Army and college. Wars and hockey. Suddenly, tonight's game is ridiculously inconsequential.

"Ethan."

It's a girl's voice. Innocent. Almost gentle.

I turn. The sliding door's about twelve inches ajar, and Danit's peeking her head through the opening.

"Hi," I say, staring at her ebony eyes which oddly gleam beautiful.

"I'm—I'm sorry," she mumbles as she steps across the threshold and inches toward a plot of vacant balcony.

This is insanely tense.

And sweet.

Look, Danit and I have been through emotional battle for the past four days. We've shared this tiny apartment, argued incessantly, and even escaped a Lebanese rocket.

So I think I'll take the high road with this one.

"It's okay," I say. "Really. Lior helped me understand."

"I don't believe—"

"I'm serious."

"*B'emet?*"

I nod. "You've opened my eyes, Danit. I mean, I always thought that visiting and showing support pretty much fulfilled our obligations as American Jews. But this trip's been different. Spending a week in Kiryat Shemona has definitely shown me the truth."

"Truth?"

"That vegging in five-star hotels and parading through Jerusalem's holy sites behind armed guards is just cheap insulation from gritty reality."

Her cappuccino lips purse into a half-smile. "You mean this, Ethan?"

I suck in a long breath, afraid to admit that whatever I just said makes a whole lot of sense.

"Yeah, Danit."

Now her smile's wider than the Golan. It's like, she knows I meant every word.

And I know it too.

"Look, Ethan," she says, running her fingertips across my right shoulder as we both lean against this rusty railing like it's a scenic lookout over the Grand Canyon. "This city may look like a *balagan* (that's *mess*), but if you focus hard, you can really find everything you're looking for. Even if you never knew it."

Wow. I think she's coming on to me or something, which is extremely weird since there's nothing going on between us. At least I didn't think so.

"Ethan?"

"Really beautiful, Danit. Never thought of it that way."

She nods, the sunlight sparkling off her liquorice hair like a thousand tiny disco balls.

"Lots of kids say they want to leave after IDF, Ethan. They all talk about living in the States. Some go and never come back."

"I know, Danit. But at least it's a free country and everyone's got a choice."

She sweeps her dark hair sideways, and that's when I see her forehead glistening with sweat. I think *Danit's* nervous.

"I'll never leave," she huffs. "Maybe I'm not so religious, but I know God wants me to stay. I hope to get nicer apartment after I'm married, but I don't ever leave Kiryat Shemona."

I nod and shoot her a quick smile. Danit—so tough on the outside, yet masking this incredibly fragile soul. Guess I had her all wrong. I go back to comparing her to Shoshana, and trust me, Shosh doesn't have it in her to wax eloquent the way Danit Borochov just did.

There's this total silence. Everything's kind of awkward. Suddenly, Danit moves her face a couple inches closer to mine, and my chest starts quivering. Oh God, I'm not sure what's about to happen, but I'm thinking she wouldn't dare do what it looks like she's about to do. Not here in the open.

Our gazes lock. For the first time, I'm noticing how the ends of her long, dark lashes curl up perfectly, just like my cousin Rachel's American Girl dolls. I like it.

Danit inhales, and my heart's pounding through my chest. This is total tension. My whole body's shaking.

And then, she turns away, like she's done waiting for me to make the first move, which I wasn't going to do anyway.

"I'll see you later," she chirps, stepping away from the railing.

"Yeah."

I watch as she drags inside, and then I let out this giant exhale of relief. That was too weird. But I somehow kept my cool. You know, nothing stupid that I would have totally regretted. I mean, this trip's been complicated enough, like an AP psych class from hell.

But what I'm beginning to understand, and what Danit

will never know, is that she's helped transport my conscience from the shallowness of Rogers Park narcissism, to the depths of gritty, Jewish truth. Suddenly, I hate who I was.

I hear the door close, and it's great to be alone again with my thoughts. My sweaty hands are gripped tight around the balcony's metal rail, and when I turn back toward the urban vistas of Kiryat Shemona, I'm promising myself to stop judging the locals by their gruffy manners.

And I'm praying that they'll stop judging me as an American arrogant.

You've elevated my soul, Danit Borochov.

Chapter Seventeen

BY THE TIME LIOR AND I ARRIVE at the pool, the place is totally packed, which surprises me since it's just 10:15 in the morning.

"Let's go," shouts Lior, dashing like a fullback toward the sun-bleached corner near the deep end.

"There's nothing there," I protest, figuring there's no chance he's spotted any vacant chaise lounges, because all the ones we pass are sprouting dirty towels or ugly pool bags, kind of like Chicago winter dibs when everyone's dumping folding chairs in shoveled-out parking spots along California Avenue.

"Next to high-dives!" he hollers.

Okay, Lior's definitely got the eyes of a Druze scout. No chance I would have seen those two ratty lounges secreted behind the high-dive's concrete pillar.

"Great spot, Lior. And no crying kids."

"You like?" he says, dumping his pool bag onto the faded-orange plastic fabric.

"Excellent."

"And you come in this time, Ethan."

"Yeah," I say, and then I start spreading this nubby towel over my lounge like it's a try-out for a Motel 6 maid job.

"Lior!" shouts this scruffy voice from the deep end, and when I look up, there's this smiling guy donning a tiny, black beach thong that should have been outlawed in the 1990s.

Lior turns. "Yossi! Be right there."

"Go ahead," I say to Lior, as I fish my bag for a tube of Banana Boat. Not looking to be traipsing around with Thong-Guy anyway.

Lior smiles. "Okay, meet you soon," he says, and in a Michael Phelps second, he disappears behind this ridiculously-long line of bodies snaking from the waterslides' stairs.

I yank off my White Sox t-shirt and park myself on the edge of this lounge. The entire place is echoing with shouts and laughter, and I'm guessing there's a couple hundred people here, swimming, sliding and tanning. It's so weird. I mean, by Chicago standards this place needs to be condemned. There's litter and smoke everywhere. And grungy groups of teens are still openly sucking hits from these crazy looking water pipes. Incredible.

My tube of sun screen's practically on fire as I spin off the lid and start squeezing warm globs of cream onto my shoulders. Look, we've got a championship game tonight, and I'll cake all eight ounces of this stuff over my body if that's what it takes to stop a Middle-East sunburn. Ethan Conners isn't taking chances.

My back always fries quick, so I rotate my neck and splotch oozy wads of cream up and down my spine. When my fingers glide across my shoulder blades, I can still feel these tiny scabs from yesterday's splinters. That gets me wondering. I mean, there's *no* security here. It's not like I'm looking to get paranoid or anything, but I can't help myself from suddenly scoping everywhere, staring at the sky for arcing rockets and scanning the pool deck for unattended bags or guys wearing bulky shirts. Never had to do that back home.

"Ethan!" screams Lior, desperate for attention as he plunges down the straight slide.

I shoot him a smile, and watch him disappear into this watery foam at the bottom of the run. Looks real fun.

I go back to smearing every square inch of exposed skin with this creamy sun block. I'm wet and sticky all over, and I feel like if I take a running start, I could pretty much slide all the way to Damascus.

I decide to dab a little extra protection along my ankles, and then I toss the crumpled tube into my bag and slip off my plastic beach tongs. Of course, as soon as I stand up, I get this shooting pain through my naked soles since the concrete's blistering-hot. I start hopping on my toes, and I feel like one of those circus-act guys stepping over a path of burning coals as I hustle toward the pool's edge where there's standing water to ease the pain. My feet sizzling in agony, I'm debating whether to go airborne into the four-foot section when I happen to glance over at the kiddie pool about one hundred feet to my left.

Brain cramp, fantasy-style.

Maybe she's there, I think to myself, as I stop, turn, and start staring at the very spot where I'd met Shayna the day before yesterday.

Now, I'm insanely curious, so I quickly dip my feet into the water and then bust around the shallow end, scanning the grassy sections near the fence by the kiddie pool. I'm dodging bodies the entire way, and it's kind of hard to get a good read through the crowd, but I'm pretty sure Shayna's not there. Whatever. I know I'll be hunting for her all morning.

"Ethan!" shouts Lior from the edge of the deep section, and there's Ron standing next to him and no Thong-Guy anywhere.

I rush forward, dive into an open lane and then stroke toward the other side.

"Water's nice," I say, popping my head over the tiny, blue waves.

"Good thing you leave expensive stuff at home this time," smirks Ron. "You try high slide?"

"Let's go, guys," I say, as I drag myself over the ledge and follow Lior and Ron to the end of the snaking line.

"Hey, Ethan!"

I shoot a glance behind me. *No way!* It's Bloom and Zuckerman, sticking out like a pair of vanilla ice cream cones amongst all these tanned Israelis. I'm probably looking just as pale.

"Dude, there's hot babes all over," croons Zuckerman, like he's never been here before, which is probably true.

Lior's eyes bulge. "You know these guys?" he asks, as Bloom brings up the rear of the slide line.

"They're from Team USA," I say, and now Zucks is looking at me like I'm weird for hanging out with locals.

"Ethan stays with us," brags Lior.

"Cool," utters Bloom.

Zuckerman smiles. "Ethan's the only guy not staying with family. But I'm thinking it's more fun hanging with friends."

"Yeah, we show him around," says Lior. "Now he knows

everything about Kiryat Shemona."

"Hey!" screams Bloom, as these two skinny, junior-high punks cut in front of us.

"*Mah yesh?*" bawls the smaller kid, like he's done nothing wrong. Then he tries staring down Bloom. Stupid.

Look, Bloom's an American monster, and he's definitely pissed. I see him suck this long hit of air which totally expands his chest, and then he takes a half-step toward the teenage interlopers. That totally scares the stuffing out of them, and we're all laughing as the brats turn quick and beat feet out of sight.

I smile. "No one messes with Jeremy. Trust me, I've got the sore ribs to prove it."

Zucks and Bloom chuckle at the inside joke. Even Lior and Ron are nodding.

"You guys tough," chirps Ron. "I like it."

"Just hope we're tougher than Team Canada," wanes Zuckerman, his blue eyes radiating concern. "Gonna be a real war tonight."

"Tell me about it," I hiss.

Lior turns, just as he's about to start climbing the concrete ladder. "Maybe we come see you tonight," he says to Bloom and Zuckerman. "I think I should check out this game."

"Bring everyone," laughs Bloom, as he watches Lior ascend the steps. "Especially girls!"

"You gotta check out his sister," I say. "She's a whole lot meaner than anyone on Team Canada."

"Really?" blurts Zuckerman who's obviously interested.

I nod. "Let's just say she can *stare* away a Lowenstein slap shot."

"Cool," buzzes Bloom.

Lior's about fifteen feet above me, and then this totally bored slide attendant waves me forward without even looking. "Okay, you next up ladder, *Amerikayi*."

"Catch you guys tonight," I holler to Bloom and Zucks.

"Eight hours to gold!" they shout back, but I'm already halfway up the ladder, so I just flick my hand in approval.

Ten seconds later, I'm standing thirty feet high, right

behind Lior who's lying sideways in the chute, waiting to be released.

"Catch ya at bottom," he mumbles into the air.

I give him a quick nod, then turn away and start scanning everywhere, like a prison guard at the Cook County clink. The view's great from this concrete perch and I'm taking full advantage, hoping for a glimpse of Shayna below. It's probably futile, but just the same, I'm zoning on every dark-haired female donning a skimpy black bikini, which basically describes half the girls here.

"Go!" mutters Slide-Guy.

Lior swings his body forward, and I gaze down at his descent. Looks fast and fun. I'm next, so I squeeze myself inside the blue, plastic channel, while the soles of my feet luxuriate in the cool water flowing down the slide's bottom.

I see Lior disappear into this explosion of white foam below, and now, I'm impatient for my turn. Meanwhile, time seems like it's standing still as I pick my head up and stare toward the forested Manara cliffs to the west. It's weird how my eyes are being totally drawn to these crooked sections of clear-cut scarring the lush, green slopes. Real ugly remnants from the 2006 Hezbollah war, just the way it looked on CNN when I was a grade-schooler watching the six o'clock news.

That starts me thinking about the townspeople. It's amazing how they persevere through it all, and now, I'm spilling puddles of spiritual guilt, knowing I'll be safe in the States next week while these Kiryat Shemonans stay here to fight Israel's enemies.

I'm still waiting for Slide-Guy to release me, but the fun's already been sucked from my conscience. Suddenly, I don't even want to go down this slide. It's like, I'm sitting here frying my brains out and feeling totally worthless, because I've spent the past week enjoying Israel's ice rinks and pools without having to pay the kind of serious admission fee that a guy my age ought to pony up if he has a shred of self-respect.

I swear, Danit was so right. I'm just this perfect poster-boy of a quintessential Jewish-American coward.

Nothing like a thirty-foot huff up a rutted waterslide to remind myself of the sordid truth.

Chapter Eighteen

IT'S SIX IN THE EVENING, and I'm crammed inside the Borochovs' car as Mr. Borochov motors the whole family to the Canada Centre. I did say crammed, right? One thing about Israel is that no one drives SUVs or mini-vans. It's not like Rogers Park where sedan isn't even part of the English language. Yeah, right now there's not a whole lot of personal space for Lior, Danit or myself in the back seat of this tiny Getz, but it's a nice shot of gritty reality just the same. I like it.

Truth is, I'm shocked that everyone is coming to the game. Especially Danit. Until now, she couldn't have cared less. Probably still doesn't. But my emotions are mixed. I mean, knowing everyone's here to watch the championship game is kind of special.

It's also making me nervous.

Lior reaches over his shoulder into the hatchback, and pulls out a sweaty skate from my unzipped CCM bag.

"I don't see how you balance on this tiny, steel blade," he says.

"It's all edges, Lior." Of course, he's got no idea what I'm talking about.

"Explain," he demands, as his eyes beam puzzled at my Bauer X-40.

I reach across Danit who's sitting in the middle and blasting this awful hip-hop on her MP3. She's completely oblivious as I grab the skate from Lior, and turn it upside down.

"Feel the blade," I explain, sliding my fingers sideways along the stainless steel. "Notice the sharp edges."

Lior rubs his index finger over the blade. "Yeah," he says, grimacing like he expects his skin to be sliced open by the shiny steel.

"That's how you balance," I say. "Turning causes the edges to dig into the ice. But the blades have to be sharp. Dull 'em down and even Gretzky's an ankle-bender."

"Gretzky?"

"Probably the most famous hockey player ever."

"Oh, of course," he says, like I don't know he's got no idea who Wayne Gretzky is.

Mr. Borochov peeks into the rear-view mirror. "I'm so excited to see first gold medal hockey game, ever," he winks. "Watch some Olympics on television, but never see championship game in person."

"Gonna be a hundred times more intense then our game against France," I say.

Lior nestles my X-40 across his leg. "You explain hockey to me, Ethan."

"You'll get it quick enough," I answer. "Pretty much like soccer on ice. Just watch out for flying pucks."

"Pucks?" grunts Lior.

I laugh. "Never mind."

Danit starts twisting her arms. She's got this miffed expression as she yanks out her earbuds, and I can practically feel her gaze carving out my guts.

"We there yet, *Abba*?"

"Just up the hill. *Rok shnee-ya*, Danit."

"Cool it, Danit," hisses Lior. "I told you Ron and Gila gonna meet us there. Gonna be like party."

"*Sababa*," she mutters, even though her dark eyes blaze evil, like she wants to tear the world apart. I'll never figure her out.

I grab my skate off Lior's leg and lean back hard against the seat. Suddenly, my stomach starts churning. Great. Feels like car-sickness, and trust me, now is *not* the time for this to be happening. Doesn't help that the Getz is a stick, and every two seconds Mr. Borochov's accelerating, shifting and coasting.

I'm also thinking I shouldn't have wolfed down five greasy potato *bourekas* just two hours before face-off.

Mrs. Borochov turns toward the back seat. "So I hear you'll be getting a medal if Team USA wins."

There's a battle going on in my stomach and I'm not looking to get chatty right now, but I've got to say something.

"Well, we're already guaranteed a silver medal," I explain,

fighting off some serious nausea. "But I'd love to bring home the Maccabiah gold."

"You guys got a chance?" asks Lior.

"Look, it's gonna be tough. Everyone knows that Canada *is* hockey. Not to mention we're playing at the *Canada* Centre, built by Jewish Canadians."

"So what?" mocks Danit, her tanned nose flaring indignant. "At least you get medal. Not like those other teams that travel all this way for nothing."

I roll my eyes. "Really, Danit. It's about supporting and visiting Israel. The hockey thing's just an excuse."

"Oh, *please*, Ethan," she retorts with this perfect imitation of Shoshana's whine.

"Shut up!" hollers Lior, staring fireballs through his sister. "I'm serious, Danit."

"Don't tell me what to do!" she yelps back.

"Hold it," I butt in. "Okay, this time maybe Danit's right."

There's a sudden quiet.

"Ethan —?"

"Look, Lior, hockey's a big-time rivalry between us and Canada."

"So —"

"So there's no way Team USA's not entirely focused on victory tonight. Trust me, the medal's nice, but what really matters is bragging rights. Just so you know."

Danit flicks her head at Lior. "I told you."

"Whatever," growls Lior, turning toward the side window.

Danit's forcing out this grin, and then she starts sliding her fingers across my right arm. "I want that your team wins," she whispers.

"Thanks," I mumble back, and all the time I'm thinking how much I hate the way she wears her emotions like a crazed chameleon. Yeah, Danit's a skinny piece of dynamite, and I've quit trying to figure where her head's gonna be at any moment in time.

And that's a major tragedy, because she's actually terminally cute and knows how to flash this great smile when she wants to. Seriously, if we could ever stay in sync for even ten minutes, I could really dig Danit Borochov.

But that's never going to happen, because I don't play mental mind games, and she's as stubborn as a metal goal post frozen into a fresh layer of ice.

Anyway, I'll be out of here in three days.

But it could have been great. And that's what's so darn galling.

Chapter Nineteen

THIRTY MINUTES TO PUCK DROP, and our locker room's as quiet as the Cook County morgue. Just me and a dozen other lip-zipped, peach-fuzzed poker faces hunkering over rancid hockey bags, totally focused on our mission.

No complaining.

No wisecracks.

Not even our usual analysis of the local girls.

That's because this is *the* game, and it's all business for the thirteen of us as we lace up our skates and re-tape cracked stick blades.

"Nervous?" whispers Lowey, as he watches me pull the dark-blue jersey over my head.

I shrug. "Just wish we didn't look so uptight."

"Gentlemen!" Coach Weiss hustles into the locker room with this erasable board swinging from his right hand, and that same Uncle Sam wardrobe plastered over his torso. "Perk it up. Or maybe you tough guys are scared of our Jewish Canucks to the north."

"No chance!" shouts Siegel, and that gets everyone buzzing.

Coach Weiss smirks. "Much better, boys."

"Hey, Coach, gonna be changing up the game plan?" asks Zuckerman, as he pounds his left heel snug into his Bauer 8000.

Suddenly, the room goes silent, and it looks like Zucks just ticked off Coach Weiss. I see Coach running his fingers down that ugly, cherry-red tie, and then he squints his eyes real narrow and gives us this *meaner-than-Mike Keenan* stare. I'm thinking Coach is more nervous than we are.

Lowey's probably thinking the very same thing. He turns and gives me this puzzled glance, and I give him a half-shrug back.

"Lemme make it real simple," grumbles Coach Weiss, like he's about to have a root canal or something. "Weak-side forwards, don't skate to where the puck is. Instead, figure out where the biscuit's gonna be. Are we clear?"

"That's it?" mumbles Spevak.

Coach snaps his head and spills this laser stare at Spevak, while the rest of us let out a collective sigh. We're all glaring at Coach Weiss, and it's like, everyone's impatient for an explanation.

But Coach Weiss knows how to play this group, and I can tell he's intentionally holding the moment. He grits his teeth, blinks once, and then inhales deep. "Don't try to reinvent the game," he says. "Look, you've worked hard to get here, so just continue playing our style."

"But Coach," whines Spevak, like a fifth-grader who's just earned detention. "These are the Canadians. We're not facing off against France or a short-handed Russian team."

"Meaning you were holding something back those first two games?"

"No, but—"

"Then just play your game!" blusters Coach Weiss, his unshaven face wrinkled like a cheap cotton shirt that never made it to the dryer.

Now, Lowey's springing to his skates. This is gonna be good.

"Listen up!" orders Lowey, standing tall and sporting this fiery gaze which could turn the Canada Centre's ice surface into a sheet of slush. "Coach is right. Play our game and don't worry how we got here. You think Canada's competition was any better? *Germany* and *Team Israel*. Get serious."

"Right on Lowey!" shouts Bloom, shaking his fist in the air and looking totally menacing in Team USA's blue jersey. Yeah, these visiting uniforms really *are* nice. Glad we're not white tonight.

Now, Coach Weiss is smirking real confident. "Take the ice in ten minutes," he says. "Couple laps in our end and then pepper Siegs with the cross-ice give-and-go drill. Look sharp out there. I guarantee our competition's watching."

"Maybe Ethan says a prayer for us," jokes Mills, as he fumbles to stretch his torn, blue sock over the plastic top of his CCM-200 shin guard.

"I don't waste God's time with insignificant requests," I scoff. "There's enough poverty and war around here to keep God busy."

Mills stares back at me, totally flustered. "Just—just joking," he stammers.

I catch his gaze, then nod real slow, trying to let him know it's okay. Look, I shouldn't have snapped like that. He's got no idea what's been going through my mind. No one in this room does.

"Lighten up, Conners," barks Schneider. "Save your wrath for Canada."

I give Schneider this head flick. He's right. I've got to focus on the game. Problem is, there's not a single guy in this room that's seen what I have this past week.

I pull my cotton blade guards off my X-40s and fling them listlessly to the side. Meanwhile, my mind's spinning like an overthrown, Jay Cutler spiral. Not good. Fifteen minutes to puck-drop, and my hockey head's somewhere between Touhy Avenue and the stratosphere over Mt. Hermon. *Stay sharp for gold, Ethan.*

But I can't. Maybe it's because I'm here without Mom and Dad, or maybe God has chosen this very moment to usher me away from a lifetime of American smugness. Thing is, I know something's changing. I sense it. Suddenly, I don't feel like that smooth, Rogers Park guy who's always in control. Truth is, I'm this emotional train wreck, and there's nothing I can do about it.

A gold medal game in the midst of rockets, army, and poverty. It's the cruelest joke ever.

Which is why I want to scream to the world that hockey's not so important after all.

Chapter Twenty

THE FIRST THING CUTTING through my mind when Canada's national anthem fades to eternity is that Dad's not here. I mean, this whole tournament was Dad's crazy fantasy, and even though I didn't want any part of it, the truth is that Dad not being here for Maccabi USA's championship game is like a sweaty hockey glove without the stink. It's just not right.

Coach Weiss makes up this improvised line, sending Spevak, Freedman and Klein to the center circle for the opening draw. It's an old hockey trick because we're the visitors, which means Canada gets the last change, and Coach doesn't want to show his cards by establishing his top line combinations before the game even begins. Trust me, I don't care that I'm parked on the bench for the first drop. I mean, everyone knows that me and Lowey are Maccabi USA's top defensive pairing, which is why Coach is playing blueliner head games by starting Pinsky and Gross instead.

As usual, the referee's taking forever getting the centers positioned for the opening drop. Ansty, I look up for a final survey of the stands. The place is crammed tonight. Probably fifteen hundred spectators plus dozens of standees, double the number that could ever be crushed inside the Skokie Skatium. Real cool. I'm feeling butterflies somersaulting through my chest and I haven't even touched the ice.

Play finally starts, and it's obvious both teams are content to simply feel out the competition. No big hits or odd-man rushes. About sixty seconds of boring, neutral zone hockey until the first stoppage.

"Lowey, Conners. Go."

As soon as Coach Weiss says it, my heart starts pounding through my chest. When I swing my butt over the boards and dig my blades into the ice, I get this paranoid feeling that I'm going to lose an edge and fall or something. Maybe it's because the Borochovs are watching. Or maybe it's what happens when you're just forty-five hockey minutes from Dad's gold

medal fantasy. Whatever. All I know is that I'm fighting off
these horrible jitters, and what I really need to do is cream a
white-sweatered Hoser right through the end boards to juice
up my confidence.

Face-off's in the neutral zone, just outside our offensive
blue line. Both teams made full line changes, and we've got
this power front-three with Bloom centering for Richman and
Mills. When the zebra flinches his wrist to drop the puck, I'm
nervously hoping Bloom doesn't win it right back to me.

He does.

As the biscuit rolls for my tape, my first thought is to
unload the thing. So I look up, praying for Mills or Richman
to circle open, but they're both hanging at the blue line like
they're expecting me to take it in myself, and that's just not
gonna happen. I decide to give them another half-second
before I dump the rubber into our attacking zone.

And that's when this maple-leafed bruiser figures he's
gonna set the tone by taking a blind run at me. I swear, I don't
even see the guy until he's already in full stride, speeding like
a Canadian Pacific freight train on the last mile to Saskatoon.
Startled, I unload the puck in a panic of self-preservation, and
then brace myself for total impact.

Crack! He wallops me hard, shoulder-to-shoulder. The
shock pushes my body forward across my hips, but I dig my
edges in deep and somehow maintain balance. Wow. The guy
had a clear shot of absolute momentum, but my blades didn't
budge an inch. Statement made and received.

"Way to take the body!" yells Pinsky.

Now, my adrenalin's pumping thick. I'm in this game. Big-
time.

For a split-second, everyone's still focused on the hit.
Except Richman. He's heads-up all the way, racing for the
loose puck in the Canadians' defensive corner. I read the play
and bust blades to the right point. Now, I'm holding the line
and there's no one on me.

"Back!" I yell, dying for an open shot on net. Problem is,
our forecheckers are doing a great job of keeping the puck
low, and they're not even thinking reverse pass to the blue
line.

"Point!" I holler again, trying to get Bloom's attention as he hustles to support Richman.

Useless. The rubber's stalled in the corner, and I'm figuring the ref's gonna stop play.

"Support!" bawls Coach Weiss.

Mills breaks for the net. "Slot!" he yells.

Suddenly, Bloom muscles the defender off the puck and takes control on his forehand. Spinning in front of the net on the right side, Bloomie looks for a screen and then sends this weak wrister sideways on goal, but the big Canadian defenders have expertly cleared the slot and the goalie sees the biscuit all the way. He covers up with his catcher to get a whistle, and now both teams follow with wholesale line changes.

Good start, Team USA.

Back on the bench, I'm sucking air and sweating waterfalls. Shouldn't be this winded after just a single shift. I reach behind me and cradle a half-empty bottle of Neviot into my glove. The water's warm and disgusting, but I still down the whole thing like a Russian Black-Hat at a *Simchat Torah* party.

I catch my breath and start scanning the stands. I'm purposefully honing in on sections of fans waving the American flag like it's the 2010 Olympic gold medal game or something. This is so cool.

"What d'ya think?" gasps Richman, as he flips up his helmet, grabs a nubby hand towel and starts smearing the sweat from his face.

"It's okay," I say, smirking behind the rusty wires of my CCM facemask. "Little more aggressive than the Russians, but I'm telling you, Richie, Canucks always buckle under pressure."

"Sure," he says, and I can tell he's not buying a single word of it.

"Just shoot low on this guy," orders Zuckerman from the other side of the bench. "Only way to be beat a big tender."

"Relax!" barks Coach Weiss, his voice laced with aggravation. "Plenty of game to go, but I told you guys to keep it simple. Forecheck hard and take care of our own zone first."

"Yeah," we mumble, with this big, communal groan, and then everyone parks themselves on the bench and leans anxious over the boards as Klein's line sets up for the draw in the Habs' zone.

"Win it!" whoops Lowey. I can feel him pounding the end of his blade into the rubber floor.

The attacking team's center is supposed to have his stick ready first, but Klein's taking his sweet time lining up for the face-off. I'm worried.

"The zebra's gonna drop it," I shout. "C'mon, Klein!"

As soon as I say it, Klein shows off some real Denis Savard flair. He spins his body counter-clockwise and sweeps his blade backwards, just as the referee drops the rubber.

He wins it clean back to Schneider on the right point.

"Textbook!" yells Lowey, his eyes bulging with approval.

"On goal!" wails Coach Weiss. He's standing with both feet atop the bench, and his body's stretched tighter than Rabbi Klepstein's *tefillin* straps.

Schneider's already got his stick cocked four-feet high. He's a lefty, and steps into the shot in full stride.

Whack!

We're about 150 feet from the play, but I can see rush hour traffic in front of the Canadians' net. And that means their goalie can't see a thing.

"Crash the goal!" barks Coach Weiss, spit spraying everywhere.

There's a mad scramble just outside the Habs' crease and Klein's in the thick of it, jostling for position. I've got no idea where the puck is, but the setup's right for a sloppy punch-in across the goal line.

And the instant I think that, Spevak suddenly lifts his shiny, green Bauer Flex high over his shoulder.

Then the red light confirms what everyone's hoping.

"Just what I said!" hollers Coach Weiss, smiling ecstatic. "Keep it simple."

The rest of us on the bench are high-fiving each other, glove-against-rancid glove. No one expected this. Not after three minutes.

Coach Weiss turns and nods. "Whadda I tell you?" he salvos. "Forecheck hard and clog the slot. Yeah, I'll take junk all day."

"And take care of our zone too," orders Zuckerman, his cage rattling as he nods all excited.

Simple hockey, Coach Weiss-style. That's pretty much how we play the next twelve minutes. Dumping and hustling to the corners, clearing traffic in front of Siegel, and throwing any kind of trash at the Canadians' net.

When the horn sounds to end the first period, I can't get to our bench fast enough. I'm craving a fresh bottle of Neviot, so I yank off my cage and soothe my gullet with more lukewarm hydration. Weird, I've never been in a game like this. It's like, I've been on the ice four times this period, and every shift's been absolutely nerve-wracking. Hard to catch my wind in this second-class barn, too. Guess it's because there's more bodies here than ever before. Or it's those oily *bourekas* still decomposing in my stomach like a pile of rotten vegetables. Nice.

I take a long breath, and try to psyche up by reminding myself that our mission's one-third completed. Yeah, we're heading into the second stanza nursing a 1-0 lead thanks to Klein's loose puck tap-in. And I've been playing smart. Real smart. A shot on goal and no giveaways. Nothing spectacular. Just some Zdeno Chara-style stay-at-home defense. Like Coach says, *take care of our zone first.*

"Ethan!"

That sounded like someone screaming my name from the left section of stands. I turn quick, and when I beam into the crowd, I see all the Borochovs scrunched near the top row and Ron and Gila are hanging with them too.

"Fans?" jests Lowey.

"That's the family I'm—"

"Whoa!" blurts Lowey. His mouth drops down to his shin guards, and I know it's because he's locking onto Gila. Look, even I'm giving her a double-take, because she's totally dazzling in this black spaghetti-strap that's practically painted onto her body. I mean, who dresses that way for a hockey game?

Spevak sees what's happening. "Pay attention!" he hollers, and then elbows Lowey's ribs for good measure.

"Conners! Lowey!" Coach Weiss is foaming spit. "You guys start the second."

"And keep their forwards out of my face," grumbles Siegel, not even thanking us for our great defensive work in the first.

I hop the boards and coast toward the center-ice face-off circle, anxious to get the period going.

Of course, there's another delay.

I can't really tell what's going on, but the Canadians are still huddled in front of their bench and the zebras aren't doing a thing about it. Amazing. Chicago refs never tolerate lallygagging on the ice. I'm starting to get agitated, so I try to keep my legs loose by skating wide circles around the closest neutral zone face-off dot while my eyes secretly case the crowd.

Siegel skates out from his crease. "What's going on?" he says, figuring I know something.

"Not sure," I shrug. "Just keep focused."

I watch Siegs turn back to the net, and then my eyes automatically drift toward this tanned girl standing by the far corner where the scratched plexiglass curves a soft, ninety degrees.

My stomach bottoms.

It's Shayna.

I can't believe it's her. But it is. She's standing along the glass to Siegel's left, camped next to that Israeli baboon from the pool, the one that almost drowned me with a sixteen-ounce cola.

My eyes are like ping-pong balls. And my brain's trying to figure out what she's doing here. With *him*.

"Sticks down!" yells the ref.

Oh God. The zebra's about to drop the puck at center and I'm twenty feet out of position, googly-eyeing this dark-haired *sabra* in the corner.

"Ethan!" screams Lowey. "Get in the game!"

Panicked, I'm sucking more air than a loaded 747 as I bust

to the blue line, just as the ref lays down the rubber.

Incredible luck! The puck somehow squirts between the centers' sticks and dribbles directly toward me.

Coach Weiss is already reading the play. "Conners! Take it up-ice!"

Look, Coach has made it perfectly clear that he *never* wants his defensemen rushing the puck Bobby-Orr-style off the draw. Thing is, I was already sprinting forward to get back into position, so Coach figures my momentum can take me wide around the flat-footed Hoser defense.

That's exactly what I'm planning to do.

"I'm covering point!" screams Richman from the right, as I jet past the red line. "Take it, Ethan!"

The air's whooshing like a November wind through my cage. I look up, and there's just one Hab to pass, and that's this lanky defenseman who's desperately sweeping his stick outward which forces me a couple feet closer to the right-side boards. But the guy's stone-footed, and I've got the speed, so I keep flanking wide, driving my edges deep into the ice.

"Beat him!" hollers Lowey.

It's a piece of cake to shake off the defender, and now I'm cutting back inside at a forty-five-degree angle to the goalie. Rushing through the big face-off circle, I'm about thirty feet from the net and I've got to make this split-second decision to either shoot or deke.

Total breakaway.

Total pressure.

I hear the air whistling through my helmet's ear flaps, and I'm loving how it mixes with the roar of a thousand screaming throats.

Suddenly, Zuckerman's words start pounding through my head. *Shoot low. Low!*

Twenty feet from the crease. I'm totally in the clear — even better than a penalty shot. I cock my wrists backward, my left palm low on the shaft.

I look up. *Bull's-eye.* There's this tiny opening between the goalie's catching glove and the left post. I shift my body weight to the front skate. My eyes take one last look. *Now,*

Ethan. Let it rip!

My Christian torques. The puck snaps fast and heavy off my blade and—

Thud! It's the sickening boom of the netminder's big, leather pad thrusting sideways to block the rubber.

Translation—your Ferris State scholarship guy just missed from point-blank.

But it gets worse. The rebound bounces like a tennis ball halfway to the side boards, and it's scooped up by the Canadian right-winger. He's got the dainty touch of a Russian ballerina as he picks up his head, and feathers this flat, breakout pass seventy-five feet up-ice, right to a fresh, Hab forward who must have sneaked into the game on a gutsy player change while everyone on Team USA was glued to my rush on goal.

"Challenge him, Siegs!" Coach's voice echoes paranoid since the Canadian's got a twenty-foot lead on our closest guy.

We are *so* toast. This Hoser's going in clean on Siegel, and I'm talking straight-on, not diagonally like my breakaway. Seriously, the guy's got options—like choosing either side of the net for a high-percentage shot.

Instead, the maple-leafed forward surprises everyone by faking to his backhand, and then wristing five-hole at Siegel's Mission Commander SEs.

There's a split-second of silence. No one knows if the shot's loose or frozen in the crease.

Until the puck dribbles past the goal line, and the red bulb glows like a Wisconsin trooper's mars light behind Siegs.

All tied at 1-1.

Big screw-up, Ethan.

I'm in extreme mental distress as I slouch to the bench, head bowed and confidence leaking through my pores. The worst part is that I can actually feel Coach Weiss's wrath branding blisters into my skin. I mean, he's staring right through me, and he's totally silent, which is ten-times worse than being publicly chewed out and getting the whole thing over with.

"Get'em next shift, Ethan," comforts Klein, the eternal optimist.

"Sure," I mumble, and I just want to break this tension by screaming out that it's all my fault. That if I'm not ogling Shayna, I'm in textbook face-off position, and I'm not gonna have Coach's blessing to rush the puck for a breakaway.

Which means I don't get the privilege of shooting into the goalie's pad and causing a thirty-foot rebound the other way.

Just one positive from all of this. Dad's not here. He'd have ripped my head off and left the rest of me for the Tel Chai Road sewer rats.

When the second period ends still tied at one goal apiece, I'm praying that no one's even remembering my mental washout anymore. I mean, Coach Weiss never disciplined me—didn't even bench my sorry butt for a single shift. And none of the guys ever a muttered a word. Of course, since that disaster, I've been playing totally focused on the back line, and trust me, my eyes never even twitched toward the other side of the glass.

But now, things are about to get tense. *Real* tense. Look, a single brain-freeze is all it takes to lose a low-scoring game like this, and no one wants to be the goat. One period to go and both teams are chomping for bragging rights, which means settling for silver is just a giant fail.

I check the board. The clock's winding down on the quickest three-minute intermission of my life. Barely enough time to lounge around the bench, gulp warm water and towel-off my sweaty face. Right now, I'm figuring I've got about ten more seconds of free-thinking time before Coach bears down on us with his predictable third period game spiel.

That's ten seconds for a quick scan toward the corner stands.

I suck a long drag of air. Then, I lean my head forward and shift my eyes a little to the left. I'm trying to be absolutely inconspicuous as I scout bodies behind the glass.

My throat pulses. Darn. No Shayna. The big, bad bruiser's disappeared too. This stinks. And intermission's almost over.

I fake a glance at the overhead scoreboard and scope again. They've got to be there. Somewhere. I mean, what's the point of cutting out before the third period in a tied, championship game? I feel my face turning hot, and I'm totally panicked as I beam like an Audubon birder at these narrow rows of bleachers behind the goal line that I'm thinking I might have missed. Lots of crowd movement back there, so I'm keeping my eyes glued wide as this pack of bobbing heads finally clears out.

And there she is! Without the goon.

I do a quick double-take, just to make sure. Oh yeah, that's definitely Shayna, her thick, liquorice-black hair hanging low over those petite, bronzed shoulders. Looks like she's sticking out another stanza, and I'm wondering if she even knows this is the last period.

"Huddle in!" barks Coach Weiss, and we all bunch close to the middle of the bench. He's standing on the ice with this erasable markerboard, and everyone starts half-circling around him like he's giving away Tel Aviv pizza slices after the *Yom Kippur* fast. Thing is, only a few guys in front can actually see whatever Coach is sketching.

"Keep it tight and simple," he says — *again*. "Play it just like the first two periods. Be patient. We'll get our chances."

Everyone's silent. Predictably tense. Then, Coach looks up and starts beaming my way through a semicircle of bobbing heads. "And no mental breakdowns," he huffs.

That's meant for me.

No one's saying a thing as we squeeze our helmets back on and snap our chin straps tight. I mean, we're some of the best players in the States, and we've all heard these late-game orations hundreds of times before. Just typical hockey protocol.

"Pinsky, Schneider, you're up," orders Coach Weiss, and I'm kind of relieved to be watching the first shift from the bench. Lowey's camped right next to me, but I doubt he's thinking the same thing.

"Let's go, USA!" screams Gross, as the ref positions both centers' sticks behind the dot at the middle face-off circle.

Suddenly, the fans start buzzing like they do at the United Center before the opening drop at a Hawks playoff game.

Everyone knows the entire tournament comes down to the next fifteen minutes, and you can almost feel the Canada Centre's wooden rafters buckling from the tension. *This* is pressure, and I swear to myself to keep it all business. You know, for Dad. And Ferris State. Even for the Borochovs.

I'm thinking Shayna wants a winner, too.

Chapter Twenty-One

7:45 REMAINING IN REGULATION. The score's still knotted at a goal apiece, and I'm going insane from this third period tension. So far, I've been out for three shifts, and I swear, this is one of the tightest matches ever. Lots of neutral zone trapping. Both teams refusing to surrender an inch of defensive ice. Probably boring to watch, too. Pretty obvious that it's more about not being the goat and just leave the glory to someone else, thank you. Seriously, every guy out here knows that one miscue equals a horrible twelve-hour flight across the North Atlantic, and like I predicted, nobody's looking to own that fatal, third-period mistake.

"Lowey and Conners, next out!" screams Coach Weiss from the other side of the bench.

As soon as he says it, my heart's pumping rivers of adrenalin. I hop the boards fast, figuring this could be my next-to-last shift.

Which means I've got three-and-a-half hockey minutes to finally do something positive.

My blade slices the frozen surface. Ice is rutty—pretty much all snow and chips. Whatever. I'm just thinking about the score. And the scholarship. Even next week's headline in the Chicago Jewish News—*Rogers Parker Wins Maccabiah Gold for USA.*

Wow, that's dangerous. The fantasy, I mean. *Remember that second-period brain cramp, Ethan.* Sure, I'd love the glory. But like Coach Weiss says, my job's the defensive end.

Which means leave the offensive heroics to someone else.

Face-off's in the neutral zone next to our attacking blue line. I position up about twelve feet behind the dot, close to the right-side boards. There's no face-off circle along the neutral spots, so I'm being extra careful. Got to make sure the Canadians aren't setting up a strong-side sleeper breakout since everyone's crowding the dot, and the referees haven't been enforcing the invisible fifteen-foot radius.

The zebra snaps his wrist. *Splat*, the puck's down flat. Mills ties up the Canadian center's stick, then somehow kicks the rubber back to Lowey on the left. I'm totally reading the play and see that Lowey's got nothing up front, so I drop back and get myself open for a cross-ice pass.

"Ethan!"

Lowey knows I'm all alone at our blue line, and he feathers the puck right on my tape. Beautiful. Now, I've got plenty of time to quarterback a rush since the nearest White-Shirt's at least twenty feet away. I glance ahead and survey up ice, waiting for our forwards to circle.

"Ethan!" shrieks Bloom, bursting open on the right side. "Boards!"

Bloom's crossing the red line, and incredibly, he's already slithered five feet behind the Canadians' left defenseman. All I need to do is angle the puck off the side boards with a pool shark's touch, and I'll have Bloomie in the clear.

Danger, Ethan. I'm still behind the center line, so if I overshoot him we're gonna be called for icing. And if the pass is weak, the Hab defenseman's got a rush going our way with Bloom five strides behind the play.

It's split-second calculation time.

I'm going for it.

I look up and gently bank the biscuit high off the right-side boards, leading Bloom with the puck the way Jay Cutler leads Brandon Marshall with the pigskin. It's a textbook headman pass, and Bloom's busting skates to gobble up the rubber just as he crosses the attacking blue line. Play's looking good, the puck drops down clean, and I'm grinning the entire way.

And then, the sliding puck hits this invisible ice rut, flies right over Bloom's blade, and glides harmlessly on goal where the Canadian netminder's only too happy to cover up for a stoppage. Unbelievable.

"No heroes!" scolds Coach Weiss, his husky voice reverberating like summer thunder.

"Ice sucks," huffs Lowey. He skates up to me as the Habs change lines. "I mean, how do you *not* zam after the second?"

"Tell me about it," I grunt, trying to recall the last time in the past four years when there wasn't an ice cut between the second and third periods.

"Stack the neutral zone!" hollers Coach Weiss, eyeing our forwards lining up for the draw.

Lowey turns. "That's code for another dump-and-chase," he says.

"Jewish Columbus Bluejackets," I say back. "Man, that's boring hockey."

"Just relax, Ethan," scoffs Lowey, as he skates away from me and plants himself along the left-rear of the face-off circle in the Canadians' zone.

This time, the ref hurries the centers and lays the puck down quick and crisp. But the lanky Hoser centerman times the draw perfectly, gets control of the rubber, and then blindly whisks the biscuit back to his strong-side defenseman. The defender's got time, looks up, then reverses and stalls behind the net, his eyes scanning forward as he reads the ice for a possible breakout.

I'm ninety feet away, and not taking any chances. I'm keeping this soft position near the red line, guaranteeing that no one's going home run between me and Siegel. It's a good strategy because these Canadian forwards are trying to confuse us by circling through the neutral zone like a trio of Edmonton Eskimo receivers running a complicated crisscross.

"Rush him, Klein!" screams Coach Weiss.

Klein looks up and buzzes right for the net, which means one of the Hab forwards gets released from double-coverage.

And that's just what the Canadian defenseman was waiting for. I watch the blueliner roll left and then he hoists the puck high off the glass, hoping his right-winger keeps skating on this diagonal slant pattern through the neutral zone.

It's a smart play.

And reckless, too.

I say this because the Canadian right-winger's busting insane for the biscuit, and he's taking this blind angle right into my piece of ice. I mean, I can actually see his bulging eyes following the puck's airborne flight, which means his survival mode's on vacation.

In hockey slang, that's called *recipe for suicide*.

Look, I'm a Jew, and so is this Hoser winger, but that's *before* the uniform goes on. Trust me, what's about to happen is every defenseman's dream.

I hold back for a split-second while I wait for the rubber to spiral down to earth. Meanwhile, the Canadian winger's still focused like a center fielder on the puck's descent, and he's probably thinking he's gonna pick it up clean.

That's just what I want.

I take three quick steps and start my glide. Everything's timed perfectly, so when I see the puck land flat and watch the winger busting face-down to gobble up the biscuit, I'm like a kid on the first day of Hanukkah.

Two feet. One foot. I square my chest and inhale deep.

Crash!

My shoulder pad pummels the Hab's rib cage, my body following through clean and even. There's this total explosion of cracking plastic, and the poor Hoser looks like he's just been t-boned by a runaway sleigh as his head snaps backward and his lumber goes airborne. What a hit!

The concussion jars me a bit, but I make my statement by keeping upright on my skates. Meanwhile, our bench is buzzing all excited, and when I turn to the left, I see the loose puck squirt to Bloom who's already flanking wide for a possible two-on-one.

"Just one to beat!" screams Coach Weiss, anticipating a great scoring chance.

Suddenly, the whistle blows.

And I'm about to be sick.

Look, I've been playing long enough to know this isn't good. I mean, the zebra actually stopped play while *we* had possession. That's not supposed to happen.

Unless the Hab's seriously injured. He isn't.

Or, there's gonna be a Team USA penalty, and since the Canadian winger's wobbly but still able to skate, I'm thinking the ref's about to flag me for the crunch.

"Twenty-two, Blue!" screams the official, pointing his finger at me and practically stabbing me with it. "Minor, head-check."

I'm livid. "You're crazy!" I scream back. "It was shoulder-to-chest!"

"Cool it, Ethan!" bellows Coach Weiss, standing with one foot on the bench and the other planted atop the boards. "Get your butt in the box!"

Coach is worried I'm gonna draw an extra minor for unsportsmanlike conduct, and he's probably right.

"You murdered him," smirks Lowey as he skates past me. "But you gotta zip it up."

"Whatever," I say back. He knows I'm pissed.

I glide to the sin bin, ready to explode through my helmet. These international refs — they're incompetent. That hit was two feet below the chin and perfectly legal. Coach Weiss knows it. He *has* to know it.

Oh, I've seen this before. Even in the pros. It's like that old playoff game from the 1990s when New Jersey's Scott Stevens destroys Eric Lindros at the blue line. Lindros goes down like a house league mite, and the ref thinks he saw an elbow from halfway across the ice, even though the replay clearly showed it was shoulder-on-shoulder. No matter. Stevens gets the major and game misconduct. Guess officiating hasn't changed much in twenty years.

I'm skulking to the penalty box, trying my best to stay positive. But it's going to be the sickest feeling in the world to be parked alone in the sin bin, knowing that everyone in the building figures I've just committed the dumbest penalty in championship game history. That includes my teammates, and maybe Coach Weiss, too. And Shayna and the Borochovs — now they're probably thinking I'm some kind of Modern Orthodox goon. *God, please don't let Canada connect on this power-play.*

I'm squirming. I'm emotionally panicked. And I'm hating that I can't see a darned thing from this penalty box. Wow. The panes of plexiglass above the gate probably haven't been cleaned since the Bears won Super Bowl XX. Everything's scuffed, scratched and fading, and I'm just gonna have to spot the zone of play and listen to the crowd's roar to figure out what's happening for the next two minutes.

I glance skyward. At least there's a clear view of the overhead scoreboard so I'll know when my penalty expires.

Faceoff's in the neutral zone near the scene of the crime. The puck drops, then quickly squirts deep into our defensive end. I'm dripping nervous waterfalls through the bottom of my helmet as I try to follow the action through this inch-and-a-half gap between panes of plexiglass above the sin bin door. Trouble is, my facemask stops me from pressing my eyes up close, and I'm getting dizzy peeking through these rusty rows of metal wires. At least I'm able to tell we've chewed up some precious seconds by somehow clearing the puck into the Canadians' end of the rink. *Short-hander, anyone?*

But my heart plunges like a Willis Tower elevator when play suddenly reverses and the crowd starts buzzing in anticipation of a scoring opportunity. I can tell the puck's somewhere in our defensive end, and I'm feeling this horrible nausea, just like I get when Dr. Fishbein starts jabbing my gums with his nasty instruments of pain.

"Screen!" barks Coach Weiss, and that tells me the Canadians are setting up low. "Let Siegel see it!"

I can barely make out a couple of White-Shirts camped in front of Siegel, which means the Canadians are definitely controlling the puck in our zone. I shoot a glance up at the board. Still a minute left in my penalty. I'm gonna puke.

But then, a whistle. Not sure what happened, but the crowd's kind of silent. Probably a frozen puck or high stick. No matter. Just fifty-three ticks until we're at full strength. *Come on guys, dump and forecheck. Keep the rubber away from Siegs, and get me out of here still tied.*

Talk about *anxious*. This stoppage is taking forever, and my feet are twitching wild in my skates. I'm watching both teams make wholesale line changes, my cage practically etching the glass as I stare like a Secret Service agent to figure out who we've got on the ice. Looks like Bloom and Spevak are killing the rest of the way, but I can't see who's paired in back.

Antsy, I quickly shift my gaze over the glass, beaming at these tiny heads in the top rows of the stands on the other side of ice. Man, this building's suddenly quiet. Seriously, all I'm hearing are echoes from bench doors slamming, and it's reminding me of those late-Thursday night practices at the empty Skokie Skatium, when you can practically hear a shin guard buckle dropping on the floor. How is it even possible for a thousand souls to stay so morbidly muffled?

My eyes descend back toward the ice. Face-off's to the right of our net. The ref whistles everyone to line up, and now the crowd's picking up energy.

Another clock check. Four-and-a-half minutes left in regulation. Suddenly, I hear sticks cracking. The puck's down and it looks like Schneider has control. He's stalling the play along the near boards, nicely eating up crucial seconds of penalty kill. Textbook.

Everything's happening to my right, but it's impossible to locate the puck. To keep sane, I just stand and peer at the clock every three seconds. I've got my fingers wrapped tight around the shaft of my Christian Pro-Flex, and only God knows how bad I'm itching to get back into the play.

"Ice it!" orders Coach Weiss, and from the tenor of his voice, I'm figuring the Habs are forechecking tough.

I look up. Ten seconds left and the puck's still in our zone. Darn. I've been around the game long enough to know that it's taking too long to clear the biscuit from our slot. Something's about to happen.

"Conners! Bench!" shouts Coach Weiss, as the last penalty tick disappears from the electronic board.

I bust out of the box and make ice contact with my skate. Lowey's got the bench door wide open. I jump inside, turn and lean my chest over the boards. Now, I'm getting a clear view of the play.

And it's not pretty.

What I'm seeing is this Canadian winger muscling a thirty-foot wrister through traffic in front of our crease. Like a pinball ricocheting off a pair of rubber bumpers, the puck double-deflects off a Hoser stick, and then Pinsky's skate. I lose sight of the black biscuit for a millisecond.

And then I see it squib between Siegel's big, leather pads.

The red light goes on.

I'm looking for a vomit bag.

Cuss words start flying fast and furious from our bench, and I just want to melt my sorry self right into the ice. I never did see how the play developed, but the Habs were pressuring us big-time for the past sixty seconds of the kill, and even though the penalty officially expired before the tally, everyone knows that we'd been scrambling short-handed, courtesy of Ethan Conners.

"Keep at 'em!" jaws Coach Weiss, as he practically strangles himself with that cherry-red necktie.

Brutal. 3:50 left in the game, and it's looking rough for the good guys. Meanwhile, my brain starts contriving this crazy fantasy of dysfunctional optimism. You know, that it's not really 2-1. That I didn't just put us down a man with four minutes left. That I'm gonna score two goals in my final shift for the ultimate You Tube hockey highlight.

Get real Ethan.

Face-off's at center, and even though I'm plastered on this bench with both eyes aiming toward the middle of the ice, my brain refuses to process what I'm supposed to be seeing. Seriously, I'm spacing major, just like in Rabbi Silverstein's tenth-period *Rashi* class, when he scribbles these unintelligible letters on the big, white board, and even though my desk is so close I can smell the felt marker, I'd probably be retaining just as much information if I was parked on Devon Street, wolfing down a bagel and cream cheese at the kosher Dunkin Donuts.

I try to collect my hockey bearings, but my mind's fighting me. I keep thinking about how I let Dad talk me into coming here. The way Shoshana dissed me in front of everyone. The way Danit exposed my American privilege.

I'm guessing a minute has gone by, but I'm still this emotional train wreck. It's like, I'm wallowing in a horrible dream, the kind where I've caused a one-goal deficit in an international, gold-medal hockey contest. But that could never happen to Ethan Conners.

"Conners!" screams Coach Weiss, jarring me from my

mental funk. I turn slow, figuring he's had enough Chicago nonsense and I'm about to be sent to the showers. That's fine. Right now, I can't think of anything better than skulking out of this building and swearing off hockey forever.

"Lowenstein! Connors! Next whistle!"

Wow, was I wrong.

Suddenly, I couldn't be more awake if I'd gotten an ice-cold shower from a half-melted Gatorade bucket. Energized, I crack another peek at the scoreboard, estimating we'll come in with about two minutes left. That means Lowey and I are gonna finish off the third. Coach is trusting *us* to get this game tied.

That's a big-time line change.

This is big-time pressure.

2:31 to go, and every guy on this bench is leaning tight over the boards, eyes glued like lasers toward center ice.

The puck drops and Klein wins the draw clean. He sweeps the rubber back to Pinsky who dumps it deep into the Habs' zone. Our wingers are forechecking like maniacs, trying to crash the boards and force the Canadians out of their *prevent* defense.

"Let's go!" yells Lowey, pounding his blade into the moldy, rubber floor mat.

Spevak hustles to the corner and gets the first stick on the puck, but the White-Shirts have the slot all bottled up and he's got no one to pass to. There's this big, Hoser defenseman all over him, and Spevie's struggling to shield the rubber while he waits for an open passing lane that never seems to develop. Meanwhile, the clock's ticking down fast, and my chest feels like it's going to implode from the tension.

1:52 left. Puck's still stalled in the corner. Spevak's frustrated. He looks up and kicks the biscuit soccer-style toward the crease, hoping it slips onto a Team USA stick. No chance. The Canadian netminder springs forward and gobbles the rubber into his catching glove, forcing a stoppage.

Line change.

Lowey and I hop the boards and bust to the big face-off circle in the Habs' defensive zone. There's 1:39 on the clock and we're down by a tally, so even us blueliners need to think and act like wingers and centers. That means shooting the rubber quick and accurate, and since I'm a lefty and the draw's to the goalie's right, everyone's looking at me to power a blast on net if Mills can just win the puck clean.

I look back. Siegel's already standing near the blue line, ready to change for a sixth skater once he's sure we've got extended possession in the Canadians' zone.

This is pressure.

The zebra tweets his whistle, and both centers set their sticks on the ice. *Splat!* The puck's down flat on the red dot. Mills and the Hab center have their sticks totally tied up as they duke it out for body position. Hyper, I decide to slide left and pinch a couple feet forward just in case the biscuit squibs free.

It doesn't.

"Support!" screams Coach Weiss, as precious seconds slip away. This stall's killing us and I figure someone's got to bust to the dot and free up the puck, so I dig my edges in and prepare to take out the center, but then quickly kill the operation when Mills somehow gets his stick loose and swats the puck into Canada's corner.

Now, Siegel jets for the bench and Bloom hurdles the boards as our sixth skater.

I'm watching Richman race for his life as he crashes the corner boards and snaps up the loose biscuit near the goal line. There's this big defenseman all over him, but Richie shoulders the guy off the play and then wrists the puck back to Lowey's left point. Trouble is, Lowey's got traffic all around him and he's got no choice but to quickly wrist a low-percentage shot on net, hoping for a rebound. No luck. The goalie sees the rubber all the way and covers up with just 1:23 remaining.

The stoppage is total anxiety, and the Habs' coach milks every second, waiting to see who we've got on the ice before exercising his home team's prerogative by changing all five skaters. He knows we've pulled our goalie, so he throws out his two biggest defensive goons, figuring that's the best way to clear out congestion in front of his net. It's a little scary, because one of these guys is this six-and-a-half foot monster who's probably from Saskatchewan or something, and I'm waiting for Coach Weiss to finally protest since everyone knows Jews don't grow that tall.

But then, I see these stringy, white fringes peeking out from under the right side of his uniform, silhouetted perfectly over his black hockey pants. Go figure.

Suddenly, the big guy's partner brushes my shoulder.

"Watch yourself, Yank," he grunts.

I stare back, too stunned to retort, even though I should have told him the ref screwed up, big time. Now, I'm livid, and all I care about is getting a chance to crunch that maple-leafed jerk right through these boards into Lebanon.

Both teams start lining up at the big circle to the goalie's right.

"Stack it inside," orders Mills, which means he wants three forwards to the right of the dot, just about fifteen feet in front of the Habs' crease.

Now, we've got three Blue-Shirts in front of me, and no one on the left. It's desperation time, and everyone in the building knows Mills has to win the draw clean back or we're burnt toast. My fingers are quivering inside my glove as I wait for the drop, and I'm hoping Mills can slip the puck to me off the draw so I'll have instant interference in front of the tender.

The ref puts the biscuit in play, and the Canadian center intentionally presses Mills' stick into the ice to prevent a quick pass back. I can tell Mills is frustrated as he spins his body forward and tries to protect the puck with his skates. But this time, the Canadian kicks the puck against Mills' stick, and now the rubber's bouncing on its side with no one in control. Bloom busts to his left for support, but the puck somehow squirts free toward the side boards, killing our set play.

The doomsday clock's ticking. This is panic time.

Bloom, Richie, and the Canadian Bigfoot break toward the boards, and I can tell it's gonna be a rugby match on ice. The Hab defenseman's a beast, and it's tough going for a few precious seconds, but it's two Blue-Shirts versus the Abominable Snowman, and Bloomie's finally able to punch the puck loose and take control.

Bloom picks his head up, and I can see he wants to set a play from just inside the blue line.

"Spread it!" screams Coach Weiss.

The crowd's buzzing. Just under forty seconds left, and we're playing by total instinct, so I decide to sneak in on a diagonal toward the top of the right face-off circle, figuring all five Canadians are playing too deep to notice me.

"Keep moving!" screams Lowey at our forwards, while Bloom dances along the left-side boards with the puck.

"Thirty second!" yelps Coach Weiss.

My heart's pounding marching band bass drums, and there's sweat splashing all over my facemask wires.

"Get something on goal!" hollers Mills in a panic.

Bloom skates the puck forward, then gives a slick head fake. That draws a Hab winger off Lowey. Now, Lowey's got a little space and Bloom's reading it perfectly. He peels a one-eighty and caroms the puck like a pool hustler off the boards, back to the left point where Lowey's got almost twenty feet of open ice.

"Blast it!" I scream.

Lowey's got his head down like an ostrich, and he's making sure the Canadians know it. Then, he winds up big and powerful for the slap shot which the whole northern border knows is coming. That totally freezes the defense, and while they're glued to Lowey, I sneak in closer toward the right circle. We've practiced this play all week and Lowey's got to know I'm open.

"Look!" I wail.

Lowey waits an extra split-second to sell the shot. Then, he sneaks his head up and feathers this Gretzky-like, cross-ice pass right for the toe of my blade. I glide a half-foot forward, dig my right edge deep, and cock my stick high for the biggest one-timer of my life.

Whack! I get all of it. The puck takes off like an Israeli F-16 for the upper corner, and the goalie's sliding right-to-left for all he's got.

But I know he's beat this time. My stick's already half-raised.

And then—
Pang!
It's the sickening echo of hollow metal vibrating loud and wicked.

My eyes are coming out of my head. *Where's the puck? Did it ring the inside cross-bar?* Suddenly, everything's in slow motion.

And then, I hear this mix of cheer and moan from the crowd as the biscuit somersaults to the ice and slides diagonally forward toward the big, Canadian defenseman near the left circle.

I want to scream obscenities. But there's no time. Instead, I cut my blades hard into the ice and bust chops back to the blue line.

"Press him!" rants Coach Weiss, like a certified maniac.

Too late. The goon defender swats the puck high into the neutral zone, and now it's a wild free-for-all to the loose rubber, our open net deliciously inviting.

"Nineteen seconds!" explodes Coach Weiss, as if he can't see we're totally fighting for our lives. "Dump and attack!"

Lowey's hustling to our blue line, and he's got a step on the rushing Canadian forward.

"Lowey!" I scream, trying to tell him I'm breaking to his right for support.

I see his facemask twitch and then he lunges his stick at the puck, barely chopping it out of the Hab's reach. Now, the rubber's squibbing toward my plot of ice, so I turn hard on my edges, swallow up the biscuit and ready myself for a last-second rush.

"Take it Ethan!" screams Richie.

"Dump it quick!" hollers Coach Weiss.

Twelve ticks left and everyone's hysterical.

I look up and start skating the puck across center. No time for a dump, and I can't take it solo because there's a line of Habs stacked like a Rocky Mounted roadblock at the blue line. *Do something, Ethan.*

Another quick scan. Now, there's about ten feet between me and the Wall of Quebec. Good enough. Sucking oxygen, I sneak a quick peek at the net, bury my head, then wind up for all I'm worth.

Crack! It's another rubber missile, and the nearest defenders part like the Red Sea, one guy turning sideways for his life and the other diving to his right

I'm watching the puck all the way. It's about twelve inches off the ice and gaining altitude.

"On goal," I growl between clenched teeth, hoping for a last-second rebound if the shot doesn't make it past the tender.

The goalie freezes like he's lost sight of the shot.

"Come on!" I holler, my body english guiding the rubber just inside the right post.

Suddenly, the tender makes this desperate lunge with his right leg pad.

Thud! He somehow manages to kick the shot sideways, away from traffic.

Okay, now, I'm gonna lose it. I mean, I just want to take the blade of my Christian and chop fence holes all over this rutty ice surface. Meanwhile, the puck bounces toward the corner, and the Canadian defenders start circling the rubber like a pack of starving polar bears.

Three ticks — two — one —

It's over.

I torture myself by watching the Habs throw their gloves and sticks airborne in celebration, while us losers lope over to Siegel and console him the best we can.

"Sorry Siegs," I grumble, hoping he's not sore at me for going a perfect zero-for-three on great scoring chances. Not to mention my incarceration on the Habs' power-play winner. There's this gagging in my throat, like I'm about to spill those *bourekas.*

"Great game, Ethan." Siegs gives me this half-grin, which is his way of saying the rest of us shouldn't feel like crap for giving him just a single goal to work with.

It doesn't work.

"Let you down big-time, Siegs," I say, rolling my eyes. "Especially me."

He shrugs like it's no big deal and moves on. Meanwhile, I'm thinking I played so bad that I should thank *Hashem* for even allowing me the privilege of a silver medal.

And then, my stomach bottoms to my skates.

Shayna. I've got to find her.

No time pouting over silver. If Shayna bails before the medal ceremony, I'll *never* see her again.

I turn, and cut blades hard to the corner. The crowd's already starting to clear out.

"Conners!" hollers Pinsky, probably wondering why I'm splitting from the handshake line.

Ignoring him, I hustle toward the boards, looking for a perfect head of liquorice-black hair.

But she's gone.

I lost Shayna. And the gold medal.

Right now, I'm hating myself like I never thought possible.

Chapter Twenty-Two

THIRTY MINUTES LATER, our dispirited locker room's more like the Academy's ACT testing hall as we change into our street clothes and pack up wet gear. I'm looking all around, hating that I'll never see my Maccabi mates again, and getting way too emotional about it. Seriously, my heart's as heavy as a Merkava tank, and I feel myself missing these guys like I've known them my whole life. I'm even longing for Coach Weiss's platoon-sergeant holler one last time, though I'd never admit that to anyone.

"Need a lift?" mutters Richman.

"Not this time," I say, as I cram both Maccabi USA jerseys into my bag and zip the compartment tight.

"Well, it's been real, Ethan," he says, before strutting out of the locker room with his Maccabiah silver wrapped around his wrist.

Naturally, Lowey and I are the last ones left in this filthy hole. We're both moping and moving real slow, and I'm wondering how I'm ever gonna explain second place to Dad.

I'm also wondering why Shayna didn't wait.

"Hey, it's been great pairing with you," says Lowey, slapping me across the back. "And good luck at Ferris State. You're gonna have a solid season, Conners."

I've known the guy for less than a week, but I feel my eyes welling serious emotion. I'm gonna miss Lowenstein.

"You're as steady as they come," I say. "And a real leader, too. We'll keep in touch back home."

Lowey smiles. "Sure."

And then he's gone.

The tournament's over. Reality's staring me hard in the face.

And my life seems totally out of control.

I clip on my *kippah*, grab my Christians, and slog out of the locker room, my body swaying like a bobblehead because this overstuffed gear bag's weighing my left shoulder sideways. God, I hate this bag. I feel like chucking it right over the

Manara cliffs. Let some Hezbollah lunatic suck a whiff of the rancid insides and see what that does for Middle-East peace.

Skulking through the hall, I'm feeling like an overloaded pack animal. Besides this bag, I've got both aluminums swinging like teeter-totters from my right hand, and this ugly, silver medal dangling from my neck.

I turn the corner wide.

And then I swallow hard.

Just ahead, I see the Borochovs waiting at the end of the gloomy hallway.

And Shayna's right behind them.

Okay, now my brain's spinning faster than a Sasha Cohen triple-axel. This can't be happening. I mean, Shayna was *gone.* I was sure of it. I was so sure of it that I never bothered cleaning up. Here's the sordid picture — I'm donning this ratty, black t-shirt that looks like it's been yanked from the bottom of a dollar store clearance bin, my hair's still flattened like the inside of a sweaty hockey helmet, and my green *kippah*'s clipped on hurriedly sideways.

This is bad. *Real* bad. I'm not used to getting cornered in sensitive situations. I mean, this would never happen back home. Now, I'm sweating waterfalls because I'm dressed like a pig, I'm lugging twenty pounds of disgusting hockey bag, and I'm hating that there's nothing I can do about it since Shayna's standing twenty feet down the hall and that's the only way out.

Lior shuffles right up to me. "You were great!" he boasts, and I'm wondering if he knows the blue team lost.

"Yeah, I love how you destroy that guy," laughs Danit, her eyes sparkling at me in a way I've never noticed before.

"You *do* know they beat us," I grunt, not showing any emotion.

"*Lo ech-pat lanu,*" says Mr. Borochov. "Real exciting, this game. I think about learning to skate myself."

"Can I see the medal?" Danit asks, reaching toward my neck and tugging at the silver like she owns it or something.

"Man, you're tough," brags Ron. "No one messes with you."

Lior nods. "Yeah. IDF can use guys like you," he says.

I glance down, embarrassed. Did Lior have to mention the IDF? That's like pasting *loser* in big white letters all over my scummy t-shirt. If I'm so tough, I'd be joining up instead of playing ice games for college scholarships.

"I mean it Ethan," says Ron. He's staring right through me, just like my old ACT tutor when I'd be spacing during geometry recap, which I usually was. "You're not at all like I'd expected. Man, never see *dati* religious guy as rough as you."

I peek up. I can practically feel all these eyes beaming at me, and there's tiny smiles everywhere. Look, I've never been called *sensitive*, but my heart's totally heavy, and I'm a nanosecond away from choking up emotion. It's like, these Israeli peers are suddenly looking at me as if I'm some kind of American bruiser. Like there's more under this knit *kippah* than a spoiled, religious Chicagoan.

And that's pretty cool.

I glance back up. There's Shayna, staring big-eyed through the hallway, and I'm wishing I could lose Danit and the Borochovs right now. Poor Shayna. She's probably clueless about hockey, but I'm so excited she stayed until the end. Just wish she wasn't glued to that Middle-Eastern warrior.

Danit steps away and mumbles something to Mrs. Borochov. Perfect. Now, I lock gazes with Shayna and start walking toward her, making sure I don't spear anyone with my stick blades. I'm even forcing a half-smile at the lunatic who splashed sixteen ounces of sticky cola all over my face.

"You like the game?" I say, wishing I'd opened with a bit more flair, and hating that the Borochovs are right behind me and probably wondering why I'm talking to this knockout stranger.

Shayna nods, but my mind's wandering. She's sporting this midnight-black tank-top and a tight pair of navy-blue gym shorts that ought to be outlawed inside an ice rink. When she blinks, I suddenly notice these long, dark eyelashes drawing my gaze into hers. No wonder she stole my concentration at the start of the second period.

"You are best player I see," she says, her chocolate eyes sparkling like frozen hockey pucks reflecting stadium spotlights. "I like this game."

That gets me smiling. "I'm glad you came," I say back, peeking over at Mr. Bruiser who's totally sizing up Danit. "Didn't think I'd see you again."

"*Slicha*, Ethan. I—I think you no want to meet after what happens at pool."

"But how did you know—?"

"You tell me about Canada Centre. I go here and find schedule for USA."

Now, I'm grinning. I'm also trying to keep composed. Wow. It's *so* cool to be stalked by a Kiryat Shemona girl. I can't wait to tell Ezra.

"Ethan!" Ron turns at me. "You don't introduce us?"

"Sorry," I say. "This is Shayna. We met Tuesday at the pool."

Lior's showing this toothy smile. "So now we see why you stayed with the chairs," he jokes.

Danit perks her head at Shayna. "*Na-eem ma-ode*," she grunts, like she's jealous or something, which would be pretty amazing considering the way she's treated me for most of this trip.

Shayna nods. "*Shmee Shayna v'zeh ha-ach sheli, Gilad.*"

My heart goes in cardiac arrest. "He's your brother?" I whoop, like this is the greatest dream ever.

"I'm sorry, Ethan. My older brother—he sometimes gets all *meshuga*."

"Man, you are strong," grunts Gilad in this deep and scruffy voice like he just swallowed a cactus or something. "I don't ever get alone with you in ice rink."

Now, everyone's laughing, but I'm starting to get emotionally uncomfortable, and I hope no one sees this ring of sweat lining the sides of my forehead. It's weird. Shayna came here to find *me*, and everyone can see I'm starry-eyed for her. Meanwhile, Danit's standing five feet to my left, and she's shooting me this Dracula stare like she's totally jealous. God, am I glad I kept my cool this morning when Danit and

I were alone on the balcony. I mean, this could have turned real ugly.

"You free in an hour?" I whisper to Shayna, even though everyone's standing close enough to hear me.

"Okay," she says, chucking me this perfect smile. "Like we planned for *yom shlee-shee*. We meet at canyon food court. Stays open until eleven tonight."

"*Sababa*. Let's say *reva l'eser,* 9:45."

"Nice," she nods.

My eyes start peeking over toward Gilad like I'm seeking his approval, which I probably am. Doesn't matter. Gilad's still zoning on Danit, and I'm figuring he wouldn't care if I took Shayna back to Chicago right now.

Meanwhile, Lior's looking impatient. "Let's go!" he shouts. "This moldy air's not good for *Abba* and *Eema*."

I lock gazes with Shayna. "Bye," I say, wondering if she's really going to be at the mall this time.

"*L'hitraot b-ode sha-ah,*" she chirps, telling me she'll see me in an hour, and the way her eyes twinkle, I know she means it.

Lior turns. "Come on, Ethan. Now."

I slog forward, my thoughts zoning deep, my conscience suddenly melting into a cesspool of guilt over this date with Shayna. It's like, I'm cheating on Shoshana, and I guess I probably am, but trust me, it's really nice when someone *enjoys* coming to my games.

Sorry, Shoshana. I never asked for this to happen.

But I'm glad it did.

Chapter Twenty-Three

WHEN LIOR DROPS ME OFF at the mall, I'm all nerves and butterflies. I've got my fingers curled tight into my palms, my heart's racing like a Kentucky Derby thoroughbred, and I'm practically sweating out my meticulously-styled hair I'd spent five minutes blow-drying after showering at the Borochovs'.

"Thanks for driving," I say, as I scoot out of the passenger seat.

"*Eyn baya*, Ethan. No problem. Just remember the way back. Maybe twenty-minute walk to apartment."

"Easy," I say, and then push the door shut.

Lior gives me this thumbs-up and peels the Getz forward. He's gone in five seconds.

I suck a deep breath. This is the first time I've been alone since I got to Kiryat Shemona. It's weird. No Borochovs. No Maccabi USA teammates. Truth is, I'm feeling vulnerable, like I'm out of my environment, which I definitely am.

I try to compose myself by exhaling long and slow, just like Coach Paulson made me do before my one-and-only penalty shot last year against Schaumburg. But it didn't work then, and trust me, it's not working now. God, I hate feeling this way. Right now, I'd swap my scholarship for a couple ticks of Ethan Conners' old Chicago confidence. *What am I even doing here?*

My legs feel like a pair of concrete planters, like they're permanently affixed to this sidewalk in front of the mall's entrance. I can't move. But my brain's spinning. Anxious, I look up into the western sky, and practically get myself hypnotized by these thin streaks of glowing orange strafing the Manara cliffs.

I'm thinking deep. Real deep. *Second-thoughts deep.* I mean, I'll be home in four days, so it's probably not a great idea to flounder into anything romantic.

But I'm not bailing.

Sure, it's risky. If Shayna really shows, there's no telling what my emotions are capable of, which is *so* unlike me. I don't get it. I used to be cool. And smooth. But this trip—I swear, it's been anything but simple.

I peek at my watch. Exactly 9:45. No more stalling, I gotta go inside. I gaze through the glass doors. The mall's pretty tiny by Chicago standards, and I can almost see the entire food court straight ahead.

I step forward. When I tug at the door's metal handle, a rush of de-humidified air satiates my face. There's this armed guard manning the front, and he's motioning me through the most serious-looking metal detector I've ever seen.

It takes about three seconds to clear security. I skulk a couple steps forward, and now the food court's staring me right in the eyes. I've been to Israel four times before, but I'm still shocked by all these American logos like Sbarro's, KFC and Burger King casting florescent glows all over. It's cool how everything's kosher, which gets me thinking how lucky I am to have that kosher Dunkin' Donuts back in Rogers Park.

I slog a little farther in. Then, I halt for a final vanity check, making sure my *kippah's* clipped straight, my blue polo's untucked and only three inches of *tzitzit* are showing. When I'm sure everything's good, I fill my lungs with this power drag of confidence, and start surveying in all directions for Shayna's long, coal-black hair.

"Ethan!"

I turn. There's Shayna, parked at the far edge of the food court by this square table near the Burger King side. She's smiling to Beirut, her hands fiddling with a cell phone. I'm just hoping she can't see my chest quivering as I start forward.

"Thanks for coming," I say, sliding with style into this plastic chair. "You know, to the Canada Centre."

Wow. I'm trying my best not to stare, but it's hard. Real hard. She's modeling this tight, dark-blue cotton pull-over with minuscule sleeves landing two inches past her golden-bronzed shoulders. Same shorts as before, too. You gotta believe me when I say she'd be arrested if Rabbi Klepstein caught her parading around the Academy like this.

"I'm happy you asked to see me again, Ethan. I think you get all angry after what Gilad does."

"I never thought he was your brother," I say, peeking like a Chicago detective into her mocha-brown eyes. "Figured he was your boyfriend for sure."

"Oh no." She turns away shyly. "*Ayn li chaver.*"

Jackpot.

We start trading these mile-deep gazes, and now I'm feeling stupid for once thinking that Shoshana had concocted this whole Shayna thing as some kind of crazy, international sting operation. Suddenly, Shoshana's no longer an issue, and it's like this iron anvil has been lifted off my back. Feels great.

"Can I get you something?" I ask. "Coke? Fries?"

"Maybe," she answers, kind of nervous. It's obvious she's waiting for me to lead.

"*Ani mayt lishtot,*" I say, telling her I'm dying of thirst. "Couple Cokes okay?"

"*B'seder,* Ethan," she replies, her shyness terminally attractive.

I hustle to the Burger King counter and come back with a pair of medium colas.

"*Todah,*" she says, soft and cute.

I push one of the cups toward her.

"How's summer?" I ask, then timidly suck the top of my straw.

"Summer—it's not so fun. Every day hot. Just go to pool or watch television."

"Kind of like back home," I say, lying. Look, I'm not about to tell her that most of my friends are either traveling around the world, taking AP summer school, or clowning around at five thousand-dollar overnight camps in the Catskills.

"But this is my last summer until army," she explains, practically advertising that she's seventeen.

"Exciting."

"Not so much."

I smile. "I just graduated high school last month."

"Then army?"

My gut cramps. "Uhh, not for me. I'm going to university in September."

"Nice," she says, glancing at my *kippah*. "You go to Yeshiva or something?"

"What?"

"You know. Yeshiva College in New York City. Lots of religious guys go there. It will be *so* cool."

"Um—not exactly," I sputter, my fingers fiddling like a junkie with the bottom of my styrofoam cup. "I'm going to a regular college. You know, not a Jewish school. All expenses paid, too, as long as I play on their hockey team."

She sets down her cola. "How you not attend *dati* school?" she asks, her eyes spilling shock. "You play this hockey for *goyim* instead?"

Okay, that stings. Real bad. Shayna's practically punched me in the gut with a tongue-jab of typical Israeli brashness.

"I—" My lips suddenly stick together like a pair of frozen Zamboni doors. I'm speechless and wallowing in hurt.

But I deserve the pain. I mean, what *am* I doing? You know, bragging about a full-boat scholarship to someone half-a-world removed from suburban narcissism and American privilege. Huffing arrogant to a girl who's going to be drafted into the army right after graduation. God, I'm a jerk.

"Ethan—"

Shayna's voice is hauntingly distant. That's because I'm zoning. About her. About all the other kids here. Eighteen-year-olds putting their lives on hold, fighting for Israel like Twenty-First Century Maccabees, while I spout haughty about playing sport for a secular school—trading religious heritage for a pair of new skates and Dad's dream of a $20,000.00 scholarship. Yup, I'm just a first-class Jewish-American hypocrite, and if I had an ounce of shame, I'd rip this *kippah* off my head and stuff it in my back pocket like a used kleenex.

"Ethan?"

"I'm sorry, Shayna. That's just how things are in America. Even at Jewish high schools it's all about college. And it's so darn expensive, too."

"But this college pays you to go?"

"American kids dream about scholarships. Football,

basketball, hockey — we work our entire lives for this chance."

She smiles. "You must be best hockey player in America."

"Not sure about that," I say, thinking how I pretty much cost us the game against Canada. "But thanks, anyway."

Right after I say that, she reaches across the table and couples her soft fingers around my palm. There's a sudden butterfly rush in my chest, and I'm loving how her dark skin contrasts exotic against mine.

"Come on." She starts tugging at my wrist.

"Where?"

"I want that you meet my *abba* and *eema*."

"What?"

"I tell them about you, Ethan. About coming from Chicago to play this hockey."

She stands up, pulls me off this plastic chair, and I'm going insane trying to figure out what's happening.

"I don't—"

"Please," she whines, her dark lips slacking pouty, even though she knows I'm not about to refuse. "It's only ten-minute walk from here."

That pretty much settles it. I chuck our cups into the trash and then she locks her fingers tight around mine. Weird, it's like she couldn't care less that our futures are heading in completely opposite directions.

"Let's go, Ethan."

We start walking right past this line of gritty, teenage guys hanging by the Sbarro's counter, and they're giving me these nasty once-overs, as if to say I've got no business romancing one of their own. That starts wrestling my nerves. Maybe I shouldn't be doing this.

Or maybe I should. I mean, I'm loving how my hand is melting in Shayna's, and I wouldn't even trade this feeling for another shot at Maccabiah gold. Besides, nothing permanent's gonna happen. I'll be back in the States on Sunday.

A minute later, we're standing outside the canyon's front entrance. It's 10:15, yet the summer heat's still got this sweltering death grip throughout the valley. Of course, I'm totally nervous and the humid air's not helping my confidence. There's this anxious sweat caking my temples and clamming my palms, which is really embarrassing because my left hand is practically glued into Shayna's fingers. That leaves just a single, free hand to swipe my brow, but I fake it real good, pretending to sweep back my hair, though I'm probably getting riled for nothing since it's dark outside and Shayna wouldn't have noticed anyway.

"I think you're cute, Ethan," she says out of nowhere, as we jaywalk across Tel Chai Road. "And the way you play this hockey sport. I never think *dati* American could be so strong."

"Really?" I say back, and now I want to jump in front of the next Egged bus because that was a pathetic retort.

But Shayna doesn't care. She nods soft and gives me this cute, half-smile.

"Thanks for coming to the game," I say.

Nice recovery, Ethan.

We hang a left, and now we're passing that decrepit strip mall of pizza and falafel shops hugging the east side of Tel Chai Road, the heavy, evening air fragrant with fried oils and fresh spices. Shayna's leading me fast, her bony fingers still locked like freight train couplers around my palm.

"Not so much further," she says. "But first, I take you somewhere special. Okay, Ethan?"

"Eh—sure," I answer, as if there's a choice.

"It's important you see this, Ethan." I notice her eyebrows furrowing serious, and I'm trying to figure out what I've gotten myself into.

We course right at Har Levanon Street, then start a steep ascent up a hilly sidewalk. It's a lot darker and real eerie off the main drag, as we march into this thick blackness at the edge of what looks like some kind of residential area.

Suddenly, Shayna slows and angles hard to the left, still dragging my hand. I've got no idea where we are, and all I can see is what looks like a chain-link fence and some distant silhouettes of large, rectangular objects.

"Almost there, Ethan."

I feel this massive tenseness in the air. Shayna's breathing hard, and my heart's pounding out of my chest.

"Is this it?" I say, desperate to know what's happening.

"Yeah," she hushes, leading me farther along the grass. "It's okay, Ethan?"

"Sure." What am I supposed to say? I don't even know where we're going.

I see her scanning forward and then she quickens our pace. Now, we're trudging this gravel path bearing directly toward the fence. Two seconds later, she stops, reaches for a handle or something, and I hear this groan of rusty metal like a gate swinging open.

"*Bo*," she says. "Come."

We strut farther in and I'm casing the grounds like a feral cat, trying to figure out where we are, vainly assuming Shayna brought me here to seduce me or something. *Careful, Ethan.*

"Come this way," she whispers.

I'm following right behind her, staring toward the left as we approach these weird slabs of concrete stacked in parallel rows.

And then, my stomach free-falls.

Cemetery! We're traipsing through a trail of tombs like you'd see in a horror movie.

Okay, now I'm thinking Shayna's sick. Totally psychotic. Oh yeah, I'm *so* done with this.

"Ethan?" she whines, sensing my apprehension.

"We can't be here," I snip, pulling my hand away from hers.

She ignores me and keeps walking straight ahead, like she knows I've got no choice but to follow. It's another gut-wrenching ten seconds before she finally stops, leans over this concrete slab, and then starts staring like a Torah scribe at the chiseled inscription.

"Shayna?" I mumble, my voice quivering.

She doesn't answer. She just keeps gazing forward, her body as rigid as a petrified olive tree for what seems like a mini-eternity. Then, she kneels down and carefully sweeps her left hand across the grave marking. The tension's thick, and my ears are about to explode from the incessant buzzing of invisible crickets everywhere. I hate this. I've got know what's going on.

I decide to lean my head closer. I need to see what Shayna's reading. My chin's just above her shoulders, and I can smell this lavender fragrance wafting from her hair.

Suddenly, she springs back up, locks her dark eyes into mine, and starts hugging me like I've just saved her life.

And then I hear these tiny sniffles. Oh, God. Shayna's crying.

"*Mah yesh?*" I whisper, wishing I knew what the heck's happening.

"I'm sorry," she whimpers. She hugs me tighter, resting her head on my shoulder. "This—this is my brother."

"Gilad?" I've got no idea what she's talking about, or why we're even here.

"*Tee-sta-kel,*" she says. "You see."

Now, Shayna's practically aiming my face toward the slab which I know is a grave, even though it's completely different than those ground-level headstones at Shalom Park where my great-grandparents are buried.

The silence is haunting. I'm literally staring into blackness.

"*Rega,*" she says, and then yanks out her cell phone, bends down low, and beams the display light over the stone inscription.

"*Mah zeh?*" I whisper.

"Don't you see, Ethan?" She's running her dainty finger like a harp player along the Hebrew etching. "Shai Ochana. Died at five years old, *al kiddush Hashem.*"

My whole body starts shaking to pieces. "Your brother? When? How?"

We lock gazes, the way people do when there's tragedy approaching and no one dares to admit it.

"Ethan—"

The moonlight's reflecting twin streams of tears coursing down Shayna's face. She's struggling to catch her breath and I'm feeling absolutely helpless, like she's dying right before my eyes and I can't do a thing about it. Frantic, I start stroking her soft hair. And then I wait.

"It—it happened so many years ago. You know?"

She wants me to respond. I can't.

"*Leefnay gidaltee*, Ethan. Before I am born."

"I don't understand," I tell her.

"Gilad was just a baby," she whimpers into my shoulder. "And *Shayna—Abba* and *Eema* give me this name."

This is really frustrating. I've got no idea what she's talking about. But I've got to say something.

"Your brother—?"

"*Niharg*. Killed."

That sucks the air out right out my lungs. God, I'm such a fool. I've learned about this stuff since I was a kindergartner, and it shouldn't have taken more than a millisecond to figure out how a five-year-old dies *al kiddush Hashem*.

Which means *in the name of God*.

"*Abba* and *Eema* give me this name, *Shayna*, for Shai."

The hairs on my arms are sticking up like a forest of emotional thorns.

"You understand, Ethan?"

I nod, then shake my head baffled, because I am. "I—I need to know what happened," I stutter.

Shayna slides her cheek off my shoulder, and digs this fist into my chest.

"Please, Shayna."

I hear her inhale, and then I start dancing my fingertips along the top of her arm.

"*Jihad* sneaks across border, Ethan. Always come to Kiryat Shemona."

"Terrorists?"

"Dogs! *Clabim*! Human pigs dressed as Jews. Even *kippah* and *tzitzit*. They sneak into *gan*. Shai's *gan*!"

My mouth's as wide as the Port of Haifa, my eyes bulging out of their sockets. Sure, I've heard of stuff like this, but it's always so far away. So incredibly distant. I swear, what's happening here in this cemetery right now—it's the heaviest moment of my life.

"The *yeladim* for a thousand Arabs in *beit sohar*," she says, bleeding total emotion. "Hour later, army special forces breaks in. *Abba* says Israel never makes deals with terrorists in those days. Never frees killers from jail."

She lets go of me and kneels back down at the grave.

"I'm sorry," I whisper.

She's totally silent, and I'm wallowing breathless, like this can't really be happening. But it is. And it's horrible. It's like a living tragedy right out of the Bible — the prophetic history of the Jewish people.

And it's so morbidly unjust that this beautiful, *Sephardic* daughter of Israel has to bear the gruesome weight of an eternal hatred going back to Jacob and Esau.

I brush down beside her at the tiny grave. "Tell me about Shai," I plead, fearing the answer which is probably going to hurt Shayna to say it as much as it's gonna crush me to hear it.

"Arab pigs throw grenade," she stresses real matter-of-fact, still staring at the tombstone. "Split-second later, Army shoots them dead, but grenade already kills Shai. He was the closest."

It takes a moment to emotionally digest what Shayna just told me. And when it sinks in, my fists start rolling into fleshy cannonballs filled with ordnance of white-hot anger. I mean, to actually know the family — to reflect on such barbarity right next to the grave of a five-year-old innocent. What's my own cushy life about anyway?

Shayna's still staring at the stone, and I'm thinking she's waiting for me to man-up and take control of this situation. But it's just too heavy. I can't think of anything to say. Stalling, I inhale deep and gaze holes into the blackness.

She's crying again.

I close my eyes and start contemplating deeper than I ever thought possible — until my mind starts rocketing through some kind of gray-matter twilight zone. Suddenly, I'm practically unconscious, my soul drifting towards this dark galaxy of absolute nothingness. Everything's weird. I'm scared.

And then, through my half-lucid blackness, I somehow

detect this crazy, spiritual constellation drawing together in a strange, but symmetrical formation.

I get it.

It's a sign. Yes! This *has* to be a sign. I'm talking about this trip. About coming to Kiryat Shemona. It sounds crazy, but I feel like one of those Biblical prophets being signaled by God, and I swear, I'm not leaving Israel until I figure out what my mission's supposed to be.

I look down. Shayna's head is still radar-locked on her brother's gravestone. "*Ani mitztayer,*" I say, telling her I'm sorry, and then I start caressing her left shoulder with my fingers.

She turns and peers into my eyes. "I have to bring you, Ethan."

"It's okay. It's okay," I tell her, and as I'm saying it, I'm suddenly overcome by an intense deja vu about this very tragedy. I swear, it's like I've known about it before, and not through the news or history books or anything like that. No, I'm sensing some kind of personal association with this nightmare, and now my brain's searing like a Pentium 5, trying to figure out why and how.

"Ethan!" Shayna recoils like a startled cobra, pulling me up with her arms. "*Yesh* connection. That's why I show you."

"Connection?"

"Listen. About America. Chicago."

"What?" I'm thinking she's losing it.

"Please, Ethan. I take you to *Abba* and *Eema*. They explain better. You must come!"

Like I've got a choice?

"C'mon!" she pleads, and then she does that coupling thing with her fingers through mine. She rushes me to the sidewalk, and I'm happy to get out of here, but I swear, I'll never forget these heaviest five minutes of my life. I already know that what just happened in this cemetery can never be culled from my essence.

We hustle across a parkway and cut a right at the first intersection. I'm figuring we're bearing for this quad of slum-like high-rises a couple blocks ahead.

"Almost there," she says.

She leads me on another hard right, and now we're marching into this neighborhood of compact houses seeping gloomy rays of incandescence through half-draped front windows. You know, cookie-cutter homes with clothes lines silhouetted like low-lying telephone wires across tiny front yards like it's rural Illinois or something.

Shayna drags me up this second, skinny driveway on our right. "Don't be nervous," she says, as we follow the pockmarked concrete walkway leading to the front door. When we approach the entrance, I notice a tiny *mezzuzah* affixed to the doorpost, along with this wooden plaque nailed to the front door bearing the name *Ochana*.

Shayna nudges the door until it creaks all the way open. I'm skulking behind her, hoping Gilad's not inside. We step over a rusted aluminum threshold, and now there's this short hallway with dozens of framed pictures attached to both sides of the wall like you'd see in a sports bar.

"Your family?" I'm staring at an old eight-by-ten of Shayna, Gilad and what must be her parents standing next to the Western Wall. Kind of weird to see Shayna dressed respectable.

"My *bat mitzvah*," she says, chucking me this cute smile and then pecking me a two-fingered love tap to the shoulder.

We shuffle into the open-walled kitchen. To the right, I see her parents camped on one of these '60s-style green love seats flanking a slick, flat-screen Sony. When they look up, I can totally see where Shayna gets her *Sephardic* complexion.

Her mother flicks off the television and smiles. "Shalom, Shayna," she says, and then she starts tunneling her eyes right through me. "*Me zeh?*"

"*Nah l'hakeer*," says Shayna. "You meet Ethan Conners, *Amerikayee* from Chicago."

Her father's head snaps up like a startled rabbit. "Chicago?" he says, his leathery face wrinkled like he's in a state of shock

"*Ken*," I answer, and then reach out for his hand.

"*Pagashti oto b'brichat skeeya*," says Shayna, explaining how we met at the pool. "*Hoo saken hockey kerach l'Maccabi USA.*"

Now her father's giving me this total once-over, like I'm
about to take Shayna to the prom or something.

"My *Abba* and *Eema* no speak English," whispers Shayna,
nudging her shoulder against my arm. "I tell them you play
for hockey team USA."

"*Na la-shevet*," orders Mrs. Ochana, using her palms to puff
up the cushions of the other love seat.

Shayna and I sink into the softness. We're sitting right
across from her parents, which is totally freaky, and I'm
starting to wonder what I'm even doing here.

Okay, everyone's puppy-eyed, no one's talking. Great. I'm
parked anxious, waiting for her parents to start a conversation
or something. Like, *what in the world are you doing in Kiryat
Shemona, Mr. Chicago guy?*

Instead, it's just an uncomfortable silence. And everyone's
fidgeting, too. It's like the living room is shrouded in some
kind of international secrecy. I'm nervous.

"*Rega*," utters Shayna's mom. She gets up quick and rushes
real mysterious across the hall towards another room. Five
seconds later, she returns with this framed picture clutched
tight against her heart, and when I glance over my shoulder,
Shayna's eyes resemble a pair of white ping-pong balls.

"*Lo, Eema!*" she screams.

I've got no idea what's happening.

"You see," pleads her mother, pushing the glass frame into
my hands.

My elbows stiffen. Everyone's staring at me, and I know
I've got to look at this picture. I peer down.

It's a little boy. Dark-complected, too. I don't get this.

My brain's spinning. My heart's pounding.

And then, my gut curdles when I figure it out.

It's got to be Shai.

There's this gruesome silence saturating the living room. I
mean, the toughest quiet I've ever experienced—a thousand
times worse than Coach Paulson's silent treatment after last
year's Metro playoff game when we gave up a short-hander
in double-overtime.

"*Ani mitztayer*," I hush, telling them I'm sorry. "Shayna

amrah li."

Her dad nods stoic, easing the tension. Then, Shayna's mother looks up, cracks a tiny grin, and starts rambling in the quickest Hebrew ever.

"Ani lo maveen," I blurt, letting them know I can't understand a word. But it's like they're not even listening. And when Shayna's dad starts butting in like a traffic reporter on steroids, I know it's a lost cause.

Shayna turns and leans into me. She's all smiles, her imperfect, bottom teeth naturally intriguing. "This is what I want to tell you," she chirps.

"What?" I grunt, frustrated at my Hebrew teachers for failing me when it finally counts.

Now, her parents cut off the chatter. They both turn and start making eye signals with Shayna, and it's really making me uncomfortable.

"What were they saying?" I ask.

"I already tell you," she answers, peeking at me real serious. "It happens before I'm born. But my *Abba* and *Eema* never forget about Americans."

"Before you were born? What are you talking about?"

"It happens a month after Shai. A package, Ethan."

"Package?"

"Comes from America Jews. From Chicago. A thousand *shekels* to pay for Shai's stone."

As she says it, the back of my neck turns into this petrified thicket of tiny, black hairs. My throat lumps, and when I peek fast at Shayna, I think I'm seeing her chocolate eyes melting thick drops of hurt.

"Tell to him!" screams her mother.

I freeze. Now, Shayna's choking up serious emotion, and I hate myself for not understanding. I mean, she wasn't even alive when it happened.

I hate this. I hate suspense. Seriously, the tension's so thick you couldn't cut it with a pro-sharpened skate blade. And when I gape up and see everyone staring at me like I've got some kind of connection with all of this, I start wishing I'd just stayed at the mall with Shayna.

"This is what happens," sobs Shayna, staring down at the smutty, tile floor. "Chicago Jews also send my *Abba* and *Eema* to fancy resort in Eilat."

"I don't—"

"They never stay in hotel their whole lives, Ethan. So *kol-koch* expensive. But this time away helps them grieve, and when they come back, they regain strength. Even decide to have another child."

My insides are hemorrhaging emotion. And I don't need Ezra to tell me what Shayna's about to say.

"I'm that child!" she hollers, her cappuccino lips quivering. *"Atah maveen?"*

Now I do. But I'm mentally paralyzed. This whole thing's too powerful. Hesitating, I suck an endless breath through my teeth.

And then I decide to combust the Ochana's living room with an incredible secret.

"Shayna." My voice is soft and serious. "Please—"

"Ethan?"

"You've got to tell your parents exactly what I'm about to say."

She starts chewing gorges into her bottom lip. "Okay, Ethan."

Now, I'm square on the spot. I snort a drag of courage, shoot a glance at her parents, and start getting chatty.

"Look, Shayna. When you told me about Shai, it was like I'd heard the story before." I see her parents dissecting every syllable, feeding like psychiatric piranhas off my facial expression even though they can't translate a single word. "And now I remember, Shayna. It's all about my mother."

"Mother?"

I nod. "You said there's a connection. And that's it! My mother had everything to do with the package."

Shayna's tongue curls, her eyelids flickering like strobe lights.

"I heard the story when I was small," I stress, my eyes wide and serious. "Swear to God."

Shayna hesitates. Then, she looks at her parents and starts

translating. I glance up, and feel their dark eyes boring tunnels through my skull.

"Look!" I wail. "My mom's got friends right here in Kiryat Shemona. The Borochovs — that's where I'm staying."

"We don't understand," mumbles Shayna.

That flusters me, so I decide to throw out some extra detail.

"Right after it happened, Mrs. Borochov sent us your parents' address and my mom started collecting money. I even heard that our synagogue's rabbi called the hotel to arrange the room."

Shayna stops translating. Her throat pulses twice. She skulks over to her parents, whispers something to them, and now there's these twin expressions of total disbelief radiating from their eyes.

And then, like an emotional high-stick to the head, I'm finally jarred into understanding what's really happening here. Okay, I *so* get it. Shayna — this sweet, gritty *sabra* — she's only alive because of my own mother's selfless devotion to *tzedakah*. Yeah, Mom's always giving to Israel. And now, seventeen years later, God's chosen to reveal his goodness by bringing me right into the Ochana's very living room. It's almost improbable to fathom, but there's simply no other explanation. Miracles come from God.

So I should know that my life's about to change forever.

When Shayna's done translating, the living room starts bleeding this absolute muteness. My body's quaking, and I don't know what to do or say, so I chuck a glance at Shayna, trying to steal her gaze. But she's frozen like a pillar of Sodomite salt, and I can tell she's fighting to stifle a torrent of tears.

"You okay?" I whisper.

She doesn't answer. Instead, she starts ruffling my hair, and then gives me this sideways bear hug like she couldn't care less that we're about eight feet away from her parents.

"Please, you stay for Shabbat," says Mrs. Ochana, her eyes glued like sonars at my green *kippah*, which makes me wonder if Shayna's parents realize their daughter's dressed totally inappropriate to be seen with a religious guy.

"Please, Ethan." Shayna's whine is totally out of character.

"Okay," I nod, though from the looks of this house I'm doubting the Ochanas even do Shabbat. Whatever. It's only right to let them show their appreciation.

And it's more time with Shayna, too.

Shayna's mom smiles. "*Leila tov*," she says. "Good night." Then she gets up, steps into my personal space, and plasters me with this total power hug.

"Thank you," says Mr. Ochana. He shakes my hand hard. "*Odd machar*," he utters, then follows Mrs. Ochana into the hallway.

When her parents clear the corner, Shayna reaches over her shoulder and kills the lights. *Smooth.*

"Ethan," she whispers.

It's dark, but the hall light's glowing. When she turns, I can actually see these thick rivers of passion oozing from her eyes.

"Sure you're okay?" I repeat, letting her know that even hockey goons have sensitive sides.

She doesn't answer. But her throat pulses.

"It's okay," I say, hating the silence.

She still doesn't answer.

"Shayna," I whisper.

She blinks twice. Then she buries her head into my arms, and I swear, I can feel warm tears channeling along the sides of my wrist. This is *so* deep. My brain's spinning.

"Ethan," she mumbles into my shoulder.

Look, I admit I'm not emotionally equipped for this. If this couch was a pool, I'd be drowning.

I peek down. Now, she's sniffling, and I've still got no idea what to do. God, what happened to that guy who's *always in control*?

He's back in Rogers Park. And that's a whole other universe from here.

Shanya's head starts fidgeting against my biceps. "I'm sorry, Ethan," she whispers.

She's sorry? After everything that's happened to her?

I gently stroke her hair, while this atomic cloud of flashbacks from Ethan's spoiled America mushrooms through my head. The Academy. The scholarship. The silver medal. Wow. Just three hours ago I'm lining up a Canuck at center ice, and now, I'm emotionally snared in this modern aftershock of prophetic, Jewish tragedy.

"I'm sorry," she hushes again.

Another heavy silence, and now I start getting this weird longing for Dad. It's like, there's this intense passion tormenting my conscience, which is so radical that it's actually scaring the crap out of me. I need to talk to Dad. Right now. And even though he probably won't understand when I tell him what's suddenly tearing me apart, I still have to try. I have to tell him about this trip. About hockey.

I have to tell him that chasing pucks on ice is totally insignificant.

Shayna's still nestling her head in my arms, and I can smell the outdoor humidity wafting from her hair. Everything's tense, and if I was any kind of man, I would definitely take the lead and say something.

But I don't.

A second later, I hear this soft meow coming from the floor. I crane my neck sideways, just as this dark, long-haired cat leaps into Shayna's lap.

"Barak!" she laughs. "*Hoo ha-chatool sheli.*"

"Cute," I say.

There's a melodic purr as Shayna caresses her fingertips under the cat's chin. Man, I love how this skanky-dressed *sabra* can be so gentle.

"You want to pet Barak?"

"Sure," I say, even though I don't like cats.

But Barak doesn't want any part of me. When I try to pet him, he darts out of Shayna's arms, and now she's leaning into me all over again.

"Are all Americans sweet like you?" she asks.

Don't make me answer that, I think to myself. But there's no way to ignore her. "Uhhh—"

"Ethan," she whispers, and before I know what's happening,

she suddenly scrunches her face hard against mine, and now she's pasting me with the deepest kiss possible. Not that I would really know.

"Shayna," I snap, as I come up for air, and I'm probably freaking her out by not looking happy.

"It's okay, Ethan?"

I shake my head. "Look, you — you don't know me, Shayna. I mean, I'm just this loser American guy traveling here for a stupid hockey tournament."

"Ethan! I don't understand."

I doubted she would, but whatever I just said could never be enunciated in my American-style Hebrew.

"Explain!" she scoffs.

I'm tongue-tied by this concussion of exploding emotions, and there's nothing I can do about it since my cerebral Hebrew dictionary is suddenly rotting like old Sunday Tribunes in the bottom of a California Avenue recycling truck. Total brain freeze.

So right now, how do I tell her what I really want to say? That I'm an Academy guy. That she is *so* out of my league.

I don't. And as much as I want to wrap my arms all over her tantalizing, *sabra* frame, my conscience stops me cold.

"Look, Shayna," I say real slow, fighting for the right words. "You've been through so much. Living here. Surrounded by enemies. A history of terror."

"Ethan —"

"Listen to me, Shayna." I sit up straight. "You know that rocket attack yesterday?"

She nods.

"I was there. And I was afraid to tell my parents."

"Why?"

"Because the terror seems more dangerous when you're on the other side of the globe. Because they'd make me come home."

That shocks her. "You run away?"

I shake my head. "This is what I'm saying, Shayna. Israelis are different. Serving in the army. Starting college at twenty-one. Hardship and struggle, just like the Biblical prophets predicted. Thing is, we learn about this stuff in America. But you Israelis live it. Every single day."

"Maybe so," she snips, and by the way she's staring, I know she's used to getting what she wants.

"Shayna." I'm staring back, determined to break through her stubborn, *sabra* brain. "I—I don't know how to explain this, but it's like, I just can't come here from the States and steal a girl from Kiryat Shemona. I mean, I know this sounds crazy, but I've done nothing to earn you, Shayna."

"That's *meshuga*!" she screams.

"Is it?" My brain's totally replaying Danit's sermon on the balcony. "Don't you get it, Shayna? I'm here on a sports vacation, playing games on ice as if that's actually important. Pretending to be Sidney Crosby, while Israeli guys my age are giving the best three years of their lives serving and fighting. That's what I'm talking about."

"*Lo cha-shoov.*"

"No. It's *very* important," I say back. "You see, someone like me needs to pay a price just to hold your hand. *Maveenah?*"

Her midnight eyes are spilling confusion, like she didn't comprehend a single word. Truth is, I can hardly believe the prose that just waxed emotional from the depths of my soul.

"*Cho-shevet sh'atah tee-paysh,*" she huffs, telling me I'm a fool. "You don't hear a word I say to you."

The air's dancing tension, but I refuse to respond. This time, I'm gonna make Shayna finish. And she knows it.

"*Nu*, Ethan, we may not be *dati* family," she says, her eyebrows furrowing serious. "But I know *Hashem* sends you to me. I tell you already I would not even be born if not for the Jewish peoples of Chicago. Does this not mean anything?"

As she says it, I'm watching the corners of her cappuccino lips quiver, which makes me feel like a selfish piece of crap for starting this bout of drama. Of course, I've got to say something, but my tongue's morphed into a glob of stale putty.

And Shayna's not done.

"You see how happy my *Abba* and *Eema* are that I bring you here," she says, leaning into me gentle while her hand sweeps my hair sideways across my *kippah*. "And it means a lot to them that you are religious guy."

"But you told me they're not *dati*," I protest.

"They were before. But after what happens to Shai, they stopped believing. *Nu*, I know my *Abba* and *Eema*, Ethan, and God's *shechina* stays with them anyway. And now, you bring it all back."

"Me?"

"That's why they invite you for Shabbat."

"I still don't—"

"Look." She presses her finger like a fence post into my shoulder. "We never have normal Shabbat like you do. But when they tell you to come, it's gonna mean Shabbat *masorti*. White table. *Brachot*. Just like when we go to my *saba* and *safta's* house. You, *dati* religious guy, inspire my parents again."

"Because of the package? And the hotel?"

"*Ken*," she whispers, her mocha eyes shooting flames. "Now they see it was the goodness of religious Americans. I watch *Abba's* face, Ethan. He stares at your *kippah* and *tzitzis*. It happens so quick. But I know."

I'm shaking. "Maybe you're right," I tell her.

"Yes," she says, and then she gives me the chills by sliding her fingers under my polo and gently twirling my fringes. "You see, maybe it's *me* that doesn't deserve *you*. *Ken*, Ethan, you keep God's Torah and *mitzvot*, and I and Gilad—we just live here in *Eretz Yisrael*."

"But you serve in the Army," I protest. "Fight like Joshua for God's land. Don't you get it?"

She sucks this extra-long drag of air, and I can tell she's miffed. "Listen, Ethan. Like so many Israelis, I don't learn much Talmud or Torah. My friends and I laugh at the Black-Hats and we worship American fashion. *Nu*? Look at how I dress. So maybe now I change because of you. And *Abba* and *Eema* change too. Yes, I want to learn these religious things, Ethan. Maybe I just don't know it until God brings me to you."

She's smiling moonbeams, her socially-imperfect teeth more beautiful than ever. This is *so* weird. An hour ago, I figured Shayna was just another untamed *sabra* looking for a good time. God, was I shallow. I never fathomed that this gritty, Kiryat Shemona girl would capture my soul with a spiritual insight more powerful than anything I ever soaked up from those big shot Chicago rabbis.

"That's beautiful," I say, and now it's *me* nuzzling *her* close. I swear, I'm a powder keg of emotion, and I'm suddenly thinking back to that June afternoon in my bedroom, when I was sulking about having to go on this trip. When the Scorpions' *Still Loving You* crooned slow and annoying.

Now I understand what that ballad was all about.

"Ethan." Her whisper is sweet, in a way I never thought possible.

"Thanks for taking me home," I tell her. "Mom's not gonna believe this."

Shayna starts holding me tighter. It's like her passion is slicing right through me, and in this tiny, empty instant, I sense my entire essence changing. I'm still Chicago-steel on the outside, but my heart's about to explode in a way I can't explain, and there's nothing I can do to stop it from happening.

"Ethan," she whispers again, her chin waltzing atop my shoulder. "*Ani — Ani o-hevet oat-cha*, Ethan."

God, I never expected that. As soon as she says it, my body starts convulsing like I've just stepped on the Red Line's third rail or something. Meanwhile, my soul's like this human hard drive sparking gigabytes of emotional calculation to my brain.

I'm thinking Shayna didn't mean it. She never meant to say she loves me.

How could she? She doesn't know anything about me. Like my favorite food. Or my favorite color. She's got no idea I've seen *Slap Shot* eleven times, and crave EJ's deep-dish pizza after hockey practice. I hate cats and dogs, too. Shayna Ochana doesn't know any of this.

But she doesn't have to.

I say this because Shayna and I have literally endured two years' of normal existence in just the past two melodramatic hours. Incredibly heavy, it's been a date with intensity, tragedy and some serious spirituality. No American shallowness. No prancing through the Old Orchard Mall where everyone's flashing sleek I-Phones, fake smiles and counterfeit noses. It's like, Shayna and I are these ultimate psychology-lab partners, our souls in perfect sync as we dissect the rancid guts of modern Jewish experience.

That's why Shayna Ochana had every right to say what she just did.

"B'emmet, Ethan," she whispers again. "You understand? Ani o-hevet oat-cha. I really love you."

I turn. Her eyes are still beaming these total rays of passion. That's how I know she means it. And the cool thing is, she's not afraid to tell me twice, before I could say it back even once. I know that could never happen in Rogers Park. Not a chance.

"Gam Ani o-hev o-tach," I say, in this real low voice, and when she scrunches her teary eyes once more against my shoulder and starts staining emotional puddles into the front of my cotton polo, I know I've just told her the most powerful words I've ever said to anyone in my life.

I also know that tonight was Ethan Conners' last shift forever on the blue line.

Epilogue

THIS CLEANSING AUTUMN BREEZE rustles through the woods, spilling golden-hued ash leaves like brittle confetti along the forest floor. The mountain current waltzes sweet against my cheeks, and when I glance up, there's a milky, low-angle sun teasing me with vibes of an early Midwestern winter. Wow. The scenery's postcard-perfect, just the way I always envisioned Ferris State in November.

Except it isn't.

"The Golan is prettiest before Hanukkah," says Shayna, as a browning eucalyptus leaf falls gently atop her liquorice-black hair. "*Tel Dan! Ha-makom ha-tovah b'yoter sheli.*"

"Gorgeous," I say back, as if I could possibly think otherwise after toiling most of the last three months in a sweltering army camp smack in the middle of the dusty *Negev*.

That's right. The *Negev*. As in, six-thousand miles from Ferris State University.

And there aren't any hockey rinks in the *Negev*.

Which is why telling Dad about my eccentric decision was the toughest phone call of my life.

Yeah, *the conversation*. Man was that rough. I know Dad didn't believe me at first. It was early Sunday morning after that Shabbat at Shayna's, and I remember raining showers of guilt all over my Samsung when I told Mom and Dad that Israel needed me a whole lot more than Ferris State did. That *Hashem* had suddenly gathered me home to the Promised Land, the very thing crammed down my throat for the past twelve years of Orthodox schooling. It was *so* God's calling, I told them, even though I knew they figured those visions only happen to *other* people's kids.

That wasn't a good morning for me. And it must have been a horrible *motzei Shabbat* for them.

Later that afternoon, when I should have been heading to Ben Gurion for the return flight, Dad called my cell. He asked me if I was really staying. If my decision was absolutely final.

I told him yes.

There were two seconds of silence, which melted into five. Then ten. It was hellish. I was sure Dad was going into cardiac arrest.

But he didn't. Thank God he didn't. Because Dad's response changed our relationship forever.

He said, "I'm proud of you, Ethan."

I almost lost it. Right in the Ochana's living room. I didn't care. And just thinking about it now still makes me teary all over.

The crisp wind tickles my nose as Shayna and I keep strolling the River Dan trail. The colors are spectacular, and I wish I could just soak up the scenery and stop analyzing the past, but no one's talking, so my mind starts wandering anew, until I randomly begin thinking about the Borochovs. I swear, I am totally indebted to them for letting me stay the entire summer. My hockey gear, too! Seriously, no one furrowed a brow over the extra mouth to feed. Not to mention another body sharing the apartment's tiny bathroom. They were great. Mr. Borochov even drove me to Jerusalem and helped me find this IDF program for Orthodox Americans. Nuff said.

Just one regret. That would be Danit. She was unsolvable. Oh sure, our relationship improved through the weeks, but that's probably because I was spending most of my time with Shayna. It was weird the first couple of days when I'd be hanging with Shayna until midnight, and then come back to the Borochovs for a dose of silent treatment from Danit. But Danit's attitude softened once Gilad finally sucked up the nerve to ask her on a date, and I'm giving that Israeli bruiser full credit for somehow taming Danit into a semi-tolerable human.

Still, my all-time favorite memory of Danit was on that second-to-last Wednesday in July. That's when my military paperwork was finalized, and I broke the news to the Borochovs. Seriously, I'll never forget the absolute shock exuding from Danit's sun-baked face when I told her I'd enlisted for an eighteen-month stint with the IDF. You bet that ended all her harping about Jewish-American sissies leaving the dirty work to Israelis.

Lior says she's never been the same.

Shayna turns. "It's great having you in Kiryat Shemona for the weekend," she says, her hand squeezing like a vise around my fingers, as if she hasn't seen me for nearly two months, which is pretty much true. "You sure Borochovs don't care that you spend Shabbat with my family?"

"*Al tee-da-gee*," I say real loud, so she can hear me over the roaring Dan. "Don't worry, the Borochovs are cool."

She smiles, and then leads me toward this giant boulder which is kind of like a stone bench parked on the river's bank. The Dan's frothing serious whitewater, so when Shayna sits on the rock, the bottom of her blue denim skirt gets soaked with spray. She doesn't seem to care.

I edge next to her and stare sideways, loving the way these thin streaks of autumn sunbeams are peeking through half-leafless branches, sparkling Shayna's hair with a heavenly brilliance.

No one says a word. That's fine. I always read that when you really care about someone, you can spend hours in silence. So I suck a long drag of mountain air and keep staring at Shayna. She looks *so* cute, styled in a black hoodie dangling loose over her skirt.

"*Hashem's* wonders," she says, her eyes peeking lasers at the rushing water.

"Magnificent," I say back, and then I start smiling when I see her skirt's hem dripping like a soggy sponge.

I love that Shayna's dressing modest now. Long sleeves. Even longer skirts. And she's transferred to a religious high school for senior year. Sure, I'd like to think it's all because of me, and it probably is. Cool. Shayna's giving herself to Judaism pretty much the way I'm giving myself to *Eretz Yisrael*. Guess God really did have a plan for both of us.

I hope it lasts. I mean Shayna and me. Seriously, I've got another fifteen months in the IDF, and she'll be drafted next August. Of course, Shayna's talking about the national service alternative since she'll be graduating from an Orthodox school, and that *would* be nice. For now, though, I'm done with basic, so I'll be getting one weekend of leave every month and it's supposed to be that way until Pesach, which means I'll be able to come to Kiryat Shemona every four weeks.

Yeah, basic training. A hundred times worse than those black-and-white war movies. And IDF drill sergeants — every one of them more brutal than Coach Weiss on his worst day. Anyone remember that guy who vowed he'd never join up? Hint — it's the same, socially-smooth Rogers Park blueliner who'd been busting blades his whole life for Dad's D-1 scholarship.

Hockey? Don't really miss it. Sure, I've laced 'em up a few times this summer with this group of guys calling themselves the Israel Recreational Hockey Association, which is basically a bunch of Americans organizing Thursday night scrimmage games. Shayna liked to come and watch too. Look, the ice is nice, but the truth is I wouldn't have survived Ferris State. Not after everything that happened here in Israel. I mean, when God calls, a Jew's got to answer, even if it means spoiling Dad's full-boat scholarship fantasy. Sorry, Dad. I know you had me on the college hockey fast-track since I laced up my very first pair of Bauer Junior 2000s. Forgive me.

"I think we should get back soon," says Shayna, as these weak, autumn sunbeams glisten off the tips of her charcoal eyebrows. "Shabbat comes in three hours and *Eema* needs help."

Wow. Just hearing her say that nearly turns my eyes into rivers. Shayna Ochana — anxiously guarding the sabbath — serving God with the kind of devotion you'd expect from a girl at Chabad seminary in Crown Heights.

Of course, a Crown Heights girl wouldn't be caught dead with a guy in the middle of a Golan Heights forest, but hey, it's only a forty-eight-hour leave.

I fake a hair sweep with my wrist, making sure to blot any emotional residue from my eyes.

"Ethan—"

"A couple more minutes," I say, desperately soaking up some final heartbeats of this natural essence. I mean, for three months I've been longing for forests and streams. The smell of pine. The roar of a living river. I'm *so* not in a hurry.

"Look!" hollers Shayna.

I glance up, and there's this furry, brown hyrax half-camouflaged in the branches of a giant Syrian Ash just in front of us.

"Kind of like an American ground hog," I say.

"A what?"

"Forget it," I grunt, not wanting to waste a single minute explaining.

"We go to America one day, Ethan. You show me all the parks. All the animals. Just like I watch on television."

I nod. "One day," I say, and then I picture bringing her home to meet Mom and Dad. Definitely Ezra. Maybe even Coach Paulson.

And Shoshana too.

Funny thing about Shoshana. I know she's doing her seminary gap year in Jerusalem, but we don't even talk. Look, I'm not blaming her for never calling me after I told her I wasn't coming home. Truth is, I still feel guilty about the way it went down. I suppose it feels pretty crappy when your boyfriend's supposed to be gone for ten days, and suddenly, he tells you those ten days just turned into *forever*.

"We have to go," grouses Shayna, nudging me off our rocky bench. "So happy Shabbat starts early. We have plenty of time after dinner."

I smile. "Good thing the Borochovs live just ten minutes from your house."

"I think Gilad invites Danit, too," she says.

Okay, *this* is going to be interesting.

Shayna pulls my arm and leads me back to this dirt path which snakes toward the old, wooden footbridge spanning the Dan. When I turn to chuck a peek behind us toward our rocky perch on the riverbank, I'm thinking this has to be the most beautiful forest in all of Israel, almost like the Jewish State's mini-Yellowstone. Trust me, after three months tramping around the barren sands of the southern Negev, this place is practically the Garden of Eden.

But it's more than natural beauty. The Golan is Israel's water source to the Kinneret.

And a military buffer against Syria too.

Yup, that's why I'm here. It's the reason I'm *schlepping* backpacks and uzis instead of clearing bodies away from the Ferris State crease. For sure, the training's tough. Insanely grueling. A hundred times worse than Coach Weiss's goal line-to-goal line suicide speed drills.

But through the toil, God's spirit keeps gushing through my veins, willing me forward like a Twenty-First Century Judah Maccabi. Makes me think about Rabbi Klepstein's lectures on the absolute power of faith. I mean, if you can't fight for your homeland, nothing else matters. Which is exactly what our barbaric platoon sergeant pounds through our skulls every single day.

I scope ahead. The dirt path's dissolving into this potholed parking lot, and I'm totally hating that our hike is over.

"You call your *abba* and *eema* from my house," says Shayna, throwing me her gaze.

"Thanks," I say back, and I really mean it since Dad had my cell disconnected when I told him the Army doesn't allow phones during basic. Haven't called home in nearly three weeks.

We slip inside the Ochana's ancient Datsun. Shayna's driving, even though she doesn't get her license until February, but it's not like there's gonna be any patrol cops in the Golan.

She cranks the ignition, and then flicks on *Kol Rega* FM 96. Nice. It's American rock. Alice-in-Chains, I think.

"You like this song, Ethan?"

"Yeah," I nod, my *kippah* creeping down my forehead.

Shayna's silent. It's like she's wants me to ingest these vibes of Americana leaking through the Datsun's tinny speakers. Maybe she's testing me. You know, checking me out to see if the harmony's making me homesick. It doesn't. Truth is, I've never had a pang of regret about leaving home to make the ultimate line change. I mean, I love this gritty, Middle-Eastern lifestyle, and it sure didn't take long for Israeli society to suck the suburban shallowness from my snotty essence.

Guess Dad's plan was *God's* plan all along.

And one day, I'll even tell Ezra he was spot-on. That being here *did* change everything.

The old Datsun idles rough. Shayna's waiting for the engine to warm, so she creeps her hand around the stick-shift handle and then slyly captures my wrist. It's just for an instant, but her touch chills me solid. She's amazing. She's even got my silver medal hanging from the rear-view mirror. I like that.

I know Mom would love Shayna.

I'll bet Dad would too.

"Another second," says Shayna, still waiting for the engine to settle.

I peek left, steal her profile, and smile. I swear, the way the Maccabiah trip turned out still seems so incredibly bizarre. But it's so right in my heart. That's because I really do believe that God planned to send me here. To Israel. To Kiryat Shemona.

Shayna turns. "You're spacing out Ethan," she says, boring holes through my lackluster eyes while her fingers tighten around the shifter.

"Sorry," I grumble. I turn toward the streaky windshield and start zoning at the graying, northern sky.

"Ethan—"

"Just thinking," I say, and then lose myself in deep reflection all over.

Just a four-day hockey tournament. *Right, Ethan Conners.* Blue-line traps and full-boat scholarships seem so ridiculously distant, like it was all part of another world, which it pretty much was. And now, well don't even tempt me to predict what's going to happen after the army. That's in *Hashem's* hands, and I'm just hoping to be a small part of His blessing.

I sneak another peek at Shayna, and when I do, the air starts dancing emotion. Which means your CJA smooth guy's biting his lip, fighting for all he's worth to hold back a slush pail of feelings. So I take a deep breath, then nod to myself.

This place. This Promised Land. It took five trips to Israel to really get it. To understand why *I* was called to spend half my life on the hockey fast-track.

It was all God's plan. A line change from heaven.

And trust me, it feels so right to finally come home.

Reading Group Discussion

1) Ethan worked most of his life to get the NCAA scholarship. Do you think he should have talked to his parents before deciding to quit hockey and serve in the IDF?

2) Do you think Ethan's Rogers Park life was too sheltered? Do you think Ethan really wanted to stay in Israel, or was he making his own statement of independence?

3) Have you ever felt so strongly about a particular cause that you would consider changing your entire life's direction despite the consequences?

4) Why does Ethan suddenly begin hating his upper-crust privilege? Is it because of Kiryat Shemona hardship? Guilt over not serving in the Jewish army?

5) Why is Ethan so shocked at Israeli secularism? Do you think it was fair to judge the locals the way he did?

6) Does Danit hate Ethan, or is she really hiding a romantic crush on him?

7) Think about the connection between Ethan and Shayna. Have you ever been in a situation that you knew was more than a coincidence?

8) Were you surprised by the reaction of Ethan's father when he learned that Ethan was not coming home?

9) Did Ethan really like his smug, drama-free life in Chicago? Do you think he should have socialized with Lior and Danit, or should he have simply concentrated on hockey and stayed away from the local teenage scene?

10) When Ethan says it's good to finally come home, he means living in God's Promised Land — the Jewish homeland. Do you think Ethan would have made this choice if Danit had never accused him of being an *American arrogant*?

Acknowledgments

A STORY LIKE *LINE CHANGE* only gets created through lots of inspiration and encouragement from all kinds of people and places. Like my wife, Sheryl, who selflessly supports my officiating career with the Illinois Hockey Officials' Association, even though it's meant many nights home alone for the past twenty-three years. And our daughter, Alyse, who prefers traveling Israel off the beaten path, loving gritty towns like Kiryat Shemona and Sderot. No five-star tours for that girl. And to everyone in my SCBWI Northern Illinois Chapter. Those monthly meetings push us to take our manuscripts to the next level.

To the people of Kiryat Shemona. You've welcomed my family into your houses, shops and falafel stands. And to the Elchana family somewhere on Tel Chai Road. I still cherish how our families met in 2007.

To Jewish high schools and academies in Chicago, where Zionism, Torah and learning lead eighteen-year-olds to Israel — and even a few to the IDF. Thanks for all your schools have done for the Chicago Jewish community.

To Mazo Publishers, for giving *Line Change* a shot.

And finally, to the crews at the Northbrook, Lincoln & McCormack and especially the Lake & LaSalle Starbucks. Your cafes are the perfect places for long hours of editing over ice coffee. Thanks.

About The Author

MARK LICHTENFELD LIVES IN Chicago's suburban North Shore and is a member of the North Suburban, Illinois Chapter of the Society of Children's Book Writers and Illustrators. He is a licensed, USA Hockey and American Collegiate Hockey Association referee, and has officiated nearly five thousand games over the past twenty-three years. He writes a column for Rink Life, a Midwestern hockey newspaper, and has been featured in many other publications during his career. Mark and his family have traveled to Kiryat Shemona many times, and of course, he has skated at the Canada Centre.

For more information on *Line Change*, go to the official website at www.line-change.com

CPSIA information can be obtained at www.ICGtesting.com
Printed in the USA
LVOW01s1035170414

382114LV00004B/389/P

9 781936 778539